THE WIRE AND THE LINES

Jox McNabb Thrillers
Book Five

Patrick Larsimont

SAPERE
BOOKS

THE WIRE AND
THE LINES

Published by Sapere Books.

24 Trafalgar Road, Ilkley, LS29 8HH

saperebooks.com

ISBN: 978-0-85495-601-2

For Morgan Chalmers and Graeme 'Spud' Inverarity,
both great chums of my youth who 'flew' with Jox in his adventures,
at least as inspirations.
Rest in peace my friends.
Per Ardua Ad Astra.

PROLOGUE

London, 15th November, 1992

Doctor Melanie McNabb was running late. It wasn't like her, but it had been a long week and she had allowed herself a Sunday morning lie-in. The Imperial War Museum where she worked was always busy in the run-up to Remembrance week in November, as people came to pay their respects and learn more about the men and women who had given their lives for their country all those years ago, and she had been working flat out. She rushed out of her flat in Fulham as the black hackney cab arrived to collect her and soon, they were making good progress through Richmond Park.

Not for the first time, Melanie marvelled at the herds of red and fallow deer clustered under the parkland's trees and across the grassy meadows. It was hard to believe that there were so many of the wild creatures roaming the London park, only a short walk away from the bustling town centre of Richmond upon Thames. She'd read somewhere that the deer were there because King Charles I decided to move his royal court to Richmond Palace to escape the ravages of the Great Plague, ordering the nearby park to be stocked with quarry for his hunting pleasure, and the beasts had thrived ever since, unlike the king himself, who lost his head in 1649.

It was late in the rutting season, and Melanie could see several large stags lying amongst the rust-coloured ferns, exhausted from their battles with each other and their subsequent exertions. She smiled to herself; she wouldn't mind joining them for a nap. She'd enjoyed a glass too many at her work do last night. The museum had organised a celebration for the launch of her latest exhibition, which was showcasing the experiences of prisoners of war. It had been a tough show to pull together and involved harrowing testimony from those who'd suffered. She'd been particularly affected by the recordings of former prisoners who had been inmates of Nazi concentration camps during the Holocaust, the images of starved captives of the Japanese, and the earlier transcripts of Boers, mainly civilians, who had been confined by the British in what were recognised as the first experiments with concentration camps. What she'd discovered had troubled her deeply, making the project challenging and disturbing, and for the first time in her professional career, she had not found her work enjoyable or fulfilling, but incredibly draining.

She had known that her own grandfather, Group Captain Jeremy "Jox" McNabb, had been a prisoner of war, but he had rarely spoken about that time and she was keen to learn more about what he may have experienced. In truth, there was so little of his illustrious military career that he had ever wanted to discuss with Melanie when she had asked him about it, and it was only through her own research as an adult that she had started to learn more about his achievements. Her curiosity around what he'd done during the war had in fact sparked her interest in military history, driving her to obtain her PhD, and ultimately leading to her position as a curator with the Imperial War Museum in Southwark. Over the years, since her grandfather's passing, she had uncovered some hidden details about his life, but in many ways, he remained an enigma. There was a lot to learn, for her inscrutable 'Grandpa Bang-Bang' had turned out to be a legendary fighter ace during the Second World War.

The taxi lurched over the speed bumps on Sawyer's Hill leading through to Richmond Gate, and the jolt shook Melanie from her reverie, driving the pin, with which she was trying to affix a paper poppy to her lapel, into her thumb. She yelped, and the cabbie asked, 'You all right, love?' He pulled in to the kerb. 'There you go, the Royal Star and Garter Home in plenty of time for you to catch the ceremony at the cenotaph on the telly. It'll mean a great deal to them what are in there, I can tell you.' He nodded towards the building. 'If you're visiting someone here, I'm sure it means something to you, too.'

You have no idea, thought Melanie, glancing at her wristwatch, a man's Rolex Oyster Perpetual with a blue face and a fire-damaged crystal. It was ten to ten, so still plenty of time before the eleven o'clock remembrance ceremony. Her watch had a long and checkered history. It had once belonged to an American airman and his initials, 'W.I.S.H. III' were inscribed on its back. The original owner had been William Huntington the Third, known as Billy Three Names, who had perished in his burning cockpit. The watch had survived, and her grandfather had worn it in William's honour for the rest of his war, and it had eventually made its way to Melanie.

Getting out of the cab, she paid the driver, and he put two fingers to his forehead in thanks, rather like a boy scout salute. That was when Melanie noticed the red and white Polish Air Force checkerboard badge on his lapel.

'You served?' she asked.

'No. 303 *Kościuszko* Fighter squadron. I was just a flight mechanic.'

'They couldn't have achieved much without you.' She squeezed his big, bear-like hand. 'Thank you for your service.'

He nodded, cuffing away the shine in his eye, then gunned the taxi's diesel engine. 'All right, love, thank you. Have a good day.'

Before her were the imposing doors of the Royal Star and Garter Home for Disabled Ex-Service Men and Women. Above the doors was a Red Cross medallion carved into a stone mantel that ran between a pair of towering sandstone columns and on it was the Union Jack, frozen stiff by the overnight frost. Her breath forming before her face, Melanie shivered and hurried through the familiar doors. She'd visited here often since the funeral of her honorary uncle, David Pritchard, almost two years ago now. He'd been a long-term resident at this massive stone edifice on Richmond Hill, the stateliest of care homes, reserved for the nation's heroes in their twilight years. Jox and Pritch had served together from their early days in training until their time in No. 111 Squadron during the Battle of Britain, and again in the run-up to D-Day, forging a lifelong bond until their respective deaths.

To Melanie, Uncle Pritch had always been larger than life, desperately good-looking, the epitome of a roguish, swashbuckling pirate captain, with his black eye patch and a single right arm. He and his French wife, Amandine, had always been her favourite visitors, glamourous and seeming terribly exotic to a little girl living in the Scottish Highlands with her grandfather. Childless, they'd been devoted godparents, bringing her beautiful toys when she was little and elegant Parisian fashions as she got older. When Amandine had passed away, Pritch had taken it badly and, unable to cope on his own, he'd moved into the home. When Jox had passed, Melanie had been so bound up in her own grief that she hadn't been there enough for Uncle Pritch, who had also been suffering from the loss of his dearest friend. She regretted not spending more time with Pritch in his later years, but she had recently formed a bond with the special friend and confidante he made during that time, Nancy Wake.

Today, Melanie was visiting Nancy, a near-octogenarian with a penchant for strong gin and tonic and weak Earl Grey tea. During the Second World War, she had been known to the Gestapo as the 'White Mouse' and was considered the deadliest Special Operations agent in the whole of occupied France.

The pair had become firm friends when making the arrangements for Pritch's funeral, and had grown even closer since, finding in each other the grandmother and granddaughter that neither had. Remembrance Sunday was important to Nancy, as it was to all the residents in the home, and Melanie wouldn't miss it for the world. She recognised several of the staff as she walked through the rooms, who waved greetings. She'd become something of a celebrity amongst them, with her connection to the late Squadron Leader David Pritchard and the force of nature that was Nancy.

'She's waiting for you in the television room,' said Archie, one of the stewards and a veteran of the Falklands War. 'Says she's saving you a seat at the front,' he chuckled. 'Some of the others won't like that, but I don't suppose anyone will be brave enough to challenge her.' He pointed up the corridor. 'Up the stairs, then on the left, Doctor McNabb.'

Melanie entered the room a little out of breath. Armchairs were lined up in military rows, interspersed by several wheelchairs. The seats were mostly filled by grey-haired residents with an impressive array of headgear, facial hair, regimental ties and glittering military medals.

'Mel darling, over here,' said Nancy, waving her crimson talons in the air. She too was wearing her medals, an impressive collection, which included the George Medal, in recognition of many acts of valour and bravery with the resistance and in SOE operations during the war. 'Quick, possession is nine tenths of the law and most of these old crocks are still gentlemen enough to leave you be.'

The pair exchanged quick kisses on the cheek in the French manner, before Melanie sat down.

Looking at the screen, Melanie watched the camera cut to the Whitehall balcony, draped in royal blue with gold braid. Left to right on the screen were Diana, Princess of Wales, Princess Anne, and the Queen Mother. All three were clad in black with a corsage of red poppies on their lapels. Diana wore a large-brimmed hat, Anne was hatless, her hair up in a high chignon, and the Queen Mother wore her signature style of hat with the brim turned up, so the nation could see the royal matriarch's familiar features.

'She'll always be my queen,' said Nancy, gesturing to the older woman. 'Now and during the war, but doesn't our Diana look lovely? A bit too skinny, mind.'

The camera cut to Queen Elizabeth II, dressed entirely in black, complete with a hat and handbag as she walked out of Whitehall. She was followed by her husband, Prince Philip, and her son Prince Andrew, both in naval uniforms. They took their positions before the cenotaph as assembled choirboys and the armed escort from all three services began to sing a hymn. The tall stone monument before them was actually an 'empty tomb' symbolising the devastating losses of the First World War, and dedicated to the immortal memory of 'The Glorious Dead' with no known graves.

'Wouldn't you have preferred to have been there in person?' whispered Melanie. 'I could have taken you.'

Nancy snorted. 'Out there? Not a chance. My old Aussie blood doesn't much like standing in the cold. Don't you worry, darling, I'm happy tucked up, nice and warm in this comfy armchair. Been down there often enough, freezing my tush off. You must have been, surely?'

'You've no idea,' replied Melanie. 'For Jox it was like a religious pilgrimage. He never missed it, and most of the time he dragged me along. I hated all the standing about, but I always loved meeting the old boys he'd served with. It was the only time I could ever learn a bit about what he did during the war. Uncle Pritch often came along and afterwards, they'd go off for a boozy lunch at the RAF club, while Amandine took me shopping at Harrods.'

On the screen were the faces of several dark-suited politicians. The BBC commentator suddenly stopped talking.

'Right, it's time,' said Nancy.

All of those that could stood up as the guns on the television boomed, marking the eleventh hour of the eleventh day of the eleventh month, the start of the two-minute silence marking Remembrance Sunday. As the chimes of Big Ben signalled the hour, Melanie recalled one of the rare war stories from her grandfather. He had told her that during the height of the London Blitz, he had seen the clockfaces and spike of London's most familiar landmark jutting through the swirling smoke of a thousand fires and it had given him the conviction that old London town could take whatever the Jerries threw at it.

As the silence stretched on, with the television camera panning across the multitude of bowed heads, Melanie's thoughts wandered back to her beloved Grandpa Bang-Bang.

He'd been on her mind a lot recently, especially while she'd been working on her current exhibition. The more she'd learnt about the lives of prisoners of war, the more in awe she was of his strength and ability to survive. Watching the proud servicemen on the screen in front of her, she wondered how many of them had experienced the horrors her grandfather had endured when captured in 1943.

CHAPTER ONE

5th *August, 1943*

The only way Squadron Leader Jeremy 'Jox' McNabb's Spitfire Mark IX was going was down. Its starboard wing, painted in the muted colours of a night fighter, looked as if something big and mean had taken a giant bite from it. Another massed volley of anti-aircraft fire rose towards the Spitfire from either side of the shoreline. It was inevitable that some of it had finally found its mark.

Cramped and claustrophobic in the fighter's tight cockpit, Jox struggled with knocking controls and the stink of leaking glycol cutting into the oxygen mask clamped tight over his nose and mouth. Moments earlier, he'd been in pursuit of a twin-engine *Messerschmitt* Bf 110 *Nachtjägder*, which had been attacking a helpless Dakota C-47 transport disgorging paratroopers onto the scree slopes and ash fields of Mount Etna. This was part of the final assault by Allied forces trying to breach the vaunted Etna line, Germany's last formidable defensive fortifications in northern Sicily.

In the red-hued sky, Jox once again found the silhouette of his opponent. It was throwing off sparks, gradually being engulfed by flames, growing ever brighter until it was a fiery comet streaking across the night sky. Jox's aircraft was buffeted by violent turbulence, further rattled by air bursts, until he felt a resounding bang. Instinctively, he knew it was a fatal blow.

Pursuer and quarry streaked across the blackened lava fields veined with orange until they'd reached the strip of water separating Sicily from mainland Italy, the heavily defended

Straits of Messina. Jox had nailed the *Nachtjägder* but had in turn been struck by intense groundfire coming from the most heavily defended stretch of water in Europe. Calabria lay ahead, visible as a long, pale beach edged with frothing breakers. Below him were the dark shadows of countless vessels evacuating personnel across the churning ocean.

Jox wrestled with the controls of the dying aircraft, knowing he was fighting a losing battle. Visibility was now limited to the dull glow of Mount Etna's lava fields left far behind, the pale moonlight ahead and effervescence from glowing white water churned by the countless ships. Jox tugged at his canopy, trying to get the fouled air to clear, then unclipped the Spit's side hatch to ease his eventual escape. The dial indicating the engine temperature on the control panel nudged into the red. It wouldn't be long before the gurgling Merlin engine would seize. Like it or not, he was going to get his feet wet again, unless he somehow manged to find somewhere to land, a challenging proposition in this near darkness.

He was desperate to avoid a repeat performance of his ditching into the waters of the Mediterranean on the first day of Operation Husky, south of the island. That was several weeks ago now, but he could vividly recall spending the best part of a day bobbing helplessly in his Mae West until he was finally rescued. There had followed a challenging sojourn on Sicily itself, where he'd done everything he could to avoid getting murdered by either side, not to mention escaping the clutches of the local *mafiosi* before he managed to regain Allied lines.

Jox peered into the night, searching for anywhere he might get the kite down. There was flak bursting at ground level, providing useful but deadly illumination. Thankfully, he was losing altitude fast and much of it was overshooting. He banked tightly, so his descent now ran parallel to the white beach. The shoreline appeared to be relatively smooth and shallow-watered, perhaps offering a feasible emergency landing strip. He'd tried crash landings on beaches before with varying degrees of success. It was the Spitfire's twin air scoops that made belly-landings challenging, always running the risk of tipping the aircraft over onto its nose.

Here the sand appeared wide, wet and even, so perhaps a wheels-down landing had a chance of working and he wouldn't bog down immediately and sink. Then, if he managed to aquaplane successfully, perhaps he wouldn't go arse over tit. The trick was to put the kite down on the wet sand under just a few inches of water in such a way that instead of going under, it skidded across the wet surface, reaching the beach with the last of its momentum. This of course assumed there weren't any waves or underwater currents, and that the beach wasn't mined, strewn with obstacles or wire, and that the gun crews in the pillboxes dotted along the shoreline didn't open fire as he raced past.

He chose to go wheels-down, the aircraft now rumbling through the shallows, rattling and bumping across wet ridges of sand in a way that sounded incredibly loud to his ears. The Spitfire finally came to a shuddering halt and Jox was thrown heavily against his straps, narrowly missing cracking his forehead on the instrument panel and reflector sight. He exhaled, leaning back against the headrest. Fumes began to catch in his throat, and he saw swirling trails of tracers above him, roaring upwards like flailing bullwhips of light. There was a gun emplacement not too far away, firing into the heavens.

Jox opened his canopy, clearing the cockpit fug as he unclipped his harness. He stood cautiously on the bucket seat, taking a nervous look around the wreck. Away in the middle distance, something was burning, possibly the *Zerstörer* he'd brought down. The only other light source was the gun position on the crest of a hill in the distance.

Instinctively, Jox reached for his talismans, a porcelain doll's arm he'd acquired early on in the war, and a Maltese switchblade he'd been gifted a few months ago, but he realised he'd left them behind with his batman, Corporal Shillington. This filled him with dread, his innate fighter pilot's superstition putting him in a heightened state of anxiety. He found some relief after fumbling in the depths of the cockpit and finding the antiquated Glisenti Model 1910 pistol he'd picked up on the battlefield in Sicily. It was a short-barrelled Italian version of the German Luger, prized by American troops as souvenirs. It was old but could still put a decent hole in anyone who had a go at him. He quickly loaded it before venturing out onto the wet sand of mainland Italy.

As he stole away from the wreckage, he could hear a ticking as the Spitfire cooled down. He breathed deeply to clear the glycol stink, then, crouching to cast as small a shadow as he could, he scuttled across the beach, moving from cover to cover, heading inland. He rested a few hundred yards beyond the beach, catching his breath, until he was distracted by the throb of engines overhead.

Silhouetted against the sky were some of the largest aircraft he'd ever seen. They must be *Messerschmitt* Me 323 *Gigants*, the German military transports he'd heard so much about. They'd been brought in to do the heavy lifting for the German evacuation and were the largest land-based transport aircraft flying anywhere. Each had six engines, a wingspan of over ninety feet and could carry a hundred and thirty troops or twenty-five thousand pounds of payload. Jox wondered if they were returning from dropping German paratrooper reinforcements into Sicily, or if they were evacuating personnel, reasoning it was probably both.

His thoughts were interrupted by the sound of harsh Germanic voices a short distance away. The beam of a torch swept over the bushes under which he was hiding. He decided to strike deeper into the thicket of head-height nettles which had grown prodigiously throughout that long summer. His hands and body were protected by his flight gauntlets, but his face was cruelly stung. Mere feet away there was an animated conversation, then heavy footsteps through the underbrush. A silhouetted figure paused and fumbled, and soon the sound of tinkling water came to him, as did the whiff of ammonia. *Strewth, that chap really needs to drink some water,* Jox thought.

Jox expected to be discovered at any moment. He heard louder voices from the direction of his wreckage, distracting whoever was closest to him. There was a shrill blast of a whistle, presumably raising the alarm at the discovery of a downed Allied aircraft. He froze in petrified silence. His heart sank at the sound of barking.

Christ, I've got no bloody chance now.

By some miracle, as dawn broke, Jox still hadn't been discovered. He'd even managed to snatch some sleep, tucked away in his hidden nook amongst the nettles. When he awoke, his stung skin was raw. He could have lived with that, but he was starting to get cramps in his legs from dehydration. He had to get moving, if only to get his circulation going.

Jox discovered he was well behind the beach, in a belt of rough scrubland. Above him there was a low cliff, topped by a winding road that followed the shoreline. He cautiously climbed to it, spotting that every few hundred yards along its length there was a cement-grey pillbox, gun slits facing out to sea, squat and stark against the shrubby maritime vegetation, the white sandy beach and the honeycomb colour of the rocks. Thankfully, it appeared that the gun positions were abandoned and empty.

His first dilemma was which direction he should go in. Picturing the coast from memory, he reasoned that the town he saw in the distance must surely be the seaside resort of Villa San Giovanni. It would have a small harbour; perhaps he could even pinch a boat to get back across the straits to Sicily.

As Jox considered his options, his stomach rumbled, providing further motivation to get going. He followed the exposed shore road, trying to keep to the roadside vegetation. As he approached a blind bend in the road, he suddenly heard the high-pitched whine of engines, followed by the screeching of braking tyres. Before he could throw himself into cover, a pair of sturdy *Zündapp* KS 750 motorcycle and sidecar combinations roared around the corner. The motorcyclists and sidecar passengers were clad in voluminous oilskins, with classic coal scuttle helmets on their heads and the distinctive metal gorgets of the *Feldgendarmerie*, the German military police, worn on chains around their necks.

These were the *Kettenhunde* or 'Chain-dogs' who'd most likely spent the night searching for him and were therefore in no mood for any nonsense. Each sidecar had a mounted MG 42 machine gun trained on him. The grim-faced *Feldwebel* standing astride his powerful bike swung a black-booted leg over his seat and stood directly in front of Jox. He grunted something and motioned with his MP40 *Schmeisser* submachine gun.

Jox nodded and meekly raised his hands in surrender. He was well and truly in the bag now.

'*Ach*, so, you are most fortunate, Squadron Leader,' said the black-clad lieutenant who'd been interrogating Jox for the last few hours. They'd come to an impasse, and he'd been called away to the telephone. When he returned, Jox wondered if this was a change in tactic. 'My general has invited you to breakfast.'

'Breakfast?' replied Jox, rather thrown. *What's all this?* he wondered as his stomach rumbled, answering for him.

The blond, blue-eyed lieutenant, a classic Aryan warrior if ever there was one, smiled, a stark contrast to the sinister SS runes on his black collar patches. 'I think you will enjoy the experience. *Herr General* Baade is, how you say, quite the eccentric. He requests the pleasure of meeting the famous Squadron Leader Jox McNabb.'

'Famous? Hardly, but yes, breakfast would certainly be welcome. Perhaps I should clean up a bit if I'm to be presented to a general?'

'Of course,' the lieutenant replied. 'I will get some soap and water, perhaps a mirror and a comb.' His pale eyes narrowed. 'But no razor, I'm afraid. *Es ist verboten* for the prisoner.'

Jox gazed at his scratched, red and blotchy reflection in the mirror. He looked tired, his face grimy from the crash and raised from nettle rash. Otherwise, he was holding up and was in pretty good shape, all things considered. His hands were raw and scratched, and he had an ache in his shoulders when he lifted his arms to comb his hair, trying to disguise his damned widow's peak. The *Feldwebel* who'd captured him had given him a thorough going-over, rifling through all his things. For a brief moment he'd been interested in Jox's blue-faced Rolex, inherited from a fallen comrade, but the fire damage to its face, telling of the owner's demise, made it of little interest.

Jox knew of General Baade by reputation. His good friend, Doc Ridgway, the new Intelligence Officer for No. 333 Squadron had often spoken of him. Baade was something of an expert in defensive warfare and had been tasked with holding the straits of Messina and organising the evacuation of the thousands of Axis troops in Sicily. Jox remembered that Ridgway had been rather taken by Baade's eccentricities, which included wearing a kilt and carrying a Scottish claymore sword. He also apparently amused himself during the desert war by using his flawless English to confuse Allied artillerymen, broadcasting spurious instructions and conflicting orders over the Allied radio net. Breakfast would certainly prove to be an interesting experience.

Jox was shown into the library of an elegant seaside villa to which he'd been driven in an open-topped *Kübelwagen*. The walls were lined with bookshelves, filled with leatherbound books that looked like they hadn't been touched for years. Between them were elegantly framed impressionist seascapes which to Jox's untrained eyes seemed rather good. The lieutenant escorting him indicated a flight of steps leading to double doors giving onto a sunny terrace with a fine sea view. A table was set for breakfast, complete with a vase of flowers, a white tablecloth and silver cutlery. Standing at the table was a white-jacketed waiter serving coffee and, by the smell of it, made from real coffee beans.

Seated at the table were two senior German officers, but from where he was standing, Jox could only see their black riding boots, one complete with stubby silver spurs. The lieutenant motioned that Jox should go outside, so he took the few steps, unsure what to expect and feeling distinctly scruffy surrounded by all this grandeur.

'Mr McNabb, I'm so very pleased you could join us,' said a distinctly English-sounding accent. The speaker was in his mid-forties and had a tanned face, but only from the bridge of his nose down to his chin. Jox instantly recognised the two-tone colouring from the desert, a sign of someone who'd spent time in the sun wearing a peaked cap. He had red tabs on the lapels of his tropical, tan-coloured jacket and a Knight's Cross at his throat. On his right bicep, Jox recognised a tank destroyer's stripe, awarded for the single-handed destruction of an enemy tank, not something a great many men could claim.

Both officers got to their feet and clicked their heels like pantomime Jerries. Jox saluted and they both reciprocated.

'My name is Ernst-Günther Baade,' said the man with the English accent, 'and I'm delighted that one of my gunners managed to hit such an esteemed bird as yourself, Squadron Leader McNabb. Of course, the pleasure is all the greater since you don't appear to have been too damaged in the process.' The general chuckled as he extended his hand towards Jox.

Jox realised that despite wearing a conventional *Heer* officer's uniform jacket, Baade was in fact wearing a bright red kilt. If he wasn't mistaken it was Royal Stewart tartan, the colour matching Baade's collar tabs.

Baade chuckled at the expression on Jox's face. 'My mother was a Stewart, and I wear their tartan with great pride. It's rather bright and I like that, always keen to make a good first impression. I'm not exactly a shrinking violet. I believe the McNabb tartan is equally bright, is it not?'

'Yes, that's right, sir,' replied Jox.

A black beret was on the table, stark against the starched white tablecloth and trimmed with a red tartan ribbon matching the kilt. Instead of a sporran, Baade wore a holstered pistol at his waist and there was an actual Scottish claymore leaning against his chair.

'May I introduce *Oberst* Kreg von Wella,' said Baade.

Von Wella wore a more conventional *Luftwaffe* uniform complete with an Iron Cross and pilot's badge pinned to his chest pocket. He was tall, broad-shouldered and would no doubt have been considered rather handsome, with curly blond hair, blue eyes and the hawkish look that often epitomised the model of an ideal Nazi fighter pilot. Less conventionally, he had a vivid Mensur scar on his left cheek and the right side of his face bore even heavier damage, looking like it had melted. Over his right eye, he wore a black eyepatch and he was holding his right arm stiffly, the hand in a black leather glove. He smelt strongly of Eau de Cologne.

'I make quite an impression too, don't you think?' said von Wella in a German accent, his single blue eye hard and shiny, and not at all kindly like Baade's. 'I have you Tommies to thank for this after the raid on Dieppe. Your *Kameraden* stole my looks and my flying brevet, so I am not so kindly disposed to *Englanders* as perhaps the General is.' The iciness in his words was quite evident.

'Squadron Leader McNabb is no Englishman, he's a Scotsman,' said Baade. 'There's a big difference. That would be like me calling you Austrian, Kreg. I don't think you'd appreciate that much.'

Von Wella bristled. '*Der Führer* is Austrian, or at least he was.'

'Well, there are always exceptions to the rule,' replied Baade. 'Come, you must behave now, Kreg. We are still gentlemen, despite the recent unpleasantness across the water.' He sighed and broke some bread with his fingers. 'I do so miss the cleanliness of war in the desert, when we still fought like gentlemen. Please, let's sit down and try to enjoy some breakfast like the civilised men we are.' He looked across at Jox. 'Would you care for some coffee, McNabb? My orderly Hans is a wizard at acquiring things that are meant to be impossible to find.'

At the mention of his name, the white-tunicked waiter came to attention and asked, '*Kaffe, mein Herr?*'

'*Viel danke,*' replied Jox.

'So, you speak German,' said von Wella. 'You will find that useful in the camp.'

'Only a little. Camp? What camp?'

'Why, my camp. It's a temporary *Stalag Luft* established to cope with the high number of Allied aircrew that keep falling out of the skies as a result of your incessant bombing.'

'Come, never mind that,' said Baade impatiently. 'Let's eat. I've a special treat for you. Hans has made Scottish potato scones with some Lorne sausage from an old family recipe that I have taught him. He's a most resourceful man and has even managed to find us some eggs to scramble.'

'Scramble, that's the RAF term for *alarm*, is it not? Appropriate, don't you think, Squadron Leader?' said von Wella, as their food arrived.

Jox frowned.

'So then, Jox, may I call you Jox?' asked Baade. 'I believe that's what your *Kameraden* call you.' He smiled at Jox's surprised expression. 'I understand you were at El Alamein.'

'I don't wish to be ungrateful for your hospitality, sir,' replied Jox, 'but all I am required to provide is my name, rank and number.'

With a reptilian glint in his single blue eye, von Wella interrupted, 'Oh, we know all about that. We have quite the dossier on you, Squadron Leader Jeremy Argyll Easton McNabb, number: 41276. We're fully up to speed with your adventures in Libya, Tunisia and more recently in Sicily. We even have some friends in common, who told us all about your little sojourn in Ragusa before Operation Husky took hold properly.'

Jox was dumbstruck by how much they knew.

'You appear surprised,' said Baade. 'Our intelligence service don't often make mistakes.'

'You didn't expect your *cosa nostra* friends to be loyal, did you?' added von Wella. 'You'll soon discover their duplicity; playing both sides is the mafia's speciality. Those Sicilians talk so much of honour and loyalty, but I saw little of that.'

Unhappy to be on the back foot, Jox retorted, 'I knew of General Baade, of course. His reputation from the western desert precedes him.' Baade nodded at the compliment. 'I hear tell that one of your favourite pastimes is using captured British Army radio sets to broadcast spurious orders, sending our troops scurrying after their own tails.'

Baade laughed. 'There's nothing quite as amusing as causing mayhem amongst your enemies. As I recall, your Special Air Service were rather adept at that too. A strange name, since I believe they have no connection with the RAF whatsoever.'

'So, I understand,' replied Jox. 'Obviously, someone somewhere had a sense of humour. I believe at one time, they were destroying more Axis aircraft than the RAF were, which was really rather embarrassing. Things have certainly changed now.' He turned to von Wella. 'I'm afraid I've not heard of you, sir, but you seem well informed for a camp commandant.' Jox savoured the last square of Lorne sausage. The slice of Scottish spiced sausage meat was a real taste of home.

'I'm rather more than that,' replied von Wella. 'The camp is overseen by the Italians, for now at least, but I'm responsible for security and all intelligence matters in the region. Let's just say it has become a second career after my own flying days came to an abrupt halt.'

'May I ask what aircraft you were flying?'

'A *Würger, Focke-Wulf* 190.'

'An impressive aircraft. I've tangled with them more than a few times, not always coming out of it terribly well.'

'I invited you to breakfast because I was intrigued by the markings on your aircraft,' said General Baade. 'The claymore sword and the pig's head. I have a love for all things Scottish and when I discovered its pilot was the fighter ace Jox McNabb, I had to meet you. As you can see, I too have a sword, but the Black Pigs are a new name to me. *Oberst* von Wella informs me you created the unit from scratch, and they were responsible for ambushing our own General Galland's fighter escort in Sicily, despite the fact they were all *Experten*. Your men must be very skilled and will surely regret the loss of their leader.'

'They'll manage,' said Jox. 'They're all seasoned veterans.'

'Yes, I'm sure, and we had quite a battle last night, didn't we? My gunners and pilots shot down seventeen of your aircraft. Unfortunately, our losses were equally heavy, but such is the nature of war. So, do tell me, who is this Marguerite?'

'She was a little girl killed in a Stuka attack in France,' said Jox, his voice hardening.

'Ah … it is the innocents that always suffer most. There are doubtless many little Margaretes who perished in the firestorms in our own German cities.'

'No more than little Margarets who died in Coventry, Clydebank and London.'

'Yes, we are aware of the unfortunate loss of your fiancée,' said Baade. 'My sincere condolences.' He was pensive. 'I think we can all agree that both sides have suffered terribly because of this war. I myself lost my dear sister Dominika in the raids. It is the unfortunate lot of professional soldiers that we have no choice but to continue the struggle.' He sighed, then rapped his knuckles on the table. 'We have lost the battle for Sicily, but you will not find Italy so easily won. The topography of the land is against you, and even the Italians will fight for their homeland.'

'Given recent events, I'm not sure they will,' replied Jox. 'It's the sheer numbers that are stacked against you. The Soviets have endless manpower and the Americans endless materiel. I've seen their professionalism and eagerness to learn first-hand, and their progress is astounding. I fear the whirlwind is truly coming for you.'

'You may be right,' mused Baade. 'But I still think we can convince the Italians to fight. I advise you not to underestimate us, my friend.' Closing the discussion, he added, 'It is unlikely we'll meet again, but you needn't concern yourself about such things any longer. Now you will be in the care of *Oberst* von Wella and his colleagues. For you, my dear Jox, I'm afraid the war is over.'

CHAPTER TWO

Oberst Kreg von Wella had told Jox that he was bound for a *Dulag Luft* run by the Italians. He'd finally arrived and was trying to find his bearings. So far, captivity had involved a terrifying journey of almost five hundred kilometres from the Straits of Messina to Tuturano. Along the interminable, dusty, winding roads through the mountains of Italy's toe, their convoy of trucks had engaged in a deadly game of cat and mouse with what the guards called *Jabos*. From the fleeting glimpses through the truck's canvas, Jox had identified a pair of USAAF P-38s stalking them, despite the letters 'POW' clearly marked on the trucks' canopies. Lurching along the mountain roads had meant motion sickness for many of the other prisoners riding with Jox, and they were all very glad when released from their jolting torment.

Jox and the other new arrivals were herded down a corridor of barbed wire, watched intently by a diverse mob of Allied soldiers, some rather shabbier than others. There were barrels of tepid water waiting for the parched newcomers, desperate to rehydrate after the dust of the long journey.

'Wouldn't touch that if I were you, old chap,' called a voice from beyond the wire.

'Why, what's wrong with it?' asked Jox, unsure who he was actually talking to.

A scruffy fellow with the crowns of a major replied, 'One sure way of getting a dose of the Double D is by drinking that. I'd wait to get a brew on for some tea. Bit short of tea leaves, so it'll be a poor *chai*, but at least it won't give you the runs.

The camp's water is drawn from a dubious well which is rather too close to the latrines. I wouldn't touch it.'

'What on earth is Double D?'

'Diego Diarrhoea is what we call it,' grinned the moustachioed major. 'You'll all get it eventually, but there's no need to be first in line. Listen, you'd better crack on. You've got half an hour to stretch your legs and get that brew on before *appello*. After that, the camp commandant, *Colonnello* Gustavo Flavius will no doubt wish to address you.'

It emerged that the scruffy fellow had been in the camp for a long time. He introduced himself as Major Timothy Reid-Steele, an old India hand and proud battalion commander of the 1/5th Mahratta Light Infantry. A typical light infantryman, Reid-Steele was rather twitchy and constantly on the move. He was on the thin side and rather pale.

'Been in the bag since Tobruk,' he said. 'Born and bred in India, though, like my father before me. I'm a true son of the regiment.' He frowned. 'That's what makes me sick to the stomach, being separated from my boys. They get hauled back here when the Eyeties need them to do the dirty work, but otherwise, we officers are cooped up here and they're kept elsewhere. Can't for the life of me fathom why. My sepoys bleed every bit as red as the next man.' He glared at Jox. 'What d'you have to say about that?'

'Couldn't agree more,' replied Jox. 'But I'm not following you. I can see chaps from all over here, different services and ranks. Yanks, Poles, all sorts. Actually, I'd rather expected they'd keep officers and enlisted men apart, separate the air force from the army.'

'Yes, well, Jerry usually does that. They're always keen on distinctions and hierarchies. The Eyeties don't much care, shoving the lot of us together, excepting of course for that one thing.'

'What's that?'

'How pale your skin is,' growled Reid-Steele. 'Every one of my boys in the Indian Army volunteered. I don't see Jerry with hordes of devoted colonial troops. We have over two million loyal sepoys fighting by our sides, unappreciated by those tucked away in old Blighty. You ever been to India?'

'Actually, I was born there. My father's with the India Office. As a boy, I spent endless journeys on steamships between Scotland and India for the long holidays. I loved the country, its vibrancy, sights and smells, but I did find it cruel, with the caste system and poverty.'

'Been back recently?'

'Haven't seen my father for ages. I was pretty much brought up at boarding school near Stirling in Clackmannanshire. I consider myself Scottish — hard not to with a name like McNabb.'

'How funny,' mused Reid-Steele. 'We're from similar backgrounds, but in my head I'm completely Indian, despite my very English name.' He rubbed his growling belly. 'British food has never agreed with me. It all tastes the same and is the colour of mud. Personally, I can't live without the spices of India. Unfortunately, I've had to since being separated from my sepoys. It's playing ruddy havoc with my guts.' He looked crestfallen. 'Never mind all that, I'd better introduce you to Colonel du Boulay, our Senior British Officer, then get you back in time for *Colonnello* Flavius.'

'What's the colonel like?'

'Which one?' Reid-Steele asked, moustache bristling. 'Actually, they're both a pain in the arse, real sticklers for the rules. Ours is a typical guardsman with a rod up his backside, and theirs is a mildly aristocratic chap who takes himself awfully seriously. When things get tough, he's rather spineless but has a cruel streak, as you can see from those poor sods tied to the trees.'

Jox had noticed the strung-up men. Some of them had been moaning in the heat. 'Yes, I did see them. What on earth did they do to deserve that?'

'Tried to escape,' shrugged Reid-Steele. '*Colonnello* Flavius takes a dim view, sees it as a personal insult, a challenge to his authority.'

'That's outrageous,' said Jox. 'Can't a grievance be lodged with the Red Cross or something? What about the camp's escape committee?'

'Escape committee?' chuckled Reid-Steele. 'Swampy and the chaps tied to those trees are the escape committee. They got fed up with trying to convince Colonel du Boulay of their plans, so had a go on their own. I'm not suggesting anything fishy, but it seems awfully timely that the goons got wind of their schemes and nabbed them right from the off. Don't suppose they'll be trying that again.'

'You actually think our colonel could be complicit? Really?'

'Du Boulay is an Irish Guard, captured in Tunisia. He says he's related to General Alexander, who's in charge of all land forces in the Med. He takes on airs and graces, claiming he has all the gen. Quite how he could have that from behind the wire is beyond me. In any case, he is the SBO and never lets you forget it. Puts his blind faith in "Cousin Alex" and expects the Allies to rescue us any day. In the meantime, I've been sitting on my arse for two bloody years.' Reid-Steele shook his head. 'He's fixated on the idea that we must sit tight and cooperate. He's against any talk of escape, and that drove Swampy and his chums potty.'

'And who is this Swampy?'

'He's an American officer, a flyboy like you. He got shot down over France, I think. Not sure how he ended up here. He's a bit of a hothead, a real lively chap. He has just one eye but is full of beans, nonetheless. Been through a lot. I don't suppose he and his chaps will be in great shape now. Poor blighters.'

A short, dapper-looking British officer walked towards them. He wore a tall, peaked cap and a sheepskin jacket despite the mild evening. He glared at the men bound to the trees, tapping a bamboo swagger stick against his trouser leg, and then glanced up at Jox and Reid-Steele. Reid-Steele came to attention and saluted, and Jox followed suit.

'Good show, and you are...?' the man asked.

'Squadron Leader Jeremy McNabb, sir, commanding officer of No. 333 fighter squadron.'

'Squadron Leader, is it? You seem awfully young.' They shook hands. 'Piers du Boulay, Irish Guards. Welcome to the family, such as it is.' The colonel had a surprisingly high voice. 'We try to make it a home from home, don't we, Timmy?' Reid-Steele gave the pretence of a smile. 'So, tell me, how did you come to be one of us, Mr McNabb?'

'Ran into a spot of bother over the Straits of Messina,' replied Jox. 'Tangled with a night fighter, then got struck by flak in the wing. I was lucky to get her down in one piece, but I was on the wrong side of the water, so got nabbed by Jerry. Ever since I've been passed from pillar to post, ending up on a truck from Reggio to here.'

'Well, you're very welcome. We do our best to endure captivity,' said the colonel. 'It's no one's idea of fun, but it's sensible not to antagonise our hosts. They know we're winning the war, we know we are, and things will sort themselves out. We just need patience.'

Jox's face hardened. 'It's been drilled into me as a fighter pilot that my training is too valuable to waste in captivity. My duty as an officer and aviator is to escape. If that's not possible, then it's my duty to be as troublesome as I can be, to tie down the enemy's capabilities. I apologise if that makes your life as the SBO more difficult, but I give fair warning, I'll be no model prisoner.'

The colonel turned glacial. 'Squadron Leader, you *will* follow my orders!'

'I regret, sir, I cannot.'

'Damn it, McNabb, don't tell me you're another blasted hothead like that Yank over there. Look where that's got him.' Colonel du Boulay pointed with his swagger stick to one of the men tied to the trees.

The sound of iron being struck clanged across the dusty exercise yard. The entire camp was surrounded by a barbed wire fence and consisted of several rows of tents and numbered huts with corrugated iron roofs. At one end there were stone farm buildings, and at the other were gates giving onto the road. All around the camp perimeter, spaced every fifty yards, were fifteen-foot-high timber watchtowers. Each held a pair of soldiers overlooking the prisoners, one manning a Breda M37 machine gun, the other with a Beretta machine pistol across his back. Outside the farmhouse was the flag of the Kingdom of Italy waving limply in the breeze from a whitewashed pole. On a raised podium at its foot a large man stood with his hands on his hips, chin jutting skywards.

A voice was shouting commands between shrill blasts of a whistle.

'We'll speak again,' said du Boulay. 'Timmy, please tell McNabb the form. I'd better go and see what *Colonnello* Flavius has to say for himself.'

The clanging stopped and a tall Italian with stripes on his arm bellowed in his native language. He had the look of a career NCO, scowling at his men and the assembled prisoners with equal venom.

The prisoners who were familiar with the drill formed into squads, while brusque guards started roughly bundling the newcomers into place. Major Reid-Steele led Jox to the front of a squad of 'newbies', indicating that he should stand alongside officers of a similar rank. He then took his place in front of the contingent, standing behind diminutive Colonel Piers du Boulay. He was small in stature and that was accentuated by the size of the *Carabinieri* officer on the dais before him. Jox assumed this was the camp commander, *Colonnello* Flavius.

Flavius was a great bear of a man, with a shaven head and a blue-tinged five o'clock shadow on his chin and pate. He wore a grey uniform, shirt and tie, with red tabs on his lapels and decorations on his left breast. A tan-coloured Sam Browne belt ran across his chest, worn with black riding boots and a garrison cap with the flaming grenade badge of the *Carabinieri*.

He peered at the prisoners down his Roman nose and struck a martial pose. Jox recognised it as something he'd seen in newsreels, a stance often assumed by Benito Mussolini after giving a triumphal speech. It occurred to Jox that he was unlikely to be feeling terribly triumphant about anything, given the fall of Sicily, but perhaps the message hadn't trickled down here yet.

An Italian sergeant major bellowed for attention. He wore an oversized helmet and puttees wound up the legs of his grey trousers, baggy at the knee. Those used to the command smartly snapped their heads to the front. The newcomers followed as best they could, with Jox noting that Army prisoners were rather smarter than airmen.

'*Salute!*' the man shouted.

Several hundred Allied hands went up to their brows, palm outwards for the British Army and Royal Air Force, and palm down for the Royal Navy and US Armed Forces. There were a few exceptions, notably from the Poles giving their two-finger salute rather like British boy scouts. The *Carabinieri* raised their right arms in the Roman salute and the *Colonnello* pointed a dagger into the air, the ultimate Italian Fascist salute.

The men were put at ease and the Italian soldiers began checking the names of the prisoners that were already registered, whilst a young lieutenant recorded the details of the new arrivals. Waiting his turn, Jox estimated there must be a few thousand prisoners gathered together, a veritable army in waiting.

'Prisoners of Camp 85, I am *Colonnello* Gustavo Flavius, *comandante* of the camp. I am authority here. You have your officers, but here my word is law.' He spoke in a deep baritone, using excellent English. 'To our new guests, I say *benvenuto*. Here, we hope to live in peace while the war rages on. I will treat you fairly, if you behave as I expect. Officers are to set examples to the men, and there will be absolutely no escape attempts tolerated. We have all experienced how terrible war can be and should therefore be grateful to be away from it. Attempts to escape will be severely punished, understood?' He strode around the wooden platform, the timber creaking under his weight. '*Colonnello* du Boulay and I have an understanding, and I expect you all to honour it. Any breach will be severely reprimanded. You can see what happens to those who try.' He pointed his dagger towards the hooded men bound to the trees. 'I will not hesitate to use the techniques my men and I learnt in Africa dealing with the natives.' He smiled, revealing even, white teeth. 'But come, let's be comrades. Who knows where the winds of war will take us? What is most important is to survive and keep healthy. As you can see, we have extended the exercise facilities and built huts to accommodate our new arrivals. You have access to cigarettes, playing cards and newspapers, so life is not so bad. Our food is not so good, but you eat what we eat. We try to get fruit and vegetables when we can.'

Hands on his hips, he eyed the assembled men. A certain restlessness crept into the ranks under his glare. He gave a shark's smile. 'You must keep healthy. We must protect you from the dangers of a large number of men living closely together. Last winter, we had an epidemic of meningitis and lost men, yours and mine. This cannot happen again. It was because of the unclean habits of the *Askari* troops, so we cleared them out and created a separate camp. In my experience I've learned that the separation of races is the best way. All new arrivals will be disinfected, an unpleasant but necessary task. That is all.'

The prisoners dispersed from their formations across the raw earth of the newly cleared exercise yard. In the soil, Jox spotted a round pebble, then another roughly the same size. He put both in his pocket.

'You like the rocks?' asked a tall chap with dark hair standing on end. His accent sounded foreign, and Jox recognised they'd been in the same truck in the convoy. He was wearing an odd mismatch of a desert RAF uniform, shorts and a flight blouse, paired with a bright green V-neck jumper. He clicked his heels together and smiled, giving Jox the two-fingered Polish salute.

His eyes were intense and restless, and Jox could tell this wasn't an airman who would be content sitting out the war.

'Flying Officer Mieczysław Wyszkowski at your service, sir.' He laughed at Jox's reaction. 'My friends call me "Whisky". Easier to pronounce, and I developed quite a taste for it at RAF Grangemouth.'

'It's certainly easier to say. I'm Jeremy McNabb. You can call me…'

'Jox,' interrupted Wyszkowski. 'Squadron Leader Jox McNabb, yes, I've heard of you. One of my instructors, Squadron Leader Pritchard, spoke highly of his great friend, Jox.'

'You were trained by Pritch? He's one of my dearest friends. Well, it's good to meet you, so tell me, how did you come to be in this particular corner of paradise?'

'I am part of the *Polski Zespół Myśliwski*, which is the Polish Fighting Team of Desert Air Force in Tunisia. We take experienced pilots and fly together as a Polish unit to train before going back to lead more Polish squadrons. It was my bad luck to get shot down and captured in Sicily, just like you, I believe, Jox.'

'Gosh, the PFT? "Skalski's Circus?" Your lot come with a hell of a reputation. I met your CO "Stan" Skalski once, a really quiet, reserved sort of chap, terribly serious.'

'For us Poles, war is a serious business,' replied Wyszkowski. 'We all have family and friends suffering under the Nazis. This is no game for us. We have no illusions about why we fight.'

'I can assure you, I have my reasons too,' replied Jox. 'I can just picture your Skalski, balding with that hook nose. I'm told the Poles say he has the "instincts of a bird" and that the Germans call him the "flying death". That's quite a reputation.'

'He is a fine leader, but you have a reputation too. Not the sort of man, I think, who sits out the war behind a wire, whatever this Italian fool is asking of us.'

'Is it that obvious?' replied Jox, picking up another pebble.

'Takes one to know one.' Wyszkowski frowned. 'Why are you looking for stones?'

'For a game I have in mind. Something to pass the time and keep my brain active. Look for stones this size and shape. I need thirty-two.'

Wyszkowski picked up a pebble. 'Will this do? How does this game work?'

'I'll explain when I've got what I need. I'm also looking for a round board, something like a chopping board or a barrel lid.'

Wyszkowski grinned. 'A mind that keeps working, good. Come, we can do this later. Let's go check out the hut where we've been assigned bunks. I checked and we're together in B7. Apparently, it's called "The Lone Star" hut.'

'And why is that?'

'No idea, but let's find out,' said Wyszkowski. 'We can explore the camp at the same time.'

'Lead on, but wait, don't we have to be disinfected first?'

'There'll be a queue for that, and I'm told they're not very strict here, despite what that colonel was saying.' He shrugged. 'You know the Italians, *la dolce vita*, never in too much of a hurry. We can do it later. They'll start with the enlisted men. I'm certainly in no hurry to get fumigated.'

They crossed the exercise area where a game of football had begun. The men were playing with a lumpy leather ball, and the game was high-spirited, a mixture of accents interrupted by laughter, loud exclamations and ribald teasing. The players looked healthy enough, if a little underweight. The ball arched towards them and in one fluid motion Wyszkowski hooked it skilfully with his right foot, flicked it to his left, then spun around before passing it back.

'Christ mon, did ya see that?' exclaimed a scruffy Argyll and Sutherland Highlander with a broad Glaswegian accent. 'Need tae gie us a game sometime, sir.'

Wyszkowski waved. 'Maybe another time, thanks.'

'Nae bother.'

'You've played before,' said Jox.

'I played at school, then also for the Aviation Academy at Dęblin, and for Wojskowy *Klub Sportowy Legia Warszaw*, the Polish Army club before the war. In 1938, we even reached the first division play-offs but came third. Then the war came and everything was finished. You play?'

'No, not really,' Jox replied. 'A bit of cricket and rugby at school, but since I joined the service pretty young, flying became my thing.'

They reached a row of tired-looking canvas tents. Glancing through the flaps, Jox saw patched awnings with signs of leakage and bare earth covered in straw. Scattered around were stained palliasses stuffed with more straw and serving as mattresses. There were a dozen per tent, each with blankets and a grubby striped pillow. One end of the tent was evidently used as a washing station with two galvanized metal tubs for water. This accommodation was for the enlisted men, and perhaps explained why they looked so grubby.

Jox was shocked at the primitive conditions. In bad weather or during the winter, life under canvas like this would be utterly miserable. It was warm enough now, but winter was coming. He remembered how grim winter had been in Tunisia, but at least then they had been in new, watertight tents. These ragged structures were no doubt veterans of the Great War. He was surprised how rough the camp was, especially since it must have been almost two years old, as prisoners from Tobruk were here. It was clear that POW camps were well down the list of priorities, and the infrastructure was struggling to cope with the influx of new inmates.

Beyond the tents and shielded from sight, but by no means smell, were the latrines. Girding themselves before their inspection, Jox and Wyszkowski saw that the facilities were little more than a three-metre pit with lateral planks to sit upon and do your business. Apart from being far from sanitary, Jox was struck by the precarious perch the construction provided. Falling in didn't bear thinking about.

Feeling rather guilty about the conditions the rest of the men were enduring, Jox was embarrassed to discover the officers' accommodation was in much better nick. The timber huts were numbered and lettered, and they found Hut B7 easily enough. Wyszkowski knocked on the door and they entered. Inside, it was quite dark as most of the windows were shuttered. Under the pitched roof it was gloomy, and the large single room smelt of cigarettes, raw pine wood and men's feet. The flooring was rough wood, and Jox made a mental note to avoid walking with bare feet or socks in the future, since there'd be plenty of nasty splinters waiting. The boards creaked under their feet on the narrow concrete plinths that kept them off the bare earth underneath. There were about twenty bunks, and each officer was provided with a straw palliasse, a blanket and a pillow in his allocated three-tiered bunk along the walls.

There were four scruffy men in the room. One was lying on his bunk, the other three smoking and playing cards. A blond fellow looked up. '*Ja*, what the hell do you want?'

Wyszkowski bristled. 'Is that the way you usually address a superior officer?' he demanded. 'Get on your damned feet!'

The fair-haired man sighed. 'What's your problem, man?' he asked loudly in a South African accent.

'Hey, boys, cool it,' drawled one of the others, a thin-faced fellow with a big nose and a toothpick in his mouth. He pulled his companion back to his chair. 'Don't pay no mind to old Fokke. He's a bit flak-happy and cusses way too much.' He got to his feet and stretched out his hand. 'Captain Greg Carver, 98th Bombardment Group. I'm a B-24 Liberator pilot. They call me "Tex" because I'm from Galveston.'

They shook hands.

'That's quite a handshake, Tex,' said Jox. 'I'm Jox McNabb, and this is Whisky.'

'Flying Officer Mieczysław Wyszkowski at your service, sir.'

'Nice to meet you, Whisky. We sure could do with a spot of that right now.' Carver glanced back at Jox. 'Yeah, I guess we B-24 jockeys do develop strong arms lugging those flying coffins around the sky.' He grimaced. 'When we got hit, it was only me and Shooter who made it out.' He stared for a moment. 'I'm sorry, this here is "Shooter" Vollick. His real name's Bruce. He's my Bombardier and is from Texas too.'

Vollick nodded through a veil of cigarette smoke. He was ruddy-faced and wore a sheepskin B3 Bomber hat on his head. It was yellowed and a bit scorched, with brown flaps hanging over his ears. His shirtsleeves were rolled up, revealing several tattoos, the image of a pair of scissors on one hand, a cowboy's six-shooter on the other. 'Howdy.' He eyed the newcomers, then smiled. 'Full house, aces high,' he added, laying his cards on the table and picking up the three cigarettes lying there.

'God damn it, Shooter,' said Carver. 'Every time.' He sighed, then patted the arm of the blond South African in a sweat-stained Desert Air Force uniform, not unlike Wyszkowski's. 'This foul-mouthed feller is Fokke De Boer from the

Transvaal, South Africa. He can't hear too good and has got a filthy mouth on him. He don't mean it, just got his nerves frazzled some.'

'His name is really Fokke?' asked a puzzled Wyszkowski.

'Yup, like them "Butcher Birds", but spelt a bit different,' grinned Carver. 'He means no harm, just gets kinda loud and sweary. Been on edge ever since his Kittyhawk got obliterated over the western desert. He's one of them "Billy Boys" of No. 1 Squadron South African Air Force. Told us the story of how he brought down a Stuka — he was crying out their squadron's traditional war cry over the radio when he got thumped. Can't remember how he got out of the aircraft, but he woke up in the desert, nerves shot to hell, deaf as a post, just in time to get picked up by an *Afrika Korps* patrol.'

An angry voice called out from across the room, from the chap huddled under his blankets. 'For Christ's sake, would you put a sock in it? Some of us are trying to sleep.'

'Yeah, we'd better take it outside,' said Carver, lowering his voice. 'Charlie's not feeling too good. A touch of the fever.' He led them out of the hut. 'It's chow time anyhow. We'd better get going, don't want to miss it, but don't expect anything too fancy.'

As they filed through the door, Wyszkowski pointed to the symbol painted on it. 'Why the yellow star?'

'For the great state of Texas. It's just a coincidence, but half the fellers in the hut are Texans, so hey, we try to remember the Alamo. Kind of a morale thing.'

'I see,' said Jox. 'And what's Charlie's story?'

'That's Flight Lieutenant Champagne. He's feeling kinda flat at the moment. He's a night fighter, on Hurricanes out of Malta. Got shot down in Sicily on an intruder mission over an enemy airfield. Been in the bag since 1941. A solid guy, just not in great shape. Come to think of it, none of us are.'

'What's this supposed to be?' Jox asked later, peering suspiciously at the sludge in his mess tin.

'*Orecchiette nera*,' replied Carver. 'We're in Puglia, the poor, southern part of Italy. This is typical Puglian pasta, shaped to look like monkey's ears, judging by the colour.'

Jox shuddered. He hadn't had the best of experiences with monkeys, having been bitten by one in Tunisia.

'What are these green things?' asked Wyszkowski.

Carver laughed. 'Y'all better get used to it. Them's wild herbs, nettles or dandelions, whatever can be collected from the fields. Force it down. It's all you're gonna get. We get real hungry real quick waiting for Red Cross parcels to arrive. With luck, every couple of weeks they do come, otherwise it's this or nothing. You'll get used to a monophagic diet.'

'What the hell's that?'

Carver smiled, the ever-present toothpick in his teeth. 'A diet where you eat the same thing over and over again, every day. It's quite common in southern Italy, but it takes getting used to, especially if you're a Texan brought up on buttermilk and inch-thick steaks.'

'How come you know so much about it?'

'I've got plenty of time on my hands, but actually I also did a couple of years in medical school before I signed up. I guess I may get back to doctoring eventually.'

'A useful chap to have around then.'

'Maybe,' replied Carver. 'That reminds me, we need to get you two paired up and registered for Red Cross care packages. They're usually shared between two, but sometimes that can go to four or five when things get lean. Depends on how much consignments coming from Geneva get plundered on the way. This whole damned country is starving, so that happens a lot. I guess we should be grateful for what we get.' He sighed and licked his lips. 'Them parcels are all that keep us from starving.'

Jox looked around the prisoners' canteen. The dining hall was a stone building full of ragged soldiers. The footballers outside had seemed in high spirits, but in here, the grim reality of meagre rations reminded Jox of where he was.

Carver sat back and lit a precious cigarette. 'It's a good idea to buddy up with someone that's different to you. Me and Shooter didn't realise, but the parcels from Switzerland are from different countries, all trying to cater for the tastes of their nationals. Contents differ. The Brit packs are pretty good, with canned meat and sweet stuff like biscuits, pudding or tinned fruit. Our Yank ones got more tobacco, plus canned bacon, salmon, corned beef, powdered coffee and milk, sometimes even candy bars. I hear tell the Indian Army parcels are full of spices and curry powder, real precious things to make bland stuff taste better.'

Shooter Vollick joined the conversation. Talking about food and parcels was clearly a favourite pastime. 'We get some non-food stuff too, like socks and underwear, but the food and tobacco is what's important, to trade with as well as to eat. You'll find cigarettes are the currency of the camp. You can get anything if you've got enough tobacco. Do y'all smoke?'

'I don't,' replied Jox. 'How about you, Whisky?'

'Sometimes, but if it's worth more not to, then I won't.'

'Good idea,' said Vollick. 'I admire that discipline. Me and Tex ain't that smart. Tobacco's the only comfort we've got in this hellhole. If you manage to keep it up, all the better. Back to my point on parcel buddies: Fokke is paired with a Free French pilot called Merriell Perrin. We call him Muriel, cos it's kinda funny and it annoys him. He's one of the guys tied to that tree with old Swampy out back. Swampy's parcel buddy is Johnny Lorelli from Austin, Texas. He's from Italian stock and speaks the lingo, which I guess would have come in handy if they'd managed to reach open country. Their punishment is to stay there till tomorrow morning's *appello*, so we'll see what shape they're in. Anyhow, have a think on who you're gonna buddy with. By the way,' he added, 'I cut hair and do tattoos, if you're interested. Won't cost you more than a cigarette.' He smiled and got to his feet, heading for a tub of soapy water to rinse off his mess tin.

Carver stretched his back. 'I'm guessing it's time we got back to the hut. The goons don't like us out after dark. This far south sundown drops kinda sudden, like in the desert. We need to get y'all squared away with bunks and bedding before they cut the power.'

'They cut the power at night? That doesn't make a lot of sense,' Jox said.

'Sometimes it's deliberate, sometimes it ain't,' replied Carver. 'Depends on whether raids are coming over. Brindisi is to the west and Taranto to the east. They're both important ports, so get bombed regular. Come on, boys, let's go.'

The Lone Star Hut was full now. Jox and Wyszkowski were allocated a bunk, the Pole on the top tier, Jox in the middle. The bottom bunk belonged to Swampy, the leader of the escape party. They were introduced to a number of men, who nodded, waved or crossed over to shake hands. Murphy Lynch, Freddy Fell and Barry Moreno were all Texans who had arrived together and were known as the 'Three Amigos'. They had been the co-pilot, bombardier and navigator of *Little Lolita*, a B-17 brought down after a raid on Naples. They'd lost their pilot, referred to reverentially as 'Big John', who'd kept the burning aircraft level while his crew had baled out.

Colin Campbell was a tall, freckled and morose Scot, the sole survivor of his Blenheim crew. Ronald Vroom was a Kiwi, a Curtiss P-40 Kittyhawk pilot who had been shot down by the 'Star of Africa', the German ace Hans-Joachim Marseille. Ronnie Pass was a Brummie, an RAF Engineering Officer and the only non-flyer in the hut. He'd been captured by an *Afrika Korps* patrol whilst leading a convoy carrying aircraft parts across the Libyan desert. Finally, there was Second Lieutenant Neil Kennedy, who was technically Army, but served with the Glider Pilot Regiment, piloting a Horsa during the disastrous night drop on the first night of the invasion of Sicily. His co-pilot and most of the glider's paratroopers hadn't survived the impact in a gully at Ponte Grande, their objective for that night. Kennedy was as timid as a mouse, carrying his survivor's guilt like a millstone around his neck.

After lights out, the barrack room quickly quietened but outside cicadas were producing a shrill buzzing that sounded like a wire brush rubbing against the metal fuselage of an aircraft. What with a chorus of snoring, it was like trying to settle down in a lumberyard, and there was no way Jox could sleep with that racket.

From a distance came the slow, chilling whine of a siren. It grew to a crescendo, into a terrifying sound Jox had always hated. Not because it reminded him of the Blitz or Malta, but rather his earliest school days. Every term, his boarding house had held a fire drill in the middle of the night. It was the senior boys' responsibility to wake the youngsters and get them out of bed into dressing gowns, before filing from their dorms, or dorses as they were called, onto Academy Place. There, dazed and shivering, they were counted and checked against the register, before being allowed back to bed. This exercise was supposed to happen in a calm, orderly fashion, but the 'sport' for the older boys was to run screaming into the dormitories, terrifying the sleeping youngsters. Invariably, no small number returned to bed with wet pyjama bottoms. Therefore, Jox had always hated the fire drills and the sound of the hand-cranked siren.

The sound drove Jox from his bunk. He tiptoed across the hut to the shuttered window, mindful of the wooden floorboards, carefully placing his bare feet to avoid the splinters. He peered between the planks across the window, his nose pressed against them. They smelled of creosote and musty wood.

The camp's searchlights were extinguished, the cicadas hushed by the commotion. The continuous drone of multiple engines reached Jox, then the bark of flak guns, followed inevitably by rumbling serial detonations, flashing like lightning against billowing smoke and clouds. He could feel reverberations through his bare feet and he glanced at his scorched wristwatch. The luminescent hands shone through the clouded glass, indicating it was ten forty-three. Earlier, the sky had been very dark, but it was now lit by the glow of fires across the horizon. The long, sloping plain down to Brindisi provided the perfect amphitheatre for the awe-inspiring spectacle of destruction.

'I was there the night Coventry burned,' said a voice behind him. 'My entire childhood went up in flames. My granddad too, as it happens. He'd survived the whole of the last war in the trenches only to get burnt to a crisp in his own bed. Tough old sod, but he didn't deserve that.'

Jox turned and saw it was Charlie Champagne. 'Are you feeling any better?' he asked.

'Oh, I'm all right,' Champagne replied. 'A touch of the malaria; it comes and goes. Got eaten alive by the mossies on Sicily when I was on the run. The only reason they caught me was because I got so sick that they found me passed out in some olive grove, trembling and sweating.'

'Much the same as one of my men, Spud Inverarity. He got caught because he was sick in Sicily, but managed to escape from his POW camp, and ended up getting rescued after spending the best part of a week in an open boat. Sunburnt to hell. He recovered, but the last time I saw him, he'd crashed his Spit and got badly knocked about. He'll bounce back — hard as nails is our Spud.' Jox laughed. 'I'm Jox, by the way.'

'I heard,' said Champagne with a tired smile, briefly illuminated by the flash of a distant explosion. His face had an unhealthy pallor, covered in a sheen of sweat. He was hugging himself as if he was cold, despite the balmy night. 'Did you know that after they bombed Coventry, a new verb was created? To "coventrate" means to absolutely devastate a section of a city by concentrated bombing. I guess that's all that marks my granddad's death on the fourteenth of November 1940. The week before I took him to a Guy Fawkes bonfire party down at the rugby club by the cathedral. We had sausages on sticks — he loved that. Ended up getting his own, rather larger bonfire, poor old fella. There was nothing left to bury. He's why I joined up, to have a go at those bombing bastards, but now I'm stuck here. Helpless and weak as a kitten. Well, at least that lot are copping it.'

'I don't think it's Jerry getting a tanning — more likely civilians near the port.'

There was a boom, louder than the others, and the night sky turned bright orange, light enough to reveal the looming black silhouettes of several Avro Lancaster bombers with their characteristic four engines and double tails. These were area-bombing creatures of the night, as the USAAF concentrated on precision daylight raids. It seemed unlikely that this made much of a difference to the Italian civilians on the receiving end.

'Something rather big got hit there,' Jox said. 'I saw some spectacular oil fires during the Battle of Britain, causing utter devastation, everything burning up in firestorms. Looked rather like that.'

The pair stared at the distant flames. They were mesmerising. At one point the fire seemed to be flowing like a river.

'The last time I saw something like that was in Scotland,' said Jox. 'Over Clydebank. On a hill above the town, there was a huge warehouse at the Auchentoshan Distillery. It got hit and millions of gallons of whisky were set ablaze and flowed like lava into a nearby burn, where it poured downstream towards the Clyde. It was a lot more convincing as a lava field than the real thing I saw flying over Mount Etna, unfortunately just before I got shot down and captured.'

'Strewth, you've been all over,' said Champagne, then he started to cough.

'It's certainly been a long war.'

'Well, you can put your feet up now.'

'Why do people keep saying that? That's not my way, no chance. First oppo I get, I'm off.'

'Not mine either,' Champagne replied. 'This damned fever has just taken the spark from me, sapped my strength and spirit.' He was shivering. 'If you do come up with a plan, escape or otherwise, you'd better discuss it with Swampy first. We elected him as head of the escape committee, since he keeps trying to escape. Of course, that rather depends on what state he's in after getting flogged half to death and left out there overnight.' He frowned, suddenly concerned. 'Gosh, I hope they'll be all right with all this flak flying about.'

Jox peered through the planked window. 'Should be fine. It's further away than it looks.'

'Doesn't take much. I've seen the tiniest bits of flak bring down bloody great aircraft.'

'Yeah, that's true,' said Jox. 'Tell me, who's this Swampy? I keep hearing his name.'

'He's a Yank flyboy. I think he was captured in France, but for some reason he was transported here. I'm not sure how, but he lost an eye in the process. Maybe that explains why he hates Jerry and the Eyeties so much. He'll do anything to make their lives difficult. Gets into all kinds of scrapes and bother, but that never seems to stop him. The more mischief he gets into, the more the chaps adore him. Drives old Du Boulay potty. They don't see eye to eye.'

Champagne shuffled back to his bunk and after one last glance at the fiery scene outside, Jox followed him.

CHAPTER THREE

The next morning, the air outside was heavy with smoke, the chemical stink of cordite and burnt brick dust filtering into the huts. Particles had blown high into the atmosphere, seeding the clouds, and had come back to earth as red rain that was currently tapping a tattoo on the corrugated roofs of the huts, and gushing down the grooves to pour from the down pipes like arterial blood. Reaching the raw earth of the exercise yard, the rain created a muddy mire dotted with the type of pebbles that Jox had been looking for.

'Fire and water, working together,' said Jox, watching the deluge through a hut window.

'Sorry, what was that?' asked Wyszkowski, who was busy making up his bunk. Somehow, he'd been able to sleep through the night, despite all the commotion. When Jox had asked him how he'd managed it, he replied matter-of-factly, 'Never have trouble sleeping. It's an escape.'

Jox's own fatigue was scratching behind his eyelids. 'Must be the rest of an innocent man — someone with no guilty conscience.'

Wyszkowski frowned. 'Why do *you* have a guilty conscience?'

'Maybe not exactly a guilty conscience. I'm just mulling over the regrets, missed opportunities and disappointments in life. You know, the great what ifs.'

Wyszkowski ran a hand through his mass of curly hair. 'You ponder over things too much. For me, there is no think, only do. The consequences are the consequences. Dwelling on things only gets in the way of doing something about them.'

Jox smiled, admiring the brutal simplicity of that philosophy. The door of the barrack swung open with the warning of 'Goons!' Men scrambled to cover up whatever they were doing.

The tall *Carabiniere* who'd led yesterday's *appello* sauntered into the room, his heavy boots leaving muddy red footprints like a blood trail on the creaking floorboards. He was flanked by a pair of guards with bayonetted rifles, their combined weight making the rough timber creak.

'*Attenzione*, for you new ones, I am *Primo Capo Squadra* Rossetti. I look for *Capo Squadriglia* Jox McNabb.' His words were respectful, but his tone was brusque and his eyes were like those of a hungry wolf.

Jox slipped down from his bunk, inserting his stockinged feet into the flight boots underneath. He stretched his aching back. 'That's me. What is it?'

'The *Comandante*, he say you come, he wants to talk you.'

Jox nodded and followed him. Once outside, Jox and his escort crossed the muddy exercise yard. He leant down to pick up a pebble, identical to the dozen or so that were under his pillow. One of the guards shoved him for his trouble.

The tented accommodation of the enlisted men was in a sorry mess. How they'd coped with last night's raid and the subsequent downpour, God only knew. As for the poor chaps lashed to the trees, hooded and slumped, they were worryingly still. The pair reached the far end of the farm buildings, the camp's administrative block, beside the guards' accommodation. Inside, it was surprisingly luxurious, if a little dated. Jox was instructed to wait in a corridor that was wallpapered with elegant pink stripes. On the walls there were gloomy photographs of family groups of ancestral farmers. At the bottom of the corridor, a gloss-varnished door led to

Colonnello Flavius's office, as indicated by gaudy gold lettering below drawn fasces, the emblem of the Italian National Fascist Party. It consisted of an axe tied within in a bundle of wooden rods, representing the power of Roman justice over life or death.

Jox wasn't kept waiting long. A pretty young woman opened the door and smiled. She was wearing the drab grey uniform of a female auxiliary, her dark hair untidy and tumbling from a hastily placed cap. The neck tie worn loose at her pale throat seemed rather at odds with her full eye makeup and the smudged crimson on her lips. 'Please come in, Squadron Leader McNabb,' said a deep voice from within the room behind her.

Jox entered to find the colonel wiping his mouth with the back of his hand. Flavius's big feet were in riding boots, resting on the desk. He lifted them off, sat up and smiled, placing his elbows on the arms of his chair. 'The famous Jox McNabb, the British fighter ace with twenty kills to his name. The dossier provided by the *Luftwaffe*'s Military Intelligence says you're quite the prize for us.'

He stared at Jox until it began to feel awkward. 'Your presence in my camp causes me a problem.' He jutted his chin out as he spoke, like at the previous evening's parade. 'You see, I have been a loyal *soldati* and follower of *Il Duce*, from the very beginning. I have served him faithfully in Libya, Eritrea, Somalia and Ethiopia. I was there in our glorious days, fighting and bleeding in the bad times too. I have done things I'm not so proud of — things that people might misunderstand. And now, for what?' His face was grave. 'Our king's head has been turned by that traitor Badoglio and together they will extinguish the fire within our beloved Italy. We now face defeat and dishonour, and our only hope is to slip quietly into peace as history passes over us.'

He was silent for a moment. 'You see, that is why I insist that no one should attempt escape. It attracts attention and problems for us all. After the terrible things I've seen, all I want is a quiet life.' He rubbed his red eyes with large knuckles, then ran anxious hands over his shaven head. 'This is not the reawakened Roman Empire that I was promised. Instead, we must now swallow the bitter pill of compromise. If we must, then I hope to do so quietly.' He sighed. 'Now you have come, bringing attention and notoriety to this corner of Puglia, a place where I hoped to be forgotten.'

'I'm not following you, Colonel,' said Jox. 'I don't see how my presence here affects any plans you may or may not have. I'm just a prisoner, the one being held against my will.'

'Yes, but you are not alone. There are, how you say, many other "high profile" prisoners gathered here. We call you the *Prominente*. *Oberst* von Wella keeps sending me more and more, amassing a glittering collection, and I don't understand why. What I *do* know is that you are bound to attract attention and cause me problems, not at all what I want. The *Tedeschi* will surely come for you and when they do, it will be in force. You are far too important to simply be abandoned, and once they are here, I fear they will never leave. They will force us to dig in and fight, and then what becomes of my peaceful backwater? It will take centre stage, a bloody battlefield, and if that is to happen, I want to understand the reason why.'

'I'm sorry, sir, I've no idea what you are talking about.'

'Why is von Wella collecting a galaxy of bright stars? There is you, the Pole from the famous Skalski's flying circus, *Colonnello* du Boulay, who is *Generale* Alexander's cousin. *Capitano* Richard Carver is also here; he is *Generale* Montgomery's stepson.

Among the *Americani*, we have *Generale* Patton's son-in-law, *Colonnello* John Waters, captured at Sidi Bou Zid in Tunisia, plus the son of a famous Southern millionaire and industrialist. We even have a Hollywood movie star, Red Cable — you know, the one with the big ears and thin moustache. He was a gunnery officer in a B-17 of the 351st Bomb group doing some propaganda films when he was shot down with the whole of his crew.'

'It's all news to me, sir,' replied Jox. 'I only got here yesterday. All I can confirm is that I've met *Oberst* von Wella. He leaves quite an impression with all those scars and that powerful cologne. I don't think he liked me very much, but I've no idea what he may be planning.' Jox squared his shoulders. 'I give fair warning: I will not collaborate with anything that goes against my oath as a British officer.'

'Ah yes, honour, duty and sworn oaths,' sighed Flavius. 'We've had plenty of those and look where that got us.' He smiled sadly. 'Thank you for your honesty, Squadron Leader. I can see you are a man of honour. I, too, was one once.' He rapped his fingers on the surface of his desk. 'We will need to be careful, as things unfold. The *Tedeschi* are becoming unpredictable, and Von Wella is cunning and cruel. He is a fanatic and certainly up to something. We should all be concerned. You and the others are important to him, but we must find out why. If you agree, I will share what I discover, if you will do the same for me.'

'May I ask, sir, why are you discussing this with me, rather than Colonel du Boulay? Surely he's Senior British Officer here?'

Flavius shrugged. 'Yes, he is senior but is also a rather foolish man, vain and self-important. With him everything is about appearances, jealously protecting his place in the hierarchy. He says he has the interest of his men at heart, but the truth is he only watches out for himself. He is where he is, not because of any talent, experience, or expertise, but because he is well connected and related to someone important. In war, that stands for little, and it is foolish men like that who get other soldiers killed. You must surely have met such busy fools in your RAF. How you say, the pedantic, small-minded martinets. I have met many, far too many, and the brave boys that followed them lie dead in the desert sands. We must not let foolish men drag us down. Are we in agreement?'

Jox held his gaze, then nodded. 'We are.'

'Thank you, Squadron Leader. You may go now.'

Jox left Flavius brooding at his desk. The transformation from the man posturing on stage yesterday was remarkable. Now he looked utterly deflated, and Jox wondered if this might be happening right across the ranks of the Italian military leadership. He'd seen plenty of Italian prisoners in Libya, Tunisia, and Sicily, and recalled that most looked rather pleased at the prospect of captivity and the end of their war. Nevertheless, he'd always expected that Fascist resolve would harden when it came to defending their homeland.

It appeared that the opposite was happening, which must surely be good news, as the Allies made their way up Italy's 'leg' before the Germans got fully mobilised and came down to meet them in real force. Perhaps Jox's time as a prisoner might not be as long or permanent as he'd feared. Perhaps sitting tight until liberated wasn't the worst idea in the world, especially given wavering Italian sentiment. The thought did have some appeal, but Jox knew there were still plenty of hardened opponents out there. Men like General Baade and Colonel von Wella, both impressive and terrifying in their different ways. Facing tough men of that calibre told him the war undoubtedly still had a long way to go.

He'd read somewhere that the geography of southern Italy was ideal for defensive warfare and correspondingly challenging for attackers. This may in fact have explained why Hannibal, starting from ancient Tunisia, had chosen to attack Rome by going 'the long way around', over to Iberia, now modern Spain, then following the southern coastline of modern France to enter what was now Italy from the north. Of course, his troops and the legendary elephants still had to make it over the Alps to deliver battle, but it seemed no coincidence that going up the length of Italy was perceived as the worse of two evils. He wished Doc Ridgway, his friend and the squadron intelligence officer, was here to explain things.

Most of what he'd seen on the western side of the country was mountainous with narrow roads winding up steep, overlooked valleys. Beaches and prospective landing grounds were invariably narrow, dominated by heights and well within the range of hidden artillery inland. Defenders had the landscape, topography and the cover of extensive vegetation to hide in and observe from, whilst attackers were always visible and exposed out on the sea or the landing grounds. Granted, the Allies had naval and increasingly air superiority, but they had to find the enemy first before they could get at them.

From an aviation perspective, much of Italy still lay beyond the range of Allied fighters. Currently, only the P-38 Lightning had anything like the range to loiter for any useful amount of time as far up the country as Naples. Long-range bomber attacks from bases in Tunisia and Sicily were unescorted beyond there, and despite claims that tight defensive formations of Flying Fortresses could take care of themselves, the catastrophic losses amongst bomber groups were evidence to the contrary. To his chagrin, Jox had learnt how formidable the flak defences at the Straits of Messina had been, and he had little doubt they would be equally murderous as the Allies advanced northwards. He was also aware that on the other side of the western coastal mountains, including mighty Vesuvius, there were a number of large Axis aviation complexes, notably at Foggia, between Naples and the 'spur' of Italy. These were still beyond Allied range and could easily deploy a murderous intensity of fighter interceptors, not to mention a bomber force ranged against Allied shipping or seaborne landings, all within range of home airfields. Experts at defensive fortifications like General Baade were no doubt already working on successive defensive lines receding like the tide up the length of the country.

It was true that the *Luftwaffe* had received a bloody nose in Sicily, but one thing Jox had always respected was his opponents' ability to bounce back, reform, refit, and savagely counterattack. The morale of Italy's *Regia Aeronautica* might well be wavering, but he had no doubt men like General Galland and his seasoned *Experten* were still out there, and many desperate air battles lay ahead, if only he could get back in there to contribute.

He considered the many scenarios, as he made his way back to the barrack hut. Absentmindedly, he saluted Colonel du Boulay and Major Reid-Steele as he passed them. The pair were in animated conversation, but stopped abruptly when they saw him. The colonel raised his swagger stick and mumbled, 'Carry on, carry on.' Reid-Steele smiled but didn't hold Jox's gaze. It occurred to Jox that people stuck behind the wire for a long while soon started acting rather oddly. Would he go similarly batty if he stayed here long enough?

He'd missed breakfast, such as it was, because of the meeting with Flavius, so he was grateful when Tex Carver offered to share the remnants of his last American Red Cross POW food package.

'It's not much, buddy, just some dried raisins and powdered coffee. I suggest you get some boiling water, safer for your gut, then pop them both in together and let the fruit absorb the liquid and the coffee. Does taste kinda weird, but old Swampy loves it — calls it *Kriegie* Gumbo.'

Jox was boiling a kettle over the hut's woodburning stove when there was a commotion outside. He glanced up and saw the 'Three Amigos' and Fokke De Boer carrying a slumped body onto a bunk on the other side of the hut. They were followed by Vollick, Wyszkowski and the two Ronnies carrying a second figure. Barging him aside, they manoeuvred their load to the lowest cot of Jox's three-tiered bunk.

'Where's the third chap?' asked Jox, realising these must be the men who had been punished overnight. The one on Jox's bunk was still hooded. He groaned, arching a freckled, mosquito-bitten back as the blanket beneath him made contact with the raw wounds from the lash. 'Gawd darn it, that hurts,' he hissed, the hessian hood pulsing as he gasped. 'Get this damned thing off, it's choking me.'

'Here, stop wriggling,' said Vollick. 'I can't undo the knot if you don't. It's too tight and I ain't got no knife. Take it easy, Swampy. Tex, get over here and take a look at him.'

From the other cot, a tired voice asked in a French accent, 'Where is Johnny? I can hear Swampy, but where is Lorelli?' Merriell Perrin's hood was pulled from his head, revealing a dark mop of hair, a Gallic nose and several days' beard growth.

'Where *is* Johnny?' asked Vollick, addressing no one in particular.

'Outside with the goons,' replied Ronald Vroom, the Kiwi. 'Rossetti, the head goon says Johnny's bought it. Caught a piece of shrapnel in one ear, didn't stand a chance. The goons are blaming the USAAF, and taking no responsibility at all.'

'Poor bastard,' said Vollick. 'Didn't deserve that, escape attempt or not.'

'*Ja*, but Muriel, I'm glad you made it in one piece, eh!' cried Fokke De Boer rather too loudly, as was his way. 'Please, no more escapes. We sit tight and wait for the cavalry to come to our rescue.'

'I missed you too. I hear you and I don't disagree,' replied Perrin. 'I've learnt the lesson, a hard one to swallow, but I'll stay here with you.'

'How's your friend Swampy bearing up?' Jox asked Carver. 'Need a hand with that string?'

'Wait a minute, I know that voice!' said Swampy from inside the hood. 'Hurry up, get this off!'

Carver fumbled and the hooded man's hands tugged until he finally managed to whip it off.

'Well, I'll be born on the bayou, if that ain't my old buddy, Jox McNabb!'

The face was bright red and bitten all over. One eye was just an empty socket but the other stared, a vivid blue colour. There were raw lash marks on his shoulders, but there was no doubting that it was Darren 'Bayou' Beans sitting before Jox. The last time Jox had seen him was just before he went down over France during a doomed operation known as the Morlaix disaster. It was a voice back from the dead, battered and bruised, yet very much alive.

'Someone get some water,' said Carver, dabbing Beans' shoulders with mercuric oxide solution on a cotton ball. Earlier, he'd explained that the American care packages included No. 4 POW medical kits containing enough medicines to care for a hundred men for a month.

'Here, he can have my tea,' said Jox, rushing to the big American's bedside.

Beans drank thirstily, oblivious to how hot it was. He exhaled mightily, blowing like a great bull. 'God, I hate Limey tea, but thanks anyway, Jox.' He reached out with a pitted, sunburnt hand and grasped Jox's. His single, pale blue eye fixed on Jox with unnerving intensity, its partner an empty grey pocket. He squeezed Jox's hand. 'Good to see you, buddy.' Both eyes were brimming with tears. He covered them with his hands and began to sob. 'Good Lord, I made such a mess of things at Morlaix when I took over from you. We lost so many of the boys, and I was terrified you'd get the blame. All because of my damned fool behaviour.'

'Never mind that, Bayou,' said Jox. 'Let's get you patched up and back on your feet. We've plenty of time to chat after that.'

'Later, yeah, later,' Beans said, suddenly looking tired. He patted Jox's hand like an ailing old man. His wrists had deep, angry-looking rope burns that would doubtless leave scars. 'Almost makes it worthwhile, getting these stripes, just to see you again. A chance to make amends.' A tear slipped down his ravaged face, and he cuffed it away. 'I mean it, buddy.'

'Don't be so daft, Bayou,' replied Jox. 'You were never at fault.'

Beans looked back at him, unconvinced. He turned to Carver. 'Thanks for fixing me up, Tex. How are the other boys doing?'

Carver winced. 'Muriel's getting patched up now, but Johnny didn't make it.'

Beans was silent for a moment, then he looked up. 'This tea's better than I expected, Jox, but I could really murder a cup of Joe. Got any coffee left from the last package run?'

'I got some,' piped up Vollick, reaching into the pocket of his USAAF bomber jacket. 'Here you go, Jox. There's just a little twist, mind.'

'I'll make it,' offered Wyszkowski. 'You keep talking with your friend, Jox.'

'Who's your buddy with the accent?' asked Beans.

'You can hardly talk,' grinned Jox, 'Mr Yeeha, "Born on the bayou" from the great state of Louisiana. You keep it respectful, Whisky's my friend and he's a far better fighter pilot than either of us.'

'Whiskey? Hell, I'd be happy for a lick of that,' said Beans. 'My head hurts and these shoulders feel like steak on the grill.'

'That'll be dehydration,' said Carver. 'As for the sting, you're gonna have to suck it up. Can't do nothing for the pain, except give you a couple of aspirins.'

Beans' torso and arms were streaked with the yellow ointment, which covered the wounds from the whip, the rope burns on his arms and a myriad of insect bites.

'I hope you didn't get bitten by anything too nasty,' said Carver, finishing up application of the ointment. 'There's a chance of malaria, but you're lucky there's no botfly here in Italy. If you'd been left like that in your Louisiana swamps, you wouldn't have escaped them wrigglers getting under your skin. You take it easy now. Rest up, you need time to heal.'

'Roger that, Tex,' Beans replied wearily. 'I ain't gonna argue.'

It was a few days before Beans or Merriell Perrin were in any fit state to tell their story. Jox had learned that Perrin had served in Greece, Crete and the Western Desert. His Hurri-bomber was downed during the Battle of El Alamein, but he'd not been rescued like Jox and was captured instead.

The pair succumbed to raging fevers the first night, shivering and sweating for forty-eight hours. They emerged, weak as lambs, numb and confused.

In the meantime, Jox and Wyszkowski registered with the Red Cross to benefit from the next delivery of care parcels, courtesy of the Order of St John via neutral Switzerland. As advised by Carver, Jox had paired with Beans, his previous partner having been Johnny Lorelli. Wyszkowski partnered with a Polish-American airman. Once they'd buddied up, the Poles began jogging around the camp to keep fit and active, but also to scout the grounds. They kept well within the wire perimeter and clear of the single knee-height "no cross" wire. They spoke to each other in their native tongue, all the while being watched by guards in their timber towers. Whilst doing their circuits, they familiarised themselves with the surroundings, but also gathered the remaining pebbles Jox had asked them for. His hut-mates were all intrigued as to their purpose, and Jox was enjoying being mysterious.

He was actually assembling a homemade Marble Solitaire board. He'd got into the game whilst recovering from his rabies vaccinations after getting bitten by a Tunisian monkey. A kind nurse called Lucy McMahon had given him her set purchased from the local souk. The game consisted of a round wooden board with thirty-three nooks drilled out in a cross-shape within a circular holding groove. The game started with thirty-two marbles in their nooks and the objective was to eliminate all but one marble left in the centre, by jumping marbles over others, as long as there was an empty space for it. 'Taken' marbles were placed in the groove until the end of the game. Jox had played endless games to keep his mind from going to mush, a way to keep sharp and pass time. He'd left his Tunisian set with his batman, Corporal Shillington, but knowing that blighter's past form, he'd probably sold it on by now.

Jox's homemade version was rather rougher, the pebbles' positions marked in pencil once he'd got hold of the right wooden board. Here again, the Polish duo came up trumps, 'liberating' the wooden lid of an olive oil barrel, pinched when they were tasked with doing the dishwashing at the guard's *cantina*. Jox soon had his set fashioned and enjoyed playing, and it soon became a spectator sport amongst prisoners starved of entertainment. There were animated conversations over tactics taking far more time than deserved, but perhaps that was the point. Soon, several other boards were being fashioned, with half the camp's inmates scouring the grounds for suitable pebbles and wooden planks.

CHAPTER FOUR

Some days later, Jox had the chance to catch up with Beans properly. Jox came to him bearing a 'gift' from their joint package. Beans had always had a sweet tooth and was a man with a large appetite, so Jox brought him a sizeable tin of Morton's apple pudding.

'I expect you to scoff the lot,' said Jox. 'We need to put some meat back on those bones.'

Beans dug in but began to struggle after a few mouthfuls, doubtless because of a shrunken stomach and a reduced appetite from almost a year of captivity.

'Can't finish this,' said Beans. 'You want some?'

'Nope, you're on your own,' said Jox. 'I'll sit here until you get it done. Take your time. You can tell me how you ended up here. We're a long way from France, so I bet there's a story attached. The last time we were together, No. 133 squadron had spent forty-five minutes circling around the coast of Brest, wasting fuel and trying to find those damned Flying Fortresses. As I recall, you and your Yanks were getting terribly frustrated. I then heard you say, "Hot dog! Bombers down there at Angels Fifteen." We'd found at least one of the wayward bomb groups. That's when my engine started stuttering and I had to hand the squadron over to you, before heading back to Blighty. You remember?'

'Do I remember, Jox?' sighed Beans, his spoon mid-air. He placed it on the table. 'I replay that moment time and again in my head every day. From the second I said, "Yes, sir, I have command, Eagle Squadron form up on me," and the boys followed me as I led them straight into a disaster.'

'What happened was a tragedy, but that's not on you. We all share the blame.'

'Tell you the truth, it's pretty tough even talking about it. I've tried so hard to forget,' said Beans with a pained look. He took a deep breath. 'Okay, so you'd bugged out with your engine problems. We circled some more, until I found a gap in the clouds. I thought I saw what looked like south-facing clifftops and reckoned that must surely be England. We were low on fuel, so I checked in with RAGGLE Leader and he agreed. I went down after confirming that all the boys were coming with me, since we needed to land pretty urgently.'

Jox nodded. 'All I could hear on the R/T were Yank voices saying you were going down. I remember being frustrated and asking myself why the hell you were all getting involved. I didn't realise the fuel situation was critical.'

'So yeah, we're dropping through the clouds and suddenly all hell broke loose.'

'There was the sound of gunfire on the R/T.'

'Damned right! I don't know how we managed it, but we were right over the port of Brest, well to the west of our target at Morlaix aerodrome. Turns out it's one of the most heavily defended ports in occupied France and they were shooting at us with everything they had. On my portside, Gene Neville got hit first and went straight down. Didn't stand a chance. There were aircraft getting hit all over. I saw a couple of chutes before I got hit myself. I reckoned it was better to bale out and destroy the aircraft, rather than belly land and just hand over my brand-new kite to the Krauts.

'We heard later that four of the guys were killed: Neville, who I saw get hit, then Bill Baker, Lenny Ryerson and Den

Smith. The rest of us were scattered, shot down or forced to land as we'd run out of fuel. Most of the survivors were captured. I saw some of them briefly, but we got split up and interrogated separately. A couple were unaccounted for, so I hoped maybe they'd evaded capture.'

Beans hung his head, silent for a long while, suppressed memories evidently rushing back. 'That's when things got bad. Like I said, we were separated and interrogated by some real mean suckers, who already seemed to know everything about us. To start with, they wanted the usual stuff: unit details, locations, aircraft capabilities, info about our airbases and the structure of our forces. They knew most of it already. Maybe some of the other guys had already spoken up, but they sure knew their stuff. I was pretty comfortable providing the bare minimum and useless titbits, just to keep myself amused, leading them up the garden path with all kinds of tall tales. Eventually, they started getting pretty angry with me.'

Beans sighed, rapping his fingers on the table. 'Then one day, they bring in this new interrogator. Up until then, most of them were guys in civilian clothes, the type wearing long leather coats and brimmed hats. Didn't take too much imagination to work out they were Gestapo, but I always just looked at them like the bad guys in some lousy Western. Taking them down a peg or two was kinda entertaining. Anyhow, the first thing I noticed about this new guy was his powerful cologne. He was wearing a *Luftwaffe* uniform and was a major, with a pilot's badge, Iron Cross, the whole nine yards. His face was bright red, like a hog's head left too long in boiling water. On one side he had a scar, but the other was in even worse shape.'

Jox looked up, the description sounding chillingly familiar.

'He had this black eyepatch over one eye and half his face looked like raw hamburger. His one remaining eye glistened colder and meaner than a water moccasin from the Louisiana swamps. He said to me, "Well, well, if it isn't Flight Lieutenant Beans from Baton Rouge, Louisiana. You see, I know exactly who you are, and I have every confidence that you are going to be of great assistance to the Reich and the Axis war effort. Should you choose not to cooperate, it will be my great pleasure to apply my considerable skills to ensure that you comply. As you can see, I have a certain grudge that still needs ironing out. Seems only fair, after what your people did to me at Dieppe." The son of a bitch pointed at his eye patch, then looked at me with an undertaker's smile. My blood turned cold.'

'He didn't happen to be called *Oberst* Kreg von Wella? A tall, blond chap, rather mean and scarred up like you said?'

'Sure, that's the guy who took my eye. He was a major then, but that's him all right. How d'you know him? I haven't seen him since France. If I ever do, I'll put a hole in that goldarned bastard, just you watch me.'

'Take it easy,' said Jox. 'The thing is, he's probably not as far away as you might believe. He's actually in charge of *Luftwaffe* intelligence for this region, and that includes oversight of this camp and several others. *Colonnello* Flavius reports to him indirectly. Funnily enough, when we spoke, just after I arrived, he was full of questions regarding von Wella too. He thinks the colonel is hatching some scheme and is worried about it all.'

'Wouldn't be surprised. Von Wella's a snake.'

'I don't disagree, but tell me the rest of your story.'

'Well, d'you remember that gumbo I made for y'all a year or so ago?'

Jox nodded.

'Well, the thing is, shrimp is a big part of making a good gumbo. If you're from the Louisiana bayou like me, there's nothing more than swamp, mud flats and brackish tidal waters. You ain't got much choice but to fish or hunt. My ancestors chose to raise freshwater shrimp. They grow fat and juicy as long as you keep them fed.'

'Beans, why the hell are we talking about seafood?'

'Hold up, there is a point. You see, the Mississippi is full of nutrients that come off the plains, as it meanders through several southern states leaving a fertile layer in its wake. These low-lying floodplains and coastal prairies in Louisiana and parts of Texas have become the home of the majority of rice farms in the United States. You see, the thing is, despite my name, it ain't beans my family's fortune is built on, it's rice. Our converted rice product is even in the Red Cross packages we're getting here. The city of Baton Rouge was pretty much built on rice, and that's what made my daddy the state governor. It got me a place at Louisiana State University, studying for a doctorate in agriculture. My destiny was all mapped out for me, whether I liked it or not. I was to be a rice scientist and then second, I suppose, a businessman. Then, the war in Europe came along and offered me an alternative. I already had a pilot's licence from my barnstorming days at college, so I just upped and ran for Canada, joining up with the RCAF. I found myself in England, in one of the Eagle Squadrons, just in time for the Battle of Britain. A bit after that was when I met y'all.'

'Are you the son of the Southern industrialist that *Colonnello* Flavius mentioned?'

'I'm guessing that's probably me.'

'So how rich is your father?'

'Can't exactly say,' replied Beans sheepishly. 'It's not all his, more like the whole family's, but they do call him the

"Kingfish". He likes to say, "I may be a small fish in Washington, but I'm the Kingfish to the folks down in Louisiana." I wouldn't exactly say he's the richest man in the south but he probably is in the state.'

'That's unbelievable, but it doesn't explain what you're doing in Italy,' said Jox.

'Well, for start, von Wella found out that I was with No. 133 Eagle Squadron at Dieppe. You remember, you came along for the ride with us on that one sortie.'

'That didn't end terribly well for me. Got dinged by our own Royal Navy and managed to make it home by the skin of my teeth. Otherwise, I'd have been a *Kriegie* a long time before you. A bad day at the office for me, but I was lucky.'

'It was certainly a bad day for von Wella. Got shot down by a Spit bearing the letters MD, so therefore a No. 133 Squadron aircraft. When he heard that, he turned real mean. Kept talking about how we'd ruined his flying career, and he'd lost his chance for glory. Somehow, he got the idea in his head that I was the one who shot him down. As it happened, I did get a piece of a FW 190 over Dieppe, but I've no idea if it was him. Could have been, I suppose. Anyhow, he was getting more and more worked up. He was pacing around the room with this ceremonial dagger in his hand, saying, "I was presented with this by *Generalfeldmarschall* Herman Goering himself when I graduated top of my class from the *Luftwaffe* academy and received my fighter pilot's badge. Because of you, it is now worthless." He threw it point-first into the table between us. I can still see it wobbling. He said to me, "Listen *Amerikaner*, if you do not do as I ask, you will pay for that debt." His black-hatted goons grabbed me from behind. By now, he was frothing at the mouth and I could smell his cologne, he was so close. He grabbed my hair with his gloved hand and stuck me with that goddamned knife, right in the eye.' Beans slumped forward. 'It didn't hurt as much as I'd expected, but I realised straight away it was gone. Someone had taken away his flying career at Dieppe, and now he'd taken mine.' Beans got to his feet, emotion etched across his face.

'What is it, Bayou? What happened?'

'I caved, Jox. I just caved. I got scared and agreed to what he wanted. I didn't want to be a traitor, a collaborator, but he was going to blind me. I couldn't face going through life like that. Some have that strength, but I couldn't. I'm sorry.'

'What did you do?' asked Jox, with a sinking feeling in his stomach.

'It's the rice. Italy produces about half the rice grown in Europe. It's a cheap and easy way to feed people, and you know what they say about an army marching on its stomach. What I didn't realise is that the Axis, spread out as it is and fighting on several fronts, are struggling to keep people fed, especially subjugated worker populations. You only need to look at the locals around here to see that. Hell, we get better fed than they do.' Beans sat back down. 'You see, I've got quite a reputation in rice circles, so to speak, however much I've tried to escape from it. They wanted the knowledge I have about how to grow rice, and God damn it, I ended up giving it to them.' He looked utterly dejected. 'They shipped me off to Italy, with my punctured eye weeping all the way. I found myself in Lombardy first, up in the north where most Italian rice is grown. Anyway, as long as I gave them what they wanted, the Eyeties treated me well enough. I guess most of the guys I was dealing with were crop scientists rather than hardcore Fascists. I worked with them for close on a year, but I started seeing more and more bombers in the skies over the rice paddies. I'd kinda buried myself away, ashamed for collaborating, but then seeing formations of Forts and Liberators in the sky, their contrails were like claw marks on the heavens and on my guilty conscience. Something mended inside me and I stopped helping them, realising there was a war going on and I needed to get back to it. I'd lost an eye but was still determined and started trying to escape. I didn't know how and couldn't speak a word of Italian. In any case, a big redheaded kid like me kinda stands out in the Italian *campagna*. I got caught several times, roughed up on each occasion, and I started getting passed from one camp to another, with increasingly severe regimes. I guess I stopped being useful. Every move was further south, and eventually I ended up here.' He smiled. 'Despite everything, I still believe those crop scientists tried to do their best for me. They were horrified by what the *Tedeschi* did to my eye and tried to keep me hidden away from the Germans. I've little doubt that if the Krauts got their hands on me, I'd have faced a rougher justice.' He sniffed. 'I've got the evidence to prove that,' he said, pointing at his eye socket. 'Yeah, so it's all about the rice. That's what made me a traitor to my country.'

'Hold on,' said Jox, looking around to ensure they weren't overheard. 'You were being tortured. There's no telling where that could have ended. You gave away no secrets, nor did you aid the enemy militarily or divulge intelligence or sensitive material. Any damage was already done when No. 133 squadron went down, and Jerry got hold of all those new Spitfire XIs. Frankly, not all of the men were as diligent as you, choosing to ditch to destroy your aircraft rather than allowing it to fall into enemy hands. As for "divulging" agricultural expertise, well, one could argue you were providing humanitarian aid to the subjugated people of Italy and beyond.'

'I'm not sure a court martial would see it that way.'

'Well then, it's a good job that no one's going to find out.'

'You would do that for me?'

'Look, Bayou, all I see is a brave comrade who was shot down in combat, captured, tortured and did what he had to do to survive. The fact that you now lead the escape committee, and that the men look up to and trust you, speaks volumes. Seems to me there are too few chaps here with that fire in their belly. I count myself fortunate that you're one and that we've met again. I couldn't wish for a sounder friend to have by my side.' Jox gazed into Beans' single eye. 'Now, I don't want to hear this again. Are we clear, Flight Lieutenant?'

'Yes sir, Squadron Leader,' Beans replied. 'Thanks, Jox. You've no idea how much that means to me. Sharing my darkest secret and being told my future might not be as bleak as I expected, is a big deal. Of course, that assumes we make it out of here in one piece. So far, to be honest, I ain't been doing such a good job.' He brightened. 'So, how about you? How come you're here?'

'Well, like I said, after Morlaix, I was under a bit of a cloud. A new CO was brought in, a sound chap called Tony Bartley, a Battle of Britain ace. The Treble Ones were transferred to Egypt and the Western Desert. I got into a few scrapes there until I got into some real bother during the second battle of El Alamein. I spent a terrifying night out in the desert, right under an artillery barrage, but fortunately I got rescued by my old pal Ghillie in the nick of time. I got patched up in Gibraltar, then we were off on the TORCH landings and the invasion of North Africa.

'That was long, tough haul, and finally I got posted to Malta, tasked with setting up a new squadron, No. 333, the Black Pigs, from a bunch of stragglers and odds and sods that were stranded there. I bolstered the numbers with some solid transfers from the Treble Ones and some replacements. By the time Operation HUSKY was launched, I had them firing on all cylinders. Things didn't start well, but we prevailed. I was involved in a night mission towards the end, over the straits of Messina. I got hit by flak, crash-landing on the toe of Italy. I was captured and interrogated by our dear friend von Wella, amongst others, and ended up here with you.' Jox grinned. 'That, my friend, believe it or not was a long story cut short.'

'Hearing that name again is like getting socked in the face,' said Beans. 'You say he oversees this camp and others?'

'That's what he told me. It may be a recent development. I wouldn't be surprised, with the way things are unravelling for the Italian Fascist regime. Last I heard, Mussolini was deposed, and I don't think the Eyeties will be in the war for much longer. My sense is they won't last, but then things will get very dangerous, very quickly. The Germans will feel betrayed and desperate to secure their southern flank. I really suspect the Italian campaign is going to be a bloody slog and we'll be stuck right in the middle of it. I can promise you one thing: I'm not sitting tight waiting to become a hostage of the Germans. First chance I get, I'm hopping it and taking my chances in the mountains. There must surely be partisans out there somewhere.'

'I'm sure there are, but the country will also be full of disillusioned and frankly angry Fascists who'll see escaped prisoners of war as easy targets to blame for their woes.'

'I'm sure you're right, but I'll take my chances,' said Jox. 'I'm not sitting here waiting for the executioner's axe to drop. A man's got to create his own destiny.'

'Or maybe sow the seeds of his destruction,' replied Beans.

'Either way, we'll be doing something rather than just waiting. Taking our fate into our own hands — to me, that feels like the soldier's way.'

Beans nodded. 'Amen to that.'

CHAPTER FIVE

Over the following few weeks, Jox and Whisky got together regularly to compare, share and discuss their care packages. They came in sturdy cardboard boxes tied with twine and covered with labels, logos and stamps of the various bodies responsible for their supply. They'd travelled far and the contents were all tinned or wrapped in grease-proof paper. For those with a sweet tooth, there was Rowntree's cocoa, Lyle's golden syrup, and often a thick tablet of Dairy Milk chocolate or Morton's apple pudding in a tin. Savoury protein came in the form of meat and vegetable stew, labelled as Maconochie Brothers' 'M&V', then of course the ubiquitous corned 'Bully Beef'. Jox was surprised to be informed by Perrin that the name of something to quintessentially British originated from the French, *boeuf bouilli* or boiled beef. The cans were from Uruguay, courtesy of Fray Bentos, and occasionally alternated with Portuguese tinned sardines. There were also dairy products, St Ivel Cheddar cheese, Nestle's condensed milk and Redgate margarine. Dry goods included loose tea, tinned Gold Flake cigarettes, Players Medium Navy Cut leaf tobacco, and a bar of soap wrapped in cellophane. Jox had little use for the tobacco, but it was a precious commodity for trading. He was surprised at how pleased he was to have soap, seizing the opportunity to get clean for the first time in rather too long. He'd been wearing his uniform since that fateful night over the Straits of Messina and realised it was getting rather ripe, but he had no way of washing it, let alone getting it dry.

They were comparing their latest packages when a loud commotion outside the hut brought them to the window. The throaty roar of multiple diesel engines sounded, followed by an alarmed bugle call from one of the camp's watchtowers. The bugler had barely managed a few notes before a pair of mottled green SD.KFZ. 234 Puma armoured cars thundered through the rusty gates and came to a screeching halt on the exercise square.

The vehicles were huge, each carrying a four-man crew on eight shoulder-high rubber wheels that made the turrets taller than any man. Behind them was a limousine and half a dozen canvas-topped Opel Blitz lorries. A further two armoured cars brought up the rear, their KwK cannons and MG42 machine guns panning across the landscape like the proboscises of unicorn beetles sniffing for trouble.

The men sitting in the limousine all wore British anti-gas goggles over their eyes, of a type popularised by Field Marshal Rommel in the Western Desert. Vast stocks had been captured by Axis troops during the North Africa Campaign of 1940-42 and had become a popular accoutrement that identified desert war veterans. A pair of hard-faced junior officers were wearing the *fourragère* of aide-de-camps, and both scanned the camp, evaluating the topography and searching for any threats. Seated across from them, facing the direction of travel, were two senior officers, one a *Luftwaffe Oberst*, the other an *SS-Obersturmbannführer*, both with aloof and rather disdainful expressions.

One of the officers raised his goggles, and Jox instantly recognised von Wella's scarred face. The other officer's right sleeve was empty and flapped in the breeze. On his collar were the runes of the *Schutzstaffel*, at his throat the Knight's Cross, and the black band of his peaked cap gleamed with a silver *Totenkopf* death's head. Watching from inside his hut, Jox could tell these were men to be wary of, men used to being obeyed and feared. They were certainly no strangers to bloodshed, be it theirs or that of others.

With a final growl, the first two armoured cars took up positions on either side of the gates, turrets whirring as their guns rotated to take deliberate aim at two of the towers, vastly outgunning the antiquated Breda M37 machine guns that were within. Several tough-looking *Fallschirmjäger* paratroopers in bulky camouflaged smocks tumbled from the trucks, moving fast and with the single-minded determination of the elite fighting troops that they were. These were clearly veterans, known by both enemies and comrades as 'Green Devils' from the colour of their smocks, worn with thick brown leather belts and clip-edged paratrooper helmets. Some orders were called out across the exercise yard in guttural German.

Oberst von Wella climbed out of his vehicle as *Colonnello* Flavius hurried towards them, buckling his pistol belt and already sweating in his tightly tailored uniform. The two German officers followed Flavius inside to his office while most of the armed guards remained by the vehicles.

'What do you think that's all about?' Whisky asked.

'No idea,' Jox replied, 'but it can't be good.'

Half an hour later all of the prisoners were called outside, where the officers were waiting with Flavius, who was holding a sheet of paper. 'The following prisoners are to be transferred with immediate effect.' He looked up at Jox briefly before reading the names.

Jox felt a jolt when his name was read out. Then he realised that all the other names had been mentioned by Flavius previously. They were the 'bright stars' that had been collected at the camp, von Wella's '*Prominente.*'

'Life will be better in the new camp, you will see,' said von Wella's aide.

'This is an absolute outrage,' blustered Colonel du Boulay. 'And by whose authority?'

'By my authority,' said von Wella.

'And who the devil are you?' demanded du Boulay, bristling like an angry bantam.

'Good morning, gentlemen, I am Oberst Kreg von Wella. I am Colonnello Flavius's commanding officer and therefore also yours. You will soon receive instructions from my men, and cooperation in this matter would be appreciated.' He indicated the hatchet-faced officer with the pale eyes standing beside him. 'This is SS-*Obersturmbannführer* Wolfgang Steiner, my head of security. He has come fresh from the Crimea and has my full authority to deal with any unpleasant circumstances which may emerge over the next few unsettled weeks. You are to follow his orders to the letter or there will be consequences.'

Von Wella held their gaze. 'This transfer will be happening. The prisoners whose names have been called out will travel by truck and then by rail from this camp to one situated in the north.' He smiled. 'The facilities at P.G. 35 at the *San Lorenza* Charterhouse of *Certosa di Padula* are vastly superior to those here. They are certainly more "fitting" for officers of your standing and connections. It is a truly beautiful baroque monastery, set high in the mountains, south of Naples. I'm told it is the largest charterhouse in Italy, dating back four hundred years or more.' He tried to add some warmth to his smile, but his scarring failed to communicate the sincerity he was trying to evoke. 'In my view, it is the most picturesque prisoner of war camp in Europe, set amongst fruit orchards and surrounded by majestic mountains. You will be comfortable there, not to mention safer, away from the battlefront. Surely, you agree this is a good thing.'

'Well, I mean,' spluttered du Boulay. 'We've had no warning. Things must be organised…'

'Please do not get agitated,' cooed von Wella. 'It is not helpful and does you no good. The selected men will pack up their belongings and be ready for transfer at 0800 hours this coming Friday. I expect your cooperation in this matter, Colonel, and will tolerate no dissention or delay. Is that understood?'

Du Boulay began to redden again. 'Of course, but…'

'In the meantime, please accept our hospitality,' said von Wella amiably. 'Please follow me.' He led them into the prisoners' canteen, and then indicated platters of food being carried in by burly paratroopers trying their best to look jovial and unthreatening. The impact was rather spoilt by several others, stern-faced and less friendly-looking, lining the refectory's walls with *MP 40 Maschinenpistoles* at the ready. 'It is just simple soldiers' fare, smoked sausage and fresh sauerkraut, but I'm sure you'll enjoy it. It is a favourite of the Bavarians amongst my men. *Feldwebel* Schultz here is a master at its preparation.'

A large paratrooper was carrying a steaming platter. He had a grin on his face, displaying white teeth, two of which were missing. He was clearly no stranger to violence and his sleeves were rolled up, revealing ham-hock-sized forearms covered with white-blond hair. 'We have some pilsner lager and *Colonnello* Flavius has found us some passable Chianti, as I'm afraid Calabrian wine is too rough for my palate.' He waved his arms in an attempt to look welcoming. 'Come, my friends, gather round and let's take a few photographs with Schultz.' He beckoned a photographer. 'Now, raise your glasses for the photo. You will forgive me if I do not stand with you. I tend to rather spoil the picture.' He pointed at his face and laughed. 'Bravo, now please enjoy yourselves.'

'Why, you god-darned son of a bitch!' screeched an American voice from across the crowded hall. Barrelling towards the pair, like a bull charging at a red rag, was Darren Beans, heading straight for von Wella. Beans had a mad look in his eye and was frothing with fury. Still out of shape from his recent ordeal, he was slower than usual, but his roar and outstretched hands made his intentions abundantly clear.

The jovial *Feldwebel*, still carrying the hefty circular tray of sauerkraut, reacted like a jungle cat. He dropped to one knee and launched the metal disc straight at Beans, catching him under the chin at the height of his Adam's apple. Sauerkraut and sausages flew everywhere, and Beans collapsed, clutching his throat and wheezing like punctured bellows. Schultz then calmly punched him in the face, leaning on him with both knees to control his flailing limbs. In the meantime, the one-handed SS officer, Steiner, who never seemed to stray very far from von Wella, had stepped protectively between the target and threat, a black Luger appearing magically in his hand. The muzzle was aimed straight at Beans' head as he writhed on the ground.

'No ... please, don't shoot!' cried Jox, launching himself at the SS officer. Somehow, he managed to knock the outstretched arm down just as he fired. A single round thudded into the refectory floorboards. In a beat, Jox was roughly manhandled to the ground by a burly pair of paratroopers. Two more were now pinning Beans down as he continued to struggle and bellow. Both now immobilised, faces to the ground, their gasping breath blew up dust and accumulated fluff from the floorboards.

'Now, now, is that any way to greet an old friend?' said von Wella. '*Ach so*, isn't this such a treat? It's always a pleasure to catch up with old acquaintances.' He adjusted his black eye patch carefully, perhaps more unsettled by the struggle than he appeared to be. 'Good to see you, *Herr* McNabb, and of course you too, my dear *Herr* Beans. I believe the appropriate American expression is "Long time no see".'

The pair were manhandled to their feet, then bent forward, pinioned so their heads still faced the ground. Steiner still had his pistol levelled at Beans, the glint in his eyes indicating he'd be more than happy to fire again, ending this insubordination once and for all.

'Everyone, please keep calm,' said von Wella, his nerves betrayed by the tremor of his gloved hand. 'There's no harm done.' He glanced at his hard-faced colleague. 'Steiner, show some restraint, please. You're not on the *Ostfront* now.' He reached with his gloved hand and lifted Beans' chin until they locked gazes, single eye to single eye. The pale blue of each almost matched. 'Still the hothead, my *Amerikaner* friend. I had hoped you might have mellowed by now. After all, there's nothing left to struggle against; in the end you divulged everything we needed. There's no reason to make such a fuss. As for the eye, well yes, perhaps I was a little overzealous at the time, but *c'est la vie, c'est la guerre.*' He patted Beans' face with his leather palm. 'I suggest we let bygones be bygones. You behave reasonably and all will be well.' He turned to Jox, who was still in the stress position. 'Please let Squadron Leader McNabb up,' he ordered. 'He is more in control of his emotions than his companion. We are friends also, aren't we, Jox?'

'I wish I could say I am pleased to see you again, Colonel,' Jox replied. 'But given what my actual friend, Darren Beans, has told me about how you treated him, we can safely say that we are not friends.'

'It's a pity, but I can live with that,' replied von Wella. 'The lion doesn't worry about the opinions of sheep. Obedience is what is required.' He turned to Beans. 'You would do well to follow McNabb's example. Between fighter pilots there may still be a vestige of gentlemanly respect, but you will find that ideological warriors like *Obersturmbannführer* Steiner have no such foibles nor qualms. If not for the actions of your friend Jox, you would have a bullet in your brain. Wolf would certainly welcome the opportunity to put you down like a rabid dog.'

Mouth frothing and his breath wheezing, Beans was giving a decent impression of that dog.

Jox glanced up and saw that Steiner was struggling to re-holster his weapon with his one hand. The SS officer caught his eye, blinked, and reassumed his usual deadpan expression.

'I believe I've changed my mind,' said von Wella brightly. 'The reunion of three fine fighter pilots, albeit belligerents, should certainly be recorded for posterity. I take a poor photograph, but if anyone can understand why, it would be the two of you.' He looked at Beans, whose breathing was becoming more even. 'Will you behave yourself?' Beans nodded. 'Let him go,' von Wella ordered the paratroopers holding him. One of the troopers watching cocked his *Maschinenpistole*.

'Take it easy, Bayou,' muttered Jox, trying to avoid a reescalation.

'I will,' Beans replied hoarsely. 'It was the shock of seeing him. I know where he is now. "Revenge is a dish best served cold" and all that.'

'I am not familiar with this expression,' said von Wella. 'What is the meaning?'

'Best not to ask,' replied Jox. 'So, are we doing this photograph?'

Von Wella's aide fussed with Jox's collar, and von Wella pulled out a pale bone comb and tidied what was left of his hair. He looked at Beans. 'This will not do.' He reached into the inside pocket of his tunic and pulled out what looked like a black silk bowtie. 'Here, I have many. They were specially made for me by a Sicilian tailor in Palermo. Sadly, I no longer have access to him. I'll show you how to tie it.'

Von Wella reached behind his head and undid the knot at the back. When he removed the eyepatch, the scarring of his facial injury looked even more shocking. In addition to the duelling scar on his left cheek, the burns on the right side were like melted wax. A lidless, opaque white eye stared from the socket, rimmed with blue like a full moon. 'Makes me quite impactful, don't you think?' he said, retying it. 'Here, let's do the same for you.'

He reached around Beans' strawberry-blond head and used the black silk patch to cover his enucleated left eye socket, the eyelid still showing the mark of von Wella's dagger. 'This will make you less frightful.' He stood back and admired his handiwork. 'Now we are as ready for the photograph as we'll ever be. We make a fine pair.'

Later that day, Shooter Vollick had set up a chair outside the Lone Star hut. He was offering haircuts for the price of a cigarette and had a few customers who wanted to smarten up before the trip north. It made little sense, but military men often did so before a deployment.

Charlie Champagne was in the chair, looking healthier than the last time Jox had seen him. In the bright sunlight, his curly ginger hair seemed to glow, highlighting his fair eyebrows and great many freckles. He had a pipe in his mouth and was reading a book on the ancient Romans. Vollick hovered around him, scissors twitching like a steel hummingbird. In contrast to Champagne, Vollick was bare-chested, displaying his impressive array of tattoos, many more than Jox had expected, having only seen the scissors on his left hand and the cowboy's six-shooter on his right.

The only other aviator Jox knew with such an impressive array was the No. 333 Squadron's senior NCO, Warrant Officer Jimmy Waerea. Jimmy, the one-handed Māori had in many ways become the spiritual soul of the newly formed squadron, its 'keeper of the flame'. Jimmy's tattoos were tribal motifs of ferns, feathers and ocean waves blending together. Vollick's were more haphazard, as if added one at a time by tattooists of differing skill. Jimmy's torso and arms were an overall canvas, telling the story of his people, whereas Vollick's were like diary entries, a kaleidoscope of colours and motifs.

Jox had a packet of Woodbines in his pocket for trading purposes, and was considering whether it was worth sacrificing one to tidy his unruly mop. It had been several weeks since Corporal Shillington, his batman, had given him a trim back in Malta.

'You got time for another one?' he asked Vollick.

'Sure, buddy,' he replied, twitching his scissors dangerously close to unsuspecting Champagne's ear. 'Got any smokes?'

'Yup.'

'Then I'm your man,' grinned the tattooed bombardier. 'I won't be long.'

Waiting for his turn, Jox watched Shooter Vollick work. He was evidently skilled and never stopped moving. As he sweated in the sunshine, it added a sheen to his multicoloured artwork. Abruptly, he pocketed his scissors and smoothed Champagne's rebellious curls with his hands. 'That's the best I can do,' he said, now holding a hand out for payment. 'Never seen a guy with such thick hair.'

Champagne grinned. 'I'm afraid my whole family has this russet thatch. It's quite pretty on my sister but gets untidy on a man.'

'However you got it, it's blunted my irons,' replied Vollick, whipping away the tattered sheet he had around Champagne and flinging off trimmed hair the colour of autumn leaves. 'Your momma must have surely fed y'all a whole lot of greens.'

'I expect she did,' replied Champagne, handing over a single cigarette.

Vollick pocketed it, pulled out a sharpening stone and began running it along the scissor blades. 'Won't be long.'

Jox nodded, struck by the variety of Vollick's tattoos. There was a Hawaiian hula girl on one forearm, a slab-sided B-24 Liberator on his bicep and swallows of different colours dotted all over. Down one arm there was a list of women's names in different lettering. Jox could see a Jennifer, Alison, Philippa, Sue, Deborah and Annabel too. There were more. Jox pointed. 'Should I even ask?'

Vollick grinned. 'I guess some might call them notches on my bedpost, but that would be doing the ladies a disservice. Personally, I call them my "growth rings", each of them teaching me how to become a better man.'

'What's the significance of the swallows? You seem to have so many.'

'In Navy circles, they signify how far a sailor has travelled, each swallow representing five thousand nautical miles. I ain't no sailor, but I am an optimist. Every time I fall in love, I get a new swallow to represent the loyalty and devotion I feel towards that person. It don't always work out, but the swallow is proof of my optimism that it will.'

'So, how did it work out with the last lady on the list?'

'That would Jane. A real beautiful gal from Hull in England. She had a hell of an accent but was a doll. I met her before we headed out to Tunisia. Got my "Dear John" from her a couple of weeks back. I guess being a POW, and so very far away, means I'm "out of sight, out of mind." I'm sure there's a whole lick of fellers buzzing around that particular flower. It's too bad. This is her swallow, the purple one. I did a pretty good job on it, don't you think?'

'Looks great,' replied Jox. 'So, wait, you did it yourself?'

'Yeah, most of them. Using a mirror, I guess the first few were tricky, but I'm getting pretty handy now. Of course, some were done by professionals too,' he said, pointing at the hula girl and B-24. 'The scissors and six-shooter I did myself.'

'You're really quite the artist,' said Jox. 'Have you done other people?'

'Yeah, sure,' he replied. 'Tex has got a sheriff's badge on his chest and Muriel has crossed wine bottles and a castle on his forearm. You interested?'

'I like the idea. Maybe something a bit like your list, but I'm fairly sure it would be frowned upon as "conduct unbecoming to an officer and gentleman" of the Royal Air Force. I suppose the Royal Navy may be laxer, but I'm pretty sure their "airships" would take a dim view.'

'Dim, did you say?' replied Vollick. 'That kinda gives me an idea. You know, there are inks that are only visible in the dark or when illuminated by certain lights like ultraviolet. The words would be there, but only visible when you wanted them to be. What d'you think of that?'

Jox sat down and shrugged. 'Food for thought.'

CHAPTER SIX

'March,' bellowed *Feldwebel* Schultz in a voice that carried across the camp. His *Fallschirmjäger* stamped their first step and began swinging their arms in the way of German infantrymen on a fast road march.

Jox watched them pass through the gates of *Campo* No. 85, and was reminded of his own square-bashing days at RAF Uxbridge. There, a Cockney flight sergeant had made it his mission to teach 'You 'orrible little erks, that despite futures as officers, this is where you earn your stripes, right 'ere, right now.' Their poor efforts were put to shame by the precise and yet fluid movements of these paratroopers, who were now covering ground at a fearsome pace.

The armoured cars had gone ahead, scouting out the wheat fields down to Brindisi. The 'Green Devils' were marching ahead of the trucks that would be transporting the selected prisoners to the rail station. Before loading up, *Colonnello* Flavius had formed up all the inmates left in the camp, now principally consisting of NCOs and enlisted men. He'd made a great show of offering his best wishes, but for most of the men being left behind, the news that many of the officers were shipping out was good news, with expectations that discipline might relax and, more importantly, they'd inherit the officers' huts.

Flavius's own troops were also formed up. He called them to attention and led the salute. He appeared genuinely troubled that the 'cream' of his charges were being taken away. There was much back-slapping and handshaking before Jox and his companions climbed aboard. Each 1.5 tonne Opel Blitz could hold ten men, sitting on benches down either side of the rear cabin. Aboard Jox's truck were Beans, Wyszkowski, Colonel du Boulay, Major Reid-Steele, Perrin and Carver. There were several other familiar faces which Jox recognised from newspapers, whether from the society, sports or entertainment pages. Amongst them were two county cricketers, a Welsh rugby international and another from New Zealand, plus the matinee idol, Red Cable, with his trademark pencil moustache and protruding ears.

All of these selected *Prominente* appeared to be high profile. They were either relatives of the rich or famous, important somehow within the military or politics, or else perhaps had a reputation in sports, business or the arts. Why he found himself on the list rather baffled Jox, but it had eventually dawned on him that it was perhaps down to his decorations. The Germans were always rather impressed by medals and the like, so perhaps that was also why Wyszkowski was included, a member of the famed 'Skalski's Flying Circus' and the holder of the *Virtuti Militari* with four Crosses of Valour.

When they arrived at Brindisi, it was in utter chaos. The port had been extensively bombed, with the quayside piled high with rubble and the twisted remains of metal cranes lying like the beached skeletons of great whales. Jox had seen much the same in Malta and London, and realised this was the probable fate awaiting cities up and down the length of Italy.

Here, the port authorities seemed to have things in hand, albeit in a chaotic, Italian sort of way, which was clearly driving their Teutonic overseers to complete distraction. There were masses of labourers and dockers everywhere, with welders sparking and stevedores bustling around as freight swung overhead from cables, all accompanied by a deafening cacophony.

As the convoy of trucks passed through the chaos, it was like an ant colony being kicked, worker ants surging forth in every direction. There was a lot of shouting and gesticulating, in contrast to the silent *Fallschirmjäger* marching grim-faced amongst them. The masses parted before them, driven by a combination of fear and awe.

Reaching the rail yard, they found it busy, but calm, ordered and efficient, as might be expected when a site was run by the *Deutsche Wehrmacht*. The lorries parked in an orderly row and the tired paratroopers were allowed to catch their breath, loosen off their packs and take on some water. Jox and his companions tumbled from the vehicles and were ordered to form up on one of the platforms where a train was being loaded. Once their names were tallied on the *Unteroffizieren's* clipboards, they too were given water and told to sit and wait until embarkation.

Jox and a few others asked if they might relieve themselves, and were told the facilities were down the platform. They were permitted to go but warned not to dawdle. Getting to his feet, Jox caught the eye of *Feldwebel* Schultz, who pointed out the guards on the roof of each carriage, each with a clear line of sight down the platform. 'You try escape, useless, *ja?*'

The guards all wore green camo smocks and grey jump trousers, living up to their nickname, the 'Green Devils'. It struck Jox as rather amusing that their British airborne counterparts in Tunisia had been nicknamed the 'Red Devils' by their German opponents, on account of their Dennison jump smocks being dyed red by Tunisia's soil pigments. How had things turned out when both sets of 'devils' had met in battle on the hellish slopes of Etna? He suspected there would be many more such encounters to come.

Heading down the platform, Jox looked over the train that would be taking them north. He'd read somewhere that the *Ferrovie dello Stato* was Italy's pride and joy, a vital service for a nation that had generally poor roads. He recalled one of *Colonnello* Flavius's more disillusioned guards saying that he had no affection for Mussolini, but 'at least he kept the trains running'.

At the far end of the platform was the largest locomotive Jox had ever seen, hissing like a malevolent dragon. Steam and black smoke billowed as the boilers and furnace were being worked up before departure. Behind it was a tender, piled high with blocks of bluey-black anthracite, paving stone to breeze block in size. Whatever shortages there may have been in Italy, this journey was apparently important enough for the best of fuel.

To Jox's untrained eye, the train looked rather jumbled. For every windowed passenger car, there were a pair of freight carriages interspersed. On the roof with the armed guards was a party of workmen with buckets of white paint and long-handled brooms being used as brushes. What were they up to, he wondered, perhaps dallying longer than he should have. In no uncertain terms he was told to get a move on, but not before realising the workmen on the carriage roofs were painting on the letters 'POW'. He'd seen the same on top of the lorries that had brought him to the P.G. 85 but recalled the pursuing P-38 Lightnings had taken little notice. He doubted anyone would take any more this time around.

That said, the train was far from a helpless target. At three points along its length were defensive armaments intended to dissuade raiders from showing an interest. Behind the locomotive, halfway down the train and again at the rear were flatbed carriages with *Flakpanzer* IVs chained into position. Open-topped, but with an armoured nine-sided turret, they looked like giant eggcups housing ferocious quad-mounted 20mm cannons. The gunners could rotate the barrels through 360 degrees laterally and 180 degrees vertically. Jox had seen them in action in the Libyan desert, and the weight of fire they could throw up was deadly. The smoke from the stacks would certainly offer a tempting target, but these guns would ensure the train was far from defenceless.

Most of the freight cars were already loaded and sealed. Their timber doors were padlocked and tagged, the contents checked and secured. In yet another demonstration of Germanic efficiency, the door sills were papered with white sheets covered in signatures with the *Luftwaffe* eagle crest. *What on earth could merit this level of security?* thought Jox.

The last few boxcars were being loaded. Large, heavy-looking objects were carried in by struggling workmen, all wrapped in hessian fabric held in place with straps. Only their bases revealed delicately carved white marble in the form of sandaled feet. They appeared to be statues of some antiquity. Jox peered into one of the cars, finding several objects with shiny gilding, suggesting perhaps artefacts of a religious origin. Artworks were being loaded by other workers, rectangular panels which were most likely paintings. Each had been wrapped against damage, and there were dozens already stacked within the freight cars. How many more or what else the train might hold was mind-boggling to imagine.

Jox had heard of Reich Marshal Herman Goering's penchant for collecting fine art and that the Nazi elite had become equally enthusiastic collectors. As the war progressed, they'd overcome their concerns about whether certain art was deemed to be 'degenerate' or not, and the looting of artworks had begun on an industrial scale. Goering was known to be a rapacious collector, filling his vast hunting lodge, Carinhall, named after his Swedish first wife, with masterpieces stolen from across conquered Europe. Unlike most serious collectors, it was said he didn't much care for an established provenance and origin, much preferring confiscated artefacts that cost him nothing.

It was seeing the *Luftwaffe* eagle and stamps displaying the Reich Marshall's authority that made the penny drop for Jox. He suddenly realised why the prisoners selected for transfer were notable in one way or another. It was nothing to do with protecting them from the encroaching war, but rather that collectively they were the ideal human shield under which looted art could be secreted north unmolested. They were simply pawns in a game of international art theft.

Jox's dawdling had caught the eye of a guard on the platform who had a shaggy German shepherd dog on a silver chain. Without saying a word, he swung his truncheon, clubbing Jox behind the knees. The dog leapt off his lead and pounced on Jox, sinking its teeth into the heel of his flight boot. It began shaking its head with surprising strength, growling furiously with its muzzle still clamped around the leather. Jox was flung about like a ragdoll, as the handler roared with laughter. Above the din, there was a shout in German, and Jox's boot was immediately released.

Jox reached down and felt his torn, wet trousers, unsure if the damp on his fingers was blood or saliva. Still shaking from shock, he got unsteadily his feet and hobbled towards the lavatories.

'You should be more careful,' hissed Steiner. 'I believe you *Englanders* have an expression, "Curiosity killed the cat," *ja?* Come now, McNabb, we must leave soon.'

Once Jox got to the facilities, he locked himself in the cubicle and sat gasping for air. He waited for the pain in his leg to subside and for his heart to stop thumping. *God, that was terrifying. How bloody stupid to take chances with men like that, fresh from the killing fields of the Eastern Front.* He wouldn't make that mistake again. Jox limped back and was one of the last to re-join the crowd of prisoners being addressed by *Oberst* von Wella. As ever, Steiner was a sinister shadow at his shoulder.

'So, we are ready to leave,' said von Wella. 'We have not assigned specific seating for you all, but avoid the first carriage, which is reserved for my staff. Every passenger carriage will hold two of my armed men, who will be patrolling. Do not antagonise them. Our friend McNabb has already discovered that they are neither kindly nor hesitant and have been ordered not to hold back. Do not be tempted to move between carriages once we are underway. Any attempt to do so will be interpreted as an escape attempt and will be dealt with severely.'

He smiled, his pale eye surveying the gathered men. 'The journey should take only a few hours, and hopefully we will arrive before dark, of course depending on whether we attract *Jabos* or meet any structural damage to the railway infrastructure on the way. I've been assured our train has priority over all but the most vital trains, and since we are travelling in the opposite direction to trains reinforcing troops and ammunition, we will only be competing with hospital trains from the front.' He smiled icily. 'Our wounded *Kameraden* are making way for gentlemen of your importance. I do hope you are grateful, and I wish you a good trip.'

Steiner whispered into his ear.

'Ach yes, I almost forgot, we have provided some reading material to help pass the time, a selection of English-language periodicals.' He nodded to his men, who handed out magazines and newspapers. It started a frenzy amongst the prisoners, starved as they were of news, desperate to learn about the progress of the war. Jox managed to grab an English-language version of *Signal*, the *Wehrmacht's* photo journal, and Beans got a copy of *Der Adler*, the *Luftwaffe's* equivalent. Neither had time to look beyond the covers before being called to board. There followed a cacophony of '*Raus, raus*', before the hundred or so prisoners were shepherded aboard.

Jox found himself in a creaking old six-seater carriage with sealed windows, streaked with soot and smelling of damp horsehair cushions and stale cigarettes. His travel companions were Darren Beans, Wyszkowski, Tex Carver, Muriel Perrin and Tim Reid-Steele.

Initially, the novelty of a train journey and travelling freely for the first time in months kept most of the men glued to the grimy windows. Others settled down to have a rest or nibbled on the rations they'd brought along.

'How's the leg feeling?' Beans asked Jox.

'It sounded worse than it actually was,' replied Jox, rubbing his bruised calf. 'It was getting whacked with that bloody great stick that hurt more than the dog. My boot's knackered, though. Those SS fellows don't mess about. We're certainly not dealing with Eyeties anymore.'

'Glad you're all right, Jox,' said Reid-Steele. 'Anyone fancy a cracker?' He was handing out soda crackers from a Red Cross package.

Carver threatened to light a cigarette but for the good of all was asked not to by Jox and Reid-Steele. He wasn't happy about it but caved in to peer pressure and the fact that they were higher-ranking officers. He was in a bad mood about having been separated from Vollick, who was travelling in a separate carriage, and was grumbling, 'God damned Limeys, still think you rule the world.'

'Knock it off, Tex,' said Beans. 'It stinks bad enough in here, and it's only going to get worse with the six of us stuck for God knows how long. Your evil-smelling weed would only add to the fug. Here, read my magazine.' He threw the copy of *Der Adler* over to him.

Carver flicked through the first few pages petulantly, then stopped and gave a low whistle. 'Well, well, would you look at that.' He began reading out loud. '"A magnificent trio of fighter aces. Captured flyboys enjoy *Luftwaffe* hospitality." Hey, looks like you're famous, boys.'

He held the magazine open at an article with several pictures. The largest one, below the headline, showed three smiling men holding wine glasses up in a toast. What was unusual was that the picture showed two of them had on matching black eye patches.

'Aw, damn,' said Beans. 'We're in the papers, fraternising with the enemy. The whole of America's going see that, Jox.'

'It's not much better here,' said Reid-Steele, holding up a spread in *Signal* magazine with a photograph of himself, Colonel du Boulay and *Colonnello* Flavius grinning towards the camera. The headline read: *Ciao bello, captivity isn't so bad.* He shook his head. 'I can tell you the colonel's cousin certainly won't like that.'

Jox's heart sank. There he was in black and white, apparently in cahoots with the enemy. That would undoubtedly require explanation if he ever made it back to friendly lines. He could have kicked himself. How had he blundered into this? He cursed his gullibility and naivety, realising he'd been well and truly played.

Their 'celebrity' status *was* being used as a human shield to smuggle looted art and God knew what else. These stories and images of the selected men 'fraternising' with the enemy had been used to tell the Allies exactly which train they would be on, ensuring it would not be attacked. The very idea of being seen as a collaborator horrified Jox. His mind was racing. This looked bad, perhaps not Lord Haw-Haw bad, the Nazi lackey who made radio broadcasts from Berlin, but still bad.

Given just how cunning and manipulative von Wella had proven to be, it seemed likely that he would share this story with Lord Haw-Haw's equivalent in the Mediterranean — Axis Sally, who broadcast from Rome, providing the perfect way of spreading the story up the Allied chain of command. Like almost every servicemen in Tunisia and during the Sicilian advance, Jox had listened to Sally's dulcet and witheringly sarcastic tones on the radio. Her real name was Rita Luisa Zucca and she was actually Italian American, originally from Manhattan, New York. She would surely find this scenario highly amusing and would certainly capitalise on the story.

Jox groaned at the very prospect. He could just imagine her sarcastic venom after her usual greeting of, 'Hello suckers!' and before her teasing sign-off: 'sealed with a sweet kiss from Axis Sally.' He covered his eyes with his hands. God only knew how she'd spin the story, but it wouldn't be good.

The train chugged west for about an hour before Jox emerged from his foul mood. By then, the periodicals had done the rounds, read by all six in the compartment, with each successive reading resulting in expletives, harsh laughter and expressions of frustration.

'We needed that like a hole in the head,' growled Major Reid-Steele. 'I can see their "generalships" of the India Office getting in a right tizzy over this blatant fraternisation.'

'That's not what galls me. What does is being played for a fool by that damned von Wella,' Jox replied. 'I don't know if you chaps clocked all the gear being loaded into the freight cars. To me it looked like a whole bunch of artworks, antiquities, paintings and the like. Almost anything might be stashed away on this train. Von Wella isn't taking any chances with the precious cargo on board, and just to be clear, that isn't us.' He laughed bitterly. 'By splashing our pictures across the press, he's ensured that the whole world knows that we're on this train. That way, he can be sure that Alexander, Patton and Montgomery won't order an attack on von Wella's express train, since they've got family aboard. We so-called "*Prominente*" prisoners are just extra insurance. That cunning one-eyed devil has really played a blinder.' Jox hesitated. 'Sorry, Bayou, I didn't mean any offence.'

Beans shook his head, adjusted his eye patch, looked up and grinned. 'None taken, buddy. I can see why you're riled up. Von Wella's Express — kinda has a ring to it.'

'It just makes me so damned cross,' replied Jox. 'Don't know about you lot, but I'm getting sick and tired of being pushed around like a pawn in someone else's game of chess.' He rubbed his bruised leg. 'Will you look at the state of my bloody boot?' He lifted his foot; the leather was torn with clear bitemarks, and the sole was hanging off. 'That dog practically chewed my damned leg off,' he fumed. 'I don't care how flipping "beautiful" this new camp is, the first chance I get, I'm out of there. Come on, who's with me?'

'Steady on, old boy,' said Reid-Steele. 'Colonel du Boulay certainly wouldn't approve. He'll doubtless insist he has his orders and we're to sit tight until liberated. In any case, you'll have to submit your plan to the escape committee for approval. That's the agreed form.'

'Aw, come on, Tim,' said Beans. 'Me and Muriel are all that's left of the damned escape committee. I'm with Jox. How about you, *Mon-sewar* Perrin?'

The Frenchman grimaced at the atrocious pronunciation and shrugged.

'How about you, Whisky?' asked Jox.

'Yes, I'll come,' the wild-haired airman replied, nodding enthusiastically.

'I ain't gonna let you damned fools disappear without me again, so count me in,' said Carver, his signature toothpick back between his teeth. 'You can count on Shooter Vollick too.'

'Well, I don't intend to be left behind as some useless tail-end Charlie,' blustered Reid-Steele. 'All right, my boys, I'm in. Just don't tell the bloody colonel.'

'There's nothing to tell him,' said Jox. 'In any case, what he doesn't know, won't hurt him. He's perfectly at liberty to sit tight and wait for "Cousin Alex", but I'm going to be a tad more proactive. I'm not sitting on my arse, hoping for rescue.'

'Fair enough,' replied Reid-Steele. 'Still, we can't do anything until we get there, so we might as well enjoy the trip. Anyone fancy another cracker?'

The landscape of Puglia flashed past the grime-streaked window. A clear, cloudless sky provided visibility for miles, a perfect fighter pilot's sky. They were heading broadly westwards, leaving the coastal plains, towards cloud-covered mountains, some already capped with snow. In contrast, to the east, there were tantalising glimpses of the Adriatic, sparkling bright in the late summer sunshine.

Jox tried to picture where he was on the map in his head. Beyond the twinkling ocean was Albania, a country he knew little about, but which had had a powerful effect on his life. He fingered the crimson square of fabric stitched onto his tunic breast. It represented the Albanian Order of Merit which he'd been awarded by King Zog during the London Blitz. He'd never quite worked out why, but the memory of that time made him smile despite the unknown which lay ahead. He was suddenly swept up by a wave of sadness, realising that Moose Grant, his old Canuk pal had been by his side on that occasion, but had since died. There was also the inimitable Tom 'Monty' Falls who'd stepped in to provide a virtuoso doppelganger for Zog, which had gone a long way towards convincing the Axis that Sardinia was the real target for invasion rather than Sicily. General Baade and *Oberst* von Wella had confirmed as much, giving Jox some satisfaction that getting duped by the enemy wasn't a one-way street. He sighed; both of his dear friends were gone now, like so many others. He almost imagined that he could smell the tobacco fug that had always followed Monty around, and for that matter King Zog too.

The smell was too strong to be his imagination. He turned to discover that Carver had succumbed to his cravings. It immediately caused an uproar in the compartment, with several chaps ganging up to remove the source of the noxious smoke.

The irate Texan complained vociferously, but eventually put it out.

The sun-kissed countryside flashed by, one minute providing a view of verdant olive groves, the next gnarled grape vines, interspersed with fields of golden cereal crops currently being harvested. There were few signs of mechanised agriculture, and the inhabitants appeared to be living barely above subsistence level. *How will this primitive land ever bear the encroaching wrath of modern war?* Jox wondered.

Muriel Perrin, who was taking a keen interest in the passing vineyards, suddenly exclaimed, 'Look at that!'

As the train curved around a long bend, several large metallic disks appeared on the horizon. They were scattered across a bluff, all facing the same way, like giant sunflowers tracking the sun. Jox recognised them as ground-based radar tracking systems, designed to detect high-altitude bombing raids.

'Anyone who thinks Jerry is on his last legs is seriously deluded,' said Jox, gazing at the sinister giant cups. 'If they're still building infrastructure like that, and make no mistake that gear is brand new and state of the art, then they're far from being done for. With that kind of kit, they'll know all about incoming raids the minute they boil up over Tunisia or the Med. I can remember the same scenario during the Battle of Britain, when we had the advantage and prior warning when Jerry was coming. It saved us hours of stooging around, waiting for them to arrive. The tables are now turned, and not for the better.' He pulled a face. 'I can remember being on Ramrod missions in '41, when we escorted medium bombers going after ground targets like those. The radar installations Jerry built on the Channel Islands and along the Atlantic coast were similar.'

The train slowed, leaving the plains and starting the climb into the mountainous, forested region of Basilicata. With the altitude, the men's ears started to pop, a familiar sensation for the aviators amongst them. Jox found it oddly comforting, and as the gradient steepened, he admired the sweeping view of the panoramic flatlands below. Towards the Adriatic coast, there were the distinctive crossed runways of an airfield; tiny flecks of aircraft could be seen taking off. Rising through the air, they were like sparks in the sunlight as they climbed, then turned towards the train. The men began debating what kind of aircraft they were, settling finally on snub-nosed Focke-Wulf 190s, painted in the mottled green and tan camouflage pattern which the Italians reserved for the desert theatre of war. It looked like an entire *Staffel*, three separate *Schwärme* separating to take up positions to the front and rear of the train, and then high above it to provide the threat of the proverbial 'Hun in the sun'.

The direction of travel swung southwest, continuing to climb the southern Apennines. In doing so, the train was coming within reach of long-range Allied fighters out of northern Sicily — aircraft like the box-shaped P-38 Lightnings that Jox had seen days ago, but also new Republic P-47 Thunderbolts, which he knew less well. They were massive, slab-sided aircraft, the largest and heaviest single-engine fighters in the Allied armoury, which made a speciality of hitting ground targets with a particular penchant for locomotives and trains. Both types had ranges of three thousand kilometres when equipped with external fuel tanks, enough to cover the outward and return legs between Sicily and the Italian mainland. The straight-line distance between Palermo and Naples was around 320 kilometres, and between Messina and Taranto about 300, allowing for a reasonable amount of deadly dwell time on target. This was a capability that enabled the aircraft to accompany bomber raids far up the 'calf' of Italy, perhaps even as far as Rome.

These high mountains were reputedly full of caves, where bears and wolves roamed. The steep landscape had a reputation for deadly landslides and wild men who made a living from brigandage and mountain robbery. It seemed likely that they would also provide a core for the growing band of partisans that Steiner and his men were here to eradicate.

Amongst the craggy peaks and forested folds in the terrain, the train found some cover, but nonetheless was still in the danger zone with both aerial and terrestrial threats. Von Wella was taking no chances and had arranged for a personal air escort as a double insurance policy.

The first sign of trouble was the sudden buzzsaw roar of quad-mounted autocannon guns opening fire from chained positions on their flatbed carriages. As the train followed the gradient, it arched to the left, providing a brief glimpse of the locomotive and the forward gun positions as they fired. Silhouetted against the rail-side vegetation Jox saw the helmeted figure of the gun's captain peering skywards through binoculars. He raised his arm and gesticulated towards a dark shadow hurtling towards the train. The four barrels juddered, loosening off a blistering trail of fire. The gunner inside the armoured eggcup was firing using foot pedals — each firing two of the diametrically opposite barrels. They had an effective vertical range of 2,200 metres, specifically designed to protect against low-flying aircraft like these.

The aircraft in question swooped towards them, flashing in the azure sky like the silver flanks of trout glimpsed in a babbling burn. What was clear to Jox was that these slow-flying metallic slabs were nothing like the slim, sleek silhouettes of P-

38 Lightnings. Instead, they had squared-off muzzle-like front ends, chequered like a chessboard, with a large propellor spinning ahead of the white USAAF star on a blue roundel painted directly onto the shiny metal fuselage. A pair of lumbering P-47 Thunderbolts were buzzing the train, just low enough to make it obvious that they'd spotted the train but were taking no steps to engage it. With the flak gunners firing at them, this was a dangerous game of brinksmanship. Almost inevitably one of them was struck, but remarkably seemed to absorb the damage, unaffected other than giving off a thin trail of black smoke. It pulled up, revealing a number of gashes in its metal fuselage, but flew on apparently unperturbed.

Jox had heard about these great big fighters. They were much maligned by pilots of sleeker aircraft types, but beloved by their own pilots, particularly prized for their ruggedness, endurance and survivability, not to mention the weight of fire they could throw down. In the US fighter armoury, the P-38 Lightnings and P-51 Mustangs were often seen as elegant, sleek and finely engineered, in the same way as perhaps the Spitfire was. In which case, the sturdy Thunderbolt or 'Jug' might be compared to the trusty workhorse, the Hurricane. As a former Hurricane pilot himself, Jox had a lot of affection and sympathy for this perceived underdog, which in his own experience was anything but.

Unfortunately, it appeared that the pair of P-47s had been sent on a reconnaissance or perhaps an intimidation mission but hadn't counted on such a warm reception. Had it even occurred to the Yank pilots why a POW train should merit such a degree of protection?

The sky through which they'd approached the train reminded Jox of a sheet of music. The contrails of their evasive action provided the lines and the deadly black pattern of flak, the notes. He imagined they represented a piece of music with an opening duet of violinists, with the multiple tracks of deadly FW 190s coming after them like a pursuing orchestra. If so, the composition was building to a crescendo and threatening a terrible climax.

The American pair were now straining to get away from the train zigzagging between the peaks and troughs in the landscape. The FW 190s, pairs of leaders and wingmen, were after them, striking with a catastrophic number of hits. The slower, already damaged Thunderbolt lost power and fell like a brick. Perhaps the pilot was already dead as his forward momentum carried his tattered aircraft along the rail tracks behind the retreating train. Striking the ground, rails and pilings were gouged up, throwing up gravel scree, timber fragments from weathered sleepers and bright sparks from screaming metal. The wreckage came to a heaving halt by the trackside, only recognisable as roadkill that had been struck by something large and very powerful.

His partner's demise was equally spectacular. At the first sign of attack, he'd pulled up hard, skimming the sheer rockface of the mountain that loomed above the train. He'd almost made it over the top when struck by fire from the deadly FW 190s. Cannon fire punctured his fuel tanks, erupting into huge flames that swiftly enveloped the engine and cockpit. It really was as if he'd been struck by a thunderbolt, with the subsequent collision with the rockface marked by a thundering boom, discernible even over the roar of the locomotive, the double reports of the ack-ack guns and the grinding of carriage bogies along the twisting rails. On the port side of the shuddering train, lit aviation fuel slid down the rockface, setting vegetation alight and triggering multiple land slips. It was a fair imitation of the lava flow that Jox had seen from Etna's fiery yaw.

The scene was suddenly gone, as Jox was plunged into darkness. The train had entered a tunnel, bored through the very heart of the mountain, now providing shelter and escape from the maelstrom raging overhead. The brutal demise of the American airmen, clinically executed by the 'butcher bird' *Staffel* were left behind, the express trundling northwards unaffected and seemingly uncaring, with all the secrets it carried unknown but to a few.

CHAPTER SEVEN

The view from P.G. 35 at the *Certosa di Padula* was breathtaking. In the eastern portion of the stunning *Parco Nazionale del Cilento e Vallo di Diano*, the prospect of seeing out the war here, tucked safely out of the way, certainly held some appeal.

It was a vast honey-coloured complex with sagging terracotta roofs covered in lichen. Far more impressive than the modest farm buildings at P.G. 85, the monastery covered almost three acres and included the largest cloistered courtyard in the world. It was designed to provide resident monks with an open space but still keep them away from the temptations of the outside world. Its current role as a place of detention was perhaps not so different, save for the degree of enforcement and the penalty for escape.

Familiarising himself with the grounds, Jox had noticed that the large lawned courtyard showed the trace of countless feet running from one corner to the other and from side to side, creating a perfect imprint of the British Union Jack, something he felt sure would be unmistakable at altitude. It felt encouraging that the flag of the union should be there, raising the new inmates' spirits, when they were faced with the despondency of their withdrawal from advancing Allied lines.

Von Wella, Steiner and their troops were presumably occupied with securing their cargo, and the prisoners were handed over to P.G. 35's Italian authorities. Once counted, registered and checked over medically, Jox and the rest of the new arrivals were provided with a heel of bread and some chicory coffee. They were then allocated monastic cells, each sleeping four, with Jox bunking up with Beans, Wyszkowski and Perrin. The bedding provided was straw-filled palliasses and grubby striped pillows. They were then allowed to explore their new surroundings and to meet the resident *Kriegie* population.

The monastic life of *Certosa di Padula* had been designed with clear distinctions between time spent in religious contemplation and time spent working. On the one hand, there were peaceful cloisters and a vast marble staircase leading to a now empty library. The floors were covered with vivid, hand-coloured Vietri ceramic tiles, and there were several ornately decorated chapels celebrating the glory of God. Altar fronts were of spectacular 18th century *scagliola* inlaid marblework, and for men wearied by the ugliness of war and the drudgery of imprisonment, to see such beauty was a balm, lifting their spirits when most needed.

The other side of monastic life was visible in the facility's extensive kitchens and cellars filled with enormous, yet sadly empty, wooden wine vats. There were laundries, workshops and yards dedicated to many different trades, and the prisoners' work was varied, overseen by monks, local peasants and often distracted guards. There were also stables, a bakery, food stores and even a working olive oil mill.

As comfortable as their new digs were, Jox and his roommates began scouting for a means of escape, searching for any weakness in the ancient monastery's dilapidated infrastructure. Compared to P.G. 85, security was lax, but it seemed likely that this regime would change if and when Steiner's SS and *Fallschirmjäger* troops took residence, especially if the stolen artworks were also stored here. There was no shortage of cellars and other dark nooks and crannies to secrete things away.

Wyszkowski was the most gifted at spotting opportunities. He'd located a hidden manhole cover, overgrown with grass. He'd somehow managed to lift it, discovering a hidden cellar. It was a perfect hiding place and an ideal starting point for a tunnel under the outer wall. He'd also identified points in the ancient walls where it wouldn't be too difficult to scrape out the crumbling mortar to dislodge bricks and gain access to hidden spaces within.

'I don't think we'd have much trouble busting out of here,' said Beans, after they had been in the camp for a few days. 'Security is lax, and the Eyeties seem happy to tread water until the Allies get here. If we don't bug them, they'll leave us alone.'

'In a perfect world, you'd probably be right,' said Jox. 'But that's not where we live. I have little doubt that von Wella and Steiner will tighten security over the next few days. Remember he mentioned German divisions heading south? Then there's the fact that whatever we were "shielding" on the train is most likely somewhere around here and will require guarding. My view is that security will soon be ramped up, so if we plan to break out, we need to do it quickly.'

'We should consider what the prisoners already here have to say,' said Perrin. 'Most of them are Desert Rats. I spoke to some New Zealanders who have been here a long time. They say the terrain out there is rough, especially in the mountains where the weather turns quickly. We're in autumn now, and they've warned that weather conditions are starting to become treacherous and unpredictable.' He looked around to check that they weren't being overheard. 'They've built a radio of sorts and are following the Allied advance on the BBC, but they are also getting an opposite point of view from Axis Sally. The British have landed near Taranto on the stirrup of Italy in something called Operation Slapstick. The Royal Navy have disembarked the British 1st Airborne Division onto the beaches and near the port. They met little opposition, but it is reported that their commanding general was killed, so perhaps it wasn't entirely unopposed.'

'That wasn't Hopkinson, was it?' asked Jox.

'I think that was the name. According to Axis Sally, he's the first British General killed in action during the Italian campaign.'

'What a shame. I met him in Tunisia before the invasion of Sicily. He and Major-General Matthew Ridgway, commanding the US 82nd Airborne Division, caught a lot of flak for how badly the airborne operations went on the first few nights. I can imagine him wanting to stick close to his lead units, somehow trying to make amends, but then getting caught by enemy fire. It's a great pity; he was a good leader.'

Perrin nodded then continued, 'So now the Allies are advancing towards Brindisi and the Adriatic. As we speak, they have probably liberated the men we left behind at P.G. 85.'

'Of all the lousy luck,' grumbled Beans.

'The question is still whether we sit and wait or take our chances,' Perrin added. 'The Kiwis have been waiting a long time and are determined to stay put until liberated. I'm sure Colonel du Boulay and his entourage will want to do the same.'

'That would be a mistake,' said Jox. 'Jerry's reinforcements will be here well before the Allies. We all saw the mountains our chaps will need to get through before reaching us. That's before we even factor in the well defended lines they will need to breach. It could take months to reach us. In the meantime, von Wella and his attack dogs won't just sit on their hands. They'll be planning to evacuate their loot, taking us as "protective cover" with them. I suspect a trip north is already on the cards. We need to get organised before that happens.'

'I agree,' said Wyszkowski. 'Things will not be so gentlemanly when fighting the Germans. In my country, we have seen far too many atrocities to trust they will behave well when things go bad. It will be carnage.'

They were interrupted by a deep rumbling overhead. Jox looked to the heavens, where countless lines of water vapour, the white contrails of dozens of heavy bombers, appeared at altitude. The sight was mesmerising, seemingly relentless.

'I sure hope they don't use this Union Jack as a bombing grid,' muttered Beans.

'I wouldn't think so,' replied Jox. 'I'm pretty sure they'd be well briefed that there are prisoners in this monastery.'

'I wouldn't count on that, considering the number of operational SNAFUs we've seen. Hell, look at that debacle at Morlaix.'

The previously unblemished blue sky was now filled with striations, as if some monstrous cat was scratching at it. They were heading broadly north-west, most likely targeting industrial complexes. Some of the parallel lines seemed to diverge, as if something unseen was making the B-17 Flying Fortresses deviate from their flight plan. Jox could see no trace of AA fire, none of the telltale black blobs that indicated that 88 mm guns or larger calibres were firing at the bomber formations. It was logical to assume it was the impact of enemy fighters, a suspicion confirmed by fresh white lines appearing at angles to the formation's direction of travel, contrail evidence of the interceptors.

The aerial combat was too high to hear, and yet its balletic evolutions became more obvious as it unfolded. Glinting pinpricks of reflected light came off the canopies of enemy fighters as they jinked amongst the bombers. They were hard to make out, but their effect on the massed B-17s was becoming increasingly obvious. Several stricken four-engined behemoths began to drop out of position, failing engines tracing lines away from the main force. Here and there they were now black, testament to engine fires no doubt raging out of control.

Suddenly, what looked like a giant black spider formed, legs steadily lengthening. Still unheard, it was drawn vividly against the heavens, evidence that a bombload had detonated in the belly of a stricken ship. Several Forts were now falling, the flecks of jumping men seen cartwheeling away like sparks cast from a tumbling log in a bonfire. As they reached lower altitudes, parachutes blossomed and the sky resembled sea shallows full of floating white jellyfish.

There was the sudden snarl of a low-flying aircraft overhead. The roar of a Focke-Wulf 190 shook Jox from his mesmerised reverie. It climbed towards the concentration of chutes, its intentions becoming increasingly clear. To Jox's growing horror, it opened fire. First one parachute, then a second collapsed under the onslaught. There were cries of outrage rising from the quadrangle, as the watching prisoners saw the 'killer shrike' was targeting bomber boys hanging helplessly in their straps. A war crime of the worst kind was unfolding before their eyes.

Wyszkowski raged, 'Like I said earlier, no more with the gentlemanly warfare. This is what Joseph Goebbels meant when he called for "total war". That's what we're up against now. I don't expect the Germans to be any more merciful with us, before the advancing Allies. It will be even worse for the local population. The Nazis will not forget being betrayed by the Italian people.'

A few days later Jox was on a chair, bare-chested in front of Shooter Vollick, who had arrived at the monastery shortly after the men Jox had travelled with. Jox's right arm was being worked on by the Texan bombardier.

Vollick had come to Jox with a proposal. In his cupped hand, he'd held a dead scorpion, three inches long. There were myriads of them living in the cracks and fissures of the ancient monastery buildings. He'd also been carrying a medical pack in a canvas shoulder bag like something that might hold a gasmask. He pulled out a large black bulb attached to a stand and an electric lead and plug and explained that the apparatus was from a Red Cross medical pack. It was apparently designed for malnourished prisoners to strip down to their underwear, put on protective goggles and get illuminated by the 'black light' to encourage the production of Vitamin D, hopefully staving off health problems associated with poor nutrition.

'All right,' Vollick had said excitedly. 'Check this out.' They were in the dark monastic cell which Jox shared with roommates. He switched on the 'black light', and it buzzed before starting to glow, throwing off a purple-coloured light. In the beam, the dead scorpion glowed a vivid bright blue. 'There are a number of substances that fluoresce under UV light. The exoskeleton of this little feller, but also ordinary things like vinegar, honey, urine, tonic water and even a simple solution of quinine extracted from our malaria tablets. They all glow in different colours when illuminated. I could make a finely ground-up solution of some combination of those, all of which are more or less easily available here and would meet the requirements of your "officer and gentleman's" tattoo code. You see, it would be there but unseen until required. Only you would know, unless you exposed it to UV light.'

'You're definitely not sticking someone's piss into my skin,' snorted Jox.

'It wouldn't be urine anymore, just one of the components to create the dye. Everything will be sterile and clean, I promise.' Vollick was grinning, clearly excited to have cracked the challenge. His enthusiasm was infectious. 'Say, what names do you actually want inscribed?'

'Probably won't make much sense to you,' replied Jox. 'You see, I have a lucky talisman. It's a porcelain doll's arm that I picked up near Dunkirk, back in '40. My squadron had just landed in France and were getting refuelled before heading out on patrol. Over the hedge, there was a ragged column of refugees fleeing from the Germans. I befriended a little girl, whose name was Marguerite. She showed me her most precious possession, her little dolly. As we chatted, a flight of Stukas attacked. In the confusion, with everyone racing for cover, I lost track of her. The column was devastated, and I couldn't find Marguerite after that. What I did find was the porcelain arm of her doll. I've kept it ever since, and it's got me through quite a few scrapes. Marguerite's name has also been on all of my aircraft and the arm has become my talisman. She represents what I'm fighting this war for.'

Jox's eyes were blazing. He cuffed away a wayward tear. 'Since then, I've had Marguerite's name and those of two other children painted onto the arm. Elias Vella was a Maltese boy who helped pull me out of a wrecked Spitfire. The poor kid was then killed by a marauding *Jabo*. Then there's Violetta Dennini, a brave little girl who I met in Sicily. Her father rescued me from the sea, and I owe him my life.

'During all those scrapes, the doll's arm got damaged, so I sent it off to get fixed, and didn't actually have it with me for my last mission. In my head, logically or not, that's why I got shot down and captured. I had misgivings about flying without it, and so it was proven. I feel terribly exposed without it.' He looked sheepish. 'I'm hoping that getting those names tattooed onto my arm will break that jinx. We're going to need as much luck as possible if we're going to break out of here.'

Vollick grinned. 'That's as good a reason for a tattoo as I've ever heard. I surely don't want to mess with any juju you might have going on. You're a survivor, Jox, lucky too, and we're going to need a whole lot of that where we're going.'

CHAPTER EIGHT

Jox's arm was still tender when news of the armistice arrived. In truth, nothing actually arrived, it was simply that P.G. 35 awoke to find that all the Italian guards had vanished. The date was Wednesday, the 8th of September 1943.

The *Kriegies* initially reacted with wild jubilation, but this was soon replaced by a creeping anxiety and eventually fear. The men who had been incarcerated for a long time became uncomfortable with breaks from their daily routine and the confines of the small world they were used to.

The monastery's farm workers also failed to appear. Only the brother monks, clad in their pristine white habits with pointed hoods, were going about their daily tasks, unperturbed by the travails of the outside world. Most were unwilling or unable to provide any insight into current events, some because of vows of silence that had been taken decades ago, others because they'd foresworn the base matters of man.

Brother Angelo was different. Tall and skeletal, he spoke some rudimentary English and had a permanently haunted expression attributed to the horrors he'd seen as a young man, when fighting the Austro-Hungarians during the last war.

'The newspapers call it the Armistice of Cassibile, since it was signed in Sicily. *Generale di Brigata* Giuseppe Castellano signed for Italy, the King and Marshal Pietro Badoglio. He is the youngest *generale* in *Italia*,' said Brother Angelo. 'Now, we can hope for the holy peace. How you say, the massacre of the innocents is over, praise be to God.'

'What else have you heard, Brother Angelo?' Jox asked gently, knowing it wouldn't take much for him to retreat under his white hood, turtlelike into the shell of his chosen solitude.

'*Il Duce* is a prisoner like you. His Majesty and government make the peace with the English and the Americans. The *Tedeschi* soldiers must leave now.'

'Leave?' said Wyszkowski. 'The Germans will never leave. No, now it will truly begin.'

As if on cue, the roar of engines could be heard outside. It was earthbound, rather than from the heavens, but came from beyond the mountains surrounding the monastery. The noise reverberated around the valley, so it was hard to tell exactly where it came from, as the throaty growls echoed from beyond the men's line of sight. Only when the low rumbling was joined by the high-pitched squeals of armoured tracks, did Jox realise the sound was of armour on the move. There was no way of knowing which army it belonged to, but it was unlikely to be Allied. Most probably, it was a German panzer force putting on a show of strength on this day of Italian defection, advancing ostentatiously towards the Allied lines. It would be sending an emphatic message to the local populace that the *Tedeschi* were going nowhere.

'It's now or never,' said Jox at the hastily gathered meeting of those who'd shared the train carriage up to the monastery. All day, there'd been furious debates over what to do in the face of the wholesale abandonment by the prison guards. They'd simply disappeared into the ether, as if terrified by what was coming. These sentiments were shared by the ragtag band of Italian soldiers that soon appeared at the monastery gates, begging for food and water. Most were half-dressed in barely recognisable uniform, paired with civilian clothing looted along the way. Dishevelled and unkempt, they were euphoric at the news of the war ending but petrified of what the Germans would do next.

Encouraged by their joy, and strictly against the orders of the Senior British Officer, Colonel du Boulay, small groups of prisoners began venturing off into the open countryside to gather intelligence, scavenge for food and just for the sheer adventure of doing as they pleased after months, sometimes years of incarceration. Many disappeared to unknown fates, but one straggling group did return, traumatised and with two less members than they'd set off with that morning. They'd seen hordes of Italian soldiers in the villages and up on the mountains, some weapon-less, but others armed and dangerous. It appeared that some groups were ashamed, but others were angry at the news of the capitulation, and had opened fire, killing a young subaltern of the Honourable Artillery Company Regiment RHA.

'It has to be tonight,' Jox urged the group. 'We tell no one; the more discreet we are, the better. We'll travel faster at night, with less people about.' He looked from eye to eye. 'The question is which direction we go in.' He took a deep breath. 'Northwest of here is the beach that leads up to the port of Salerno. It seems like a likely spot for the Allies to attempt a landing. There's seventy miles between there and here, across some pretty arduous mountains of the Meridional Apennines. The alternative is to follow the valley and main road north, but then we're likely to run into German reinforcements coming down the *Vallo di Diano*. Personally, I don't think blundering blindly towards the front lines is a good idea. Before we reach any friendlies, we'd have to cross enemy positions and defensive lines, and they're unlikely to let us simply waltz through.'

'Jox is quite right,' said Major Reid-Steele, the only infantryman amongst them. 'We can't go charging around the countryside just because we're desperate to get home.'

'Thanks, Tim,' said Jox. 'If the information we've got is accurate, the Brits are on the Adriatic, working their way up from Taranto to Brindisi and on towards Bari. I think our best bet would be to head east. It's further to go and there are more formidable mountains to cross, but at least we wouldn't be in an active combat zone all of the way. What do you think?' There were nods all round. 'Tonight, it is,' he concluded with chilling finality.

The chosen men stole away under cover of darkness, a little before midnight. The elaborate tunnel that had been excavated and the hidden passages through the ancient monastery in the end were surplus to requirements. To escape, they simply stole out of a side gate into the darkness of the Campagna countryside.

There were seven of them: Jox, Beans, Reid-Steele, Perrin, Wyszkowski, Carver and Vollick. It was agreed that Reid-Steele was in command and would lead the way, with the rest following in pairs. Jox and Wyszkowski went second, following the major through the columned cloisters around the enclosed 'Union Jack' lawn.

Once outside, they crossed a courtyard, the leather soles of their shoes tapping noisily on the cobbles. Jox cursed his right boot, the one that had been savaged by the SS dog, which was now in a very bad state. He'd tied it up with twine, hoping it might hold together for long enough to get him through the mountains, but he was starting to doubt it would. He was very mindful of what his old mentor, Anthony Glasgow had said regarding failing footwear doing him more damage than anything else during his own 'home run' from an Austrian POW camp. Jox would need to find a solution, but in the meantime, he had no alternative but to soldier on.

Reaching a drainage ditch, the major crouched low, waiting for the rest to catch up. They followed the ditch for several hundred yards as it ran alongside the road into Padula. Passing a squeaking gate, they then crossed a dry-stone dyke and began climbing a steep field beyond. In the pale moonlight, the sound of their feet and rasping breath was impossibly loud. Reaching a grove of stunted olive trees, it dawned on Jox how unfit they'd become after months of poor nutrition and inactivity. Beans and Reid-Steele were blowing like old dray horses, the former still weak from his flogging, the latter older than the rest and out of shape from being in the bag since the summer of '42.

They had water, but limited food, as the Red Cross parcels hadn't yet caught up with them at P.G. 35. They would need to live off the land, trusting to fortune to provide. From the top of the hill, there was a good view back on the *Certosa di Padula*. Its sheer size was an indication of the fervour behind its dedication to the martyred Saint Lorenzo. Despite its vastness, little light emanated from it, just the pale half-moon bathing the valley in an eerie blue light. On the opposite side of the valley, Padula sparkled brighter, the sound of accordion music coming from the village, despite the late hour and tragic events earlier in the day. Occasionally, the crackle of gunfire interrupted the revelry, but it was unclear whether it was celebratory or retaliatory.

The Apennine mountains that could be seen from the monastery now stood before them. They'd always been a looming presence, but no one had ever really considered having to climb them. As they began the ascent, the air become decidedly colder, but Jox still found himself sweating with exertion, the salt on his skin stinging on the names tattooed across his bicep.

In the early hours of the morning, they rested in a semi-circle, struggling for breath in the thinning alpine air. Jox's night vision was ruined as the sky was suddenly torn apart by bright flashing and the rumbling of artillery fire. Where it was from and where it went was unclear, but the whooshing of shells overhead, followed by flashes beyond the high peaks were terrifying. Brilliant white detonations edged the jagged horizon in an awesome display of firepower that sapped everyone's spirits and slowed their continuing progress.

By first light, morale rose as they reached the jagged summit of their first peak. The journey had taken them on a parallel course to the sounds of the guns, rather than towards them. Ahead, there was a pass between two slopes, with signs of battle revealed by the dawn.

Reid-Steele identified the bombed-out defensive positions. 'In the Indian Army we call these sangars, typical mountain tactics used on the Northwest Frontier. Where it's too rocky to dig, we'd build defensive positions by piling up blocks of stones to provide cover. The stones can stop a bullet or grenade fragment, but if hit by a proper artillery stonk, their fragments are as deadly as any shrapnel. They're not really much protection from mortars either, as rounds go straight up and down into the positions, whereas conventional artillery hits sideways. Not ideal, but if you can't dig, there's not much of an alternative.'

He began picking his way through the shattered positions, the bottoms of which held pockets of swirling mist. As he cleared the area around his boots, a crumpled body wearing khaki battledress was revealed, surrounded by several dead

Germans. 'This chap here looks like a Gurkha,' the major said sadly. 'Plucky little fellow sold his life dearly. The Gurkhas are fearsome fighters.'

The positions had been abandoned in haste after taking a pasting. The Gurkhas had clearly been overrun and had made a fighting retreat, the Germans passing through in pursuit. The evidence was there in the ragged lines of hulking German paratroopers and the Indian Army soldiers lying side by side, unburied. The Gurkhas had been searched and most had their oversized Tommy helmets placed over their faces, their khaki uniforms stained black by wounds and the toes of their clumpy boots pointing skywards. To Jox, they looked rather like broken dolls, despite their fearsome reputation as warriors.

'Do you suppose it would be all right if I pinched the boots off one of these chaps?' Jox asked sheepishly.

Reid-Steele glared at first but softened. 'I don't suppose there's any harm in it. They won't be needing them anymore.'

Jox passed down a forlorn row until he found a potential fit. He felt like a grave robber, but knew finding a stout pair of replacement boots might well mean the difference between life and death.

'Mind you lace up your boots correctly,' said the major. 'None of this criss-crossing business like these German paratroopers. With Gurkhas lurking, you always run the risk of getting your throat sliced open if you get that wrong.'

'What d'you mean?' asked Jox.

'Gurkhas are experts at creeping about at night. They often tell friend from foe by touching the laces of a sleeping man's boots. If they feel wrong, they'll plunge one of these into the man's groin or run it across his neck.' Reid-Steele was brandishing what Jox recognised as a kukri, the Gurkhas' foot-long, bent-bladed and razor-sharp weapon of choice. 'A

Gurkha warrior would never be separated from his blade if still alive.' Reid-Steele glanced around. 'I'm rather surprised the Jerries left this one lying here. They're usually highly prized as trophies, in the same way the Yanks love German Lugers.'

Something about what Reid-Steele had just said sent a chill down Jox's spine. He froze, staring down at the litter of recent combat at his feet. He was about to say, 'Be careful what you touch,' when there was a sudden whoosh and bang. Just a few yards ahead of him, there was a bright flash from where Vollick had just exclaimed that he'd found some compo tins. From the corner of his eye, Jox saw Vollick snatched sideways and simultaneously felt like he'd been punched in the arm, exactly where he'd just been tattooed. Jox fell to the ground, grasping it tightly. In the stillness after the detonation, the air stank of cordite and the metallic tang of spilt blood.

'What the hell was that? Did anyone get hit?' gasped Beans, raising his head from behind the rocky parapet of a sangar which had protected him from the blast. Jox knew the answer before Reid-Steele replied. He'd recognised the two-stage detonation of an S-mine, a bounding anti-personnel mine, designed to launch into the air and detonate three feet off the ground, spraying ball bearing in all directions.

'Your lot call them "Bouncing Bettys",' the major replied. 'Better watch out — there's sure to be more about. For God's sake don't touch anything else.'

'Shooter's been hit!' cried Carver, his face pale as he grasped his own abdomen.

Jox's arm was burning, and he found a neat puncture hole in his flying blouse. A thin trickle of claret wept from it. Carver and Vollick's need was greater, so he scrambled over to them. Vollick had caught the full force of the blast. Much of his clothing had been stripped off, exposing his tattooed torso, blackened by the explosion, his flock of bluebirds were stilled. The flash of the explosion had been blinding, and the dimness of dawn cloaked the full extent of his injuries, but it didn't look good. They gathered around, heads bowed.

'Shooter's done for,' said Reid-Steele too loudly, deafened and stating the obvious. 'Poor chap, what rotten bloody luck.'

Carver groaned and collapsed onto his side, his arms held tightly across his lower gut. Jox dropped beside him, trying to comfort him, whilst peeling his fingers away to examine the wound. The Texan's eyes were screwed tightly shut, his face shiny with perspiration, and there was blood seeping through his fingers. He began to pant like a dog. 'I'm gut shot,' he gasped.

'Keep still,' said Jox, wanting to sound like he knew what he was doing. Carver was the closest to a medic amongst them, and it was a lousy break that he was the one hurt. 'Tell me what to do, Tex,' pleaded Jox. 'Stop thrashing, there could well be more mines around. Jerry likes to spread them in clumps.'

'Jox is right,' said Reid-Steele. 'Standard German infantry practice — an immediate counterattack after being assaulted by the Gurkhas, followed by a tactical withdrawal back to their original defensive positions having interdicted the contested area with landmines and booby traps. We need to watch out for those wooden Schü-mines especially. They're quick to scatter and are just little boxes of TNT with a detonator, but more than enough to ruin your day. They're almost undetectable and can be tucked in next to anything that catches your eye. If something looks interesting, boys, it's probably deadly.'

'Never mind all that,' said Wyszkowski, trying to get Carver to release his grip around his abdomen. There was something protruding, and a dark gush of blood ran down his trouser leg.

Carver's face glowed pale in the thin light of the morning.

'This is not good,' said Wyszkowski. 'He's been hit in the colon area. It gets pretty mucky down there — infection can spread easily. No way he can go on. If he's to stand any chance, we need to get him back to the monastery. Going back downhill will be faster than coming up. I'll go back with him. Who will help me?'

They looked at each other. Freedom held a powerful draw. It was Major Reid-Steele, who'd been a prisoner the longest amongst them, who broke the silence. 'I'm senior here, so it's my responsibility to take care of you men.' He touched Wyszkowski's shoulder. 'Thank you, Whisky, for showing me where my duty lies.' Brightening, he added to the wounded man, 'Come on, old boy. Let's see if we can't get you home, or at least what will have to serve for a little while longer.'

The pair lifted the injured Carver and said quick goodbyes to avoid prolonging things, and started half-walking, half-carrying Carver down the slope. Retracing their steps wouldn't be easy, especially for Carver, but they had a chance of preserving his life if they could make it back to the monastery in time.

Jox, Beans and Perrin stood silent, watching the other three heading down the slope. They avoided each other's gaze, each feeling guilty about how determined they'd been to pursue their freedom, rather than sacrificing themselves for the sake of a comrade. It brought with it a shame that held a painful sting.

Jox eventually said, 'Right, we'd better make a go of it, if only to make our loss and their sacrifice worthwhile. '

It was hard to believe that already over half of their number had fallen or given up their freedom. It was a sobering thought and kept them quiet as they set off again, picking their way through the battlefield of demolished sangars, discarded equipment and broken men. Like the Gurkhas before him, there was no burial for Shooter Vollick; it was simply too dangerous, so Beans simply pocketed his countryman's identity tag and quietly said goodbye to their fallen comrade.

'Wait a minute,' said Beans. 'Before we go, what about the tins? Don't know about y'all, but I'm starving.'

'They do look tempting,' said Jox. 'But that's exactly what the major warned against.'

'Yeah, but I'm famished, and I'll bet y'all are too,' replied Beans, sounding a little petulant.

'I have an idea,' said Perrin. 'I found some string here. Maybe if we tie it to a stone and place it beside the tins, we can pull whilst sheltering. If it goes boom, we are safely behind the rocks.' He weighed a rock the size of an apple in his hand. 'Something like this would do, but we must place it very carefully. We need someone precise and dainty, with the hands of a pilot.' They were looking at Jox, Beans with a pleading expression.

Jox sighed. He didn't have much choice. 'All right, I'll give it a try. Set up your equipment, Muriel. In the meantime, Bayou, will you take a quick look at my arm? I copped a piece of that mine. Didn't make a fuss earlier as the others were a lot worse off than me, but it's starting to hurt. Not exactly ideal for the delicate work you two are suggesting.'

Beans helped Jox out of his flight jacket and holed blue RAF shirt. Neither had been laundered in a long while and Jox was worried that perhaps a piece of dirty cloth may have found its way into the wound. The last thing he needed now was an infection. The big American's intake of breath once Jox's arm was revealed was concerning. Where Vollick had taped a gauze pad over the children's names he'd tattooed there, a projectile had entered the bicep right in the centre.

'Should I take it off?' asked Beans, his fingers probing the bandage. 'I can feel a lump.'

'Stop poking it and take a look,' snapped Jox.

Beans peeled back the latex holding the gauze to reveal a raised purple bruise with a black hole at its tip. It looked rather like a giant pimple. Probing gently, Beans determined that the embedded piece was the size of a redcurrant, just under the skin and in the muscle of Jox's bicep. He saw the faint outline of tattooed names, with the hole a full stop after Elias's name.

'I can get it out, but we'll need something sharp.'

Perrin had joined them and was carrying a ball of twine, to which he'd attached the apple-sized rock. He unravelled the string until there was about fifteen metres of it at his feet. 'We have what we need. Are you ready?'

'No, wait,' replied Beans. 'We need a knife to cut that thing out of Jox. Have you got one?'

'No, but wait, where is the major's kukri? Did he take it with him?'

'I think normally he would have, but he had to carry Tex, so may have left it behind. Should be around here somewhere.'

They searched the area and found the blade on the lip of the sangar where Reid-Steele had sheltered when the mine detonated. Perrin unsheathed it and ran his finger along the blade. He yelped as it drew blood. 'It is a very big blade; you think you can work with it, Swampy?'

'I can try.' Beans positioned the blade against Jox's bruised arm. 'This is going to hurt, but I'll be a quick as I can. It'll just be a little incision, no more than an inch, then I'll try to flick it out.' He paused. 'Do you want something to bite down on?'

Jox nodded. 'I suppose it can't hurt.'

Perrin found him something suitable, one of the wooden-handled eating utensils that were stuck in the kukri's leather sheath.

'Bite down on that,' said Beans. 'I'm going in. Hang in there, buddy.'

There was a sharp scratch, followed by some scraping and tugging, then the trickle of what was presumably blood snaking down Jox's arm. He made a point of not looking as he was never terribly good with the sight of blood, especially his own. He focussed instead on the compo tins, his next objective. Stacked in a tidy triangle on top of a canvas bag, they did look rather suspicious.

'It wasn't too deep,' said Beans. 'You're lucky it didn't hit any bone; it's just a soft tissue wound. The explosion must have heated the pellet, as there's little blood and the wound is practically cauterised.'

'Don't feel very bloody lucky,' said Jox through gritted teeth.

'It's out now,' said Beans. A grey metal sphere, about the size of a child's fingernail fell to the ground. 'How does that feel?'

'Not too bad, but it's getting a bit stiff,' replied Jox, flexing his fingers. For the first time in ages, he noticed the burn scars on his hands, the legacy of an aircraft fire when he was still learning to fly. His burns had been sustained in his vain attempt to save his friend George from the flames. Jox shook his head to rid himself of the memory. 'Right, let's give this a go,' he said. 'But you know, I really don't see why I'm the one doing this. Both of you are pilots too.'

'Yeah, but my flying days are over,' said Beans. 'With one eye, I have no depth perception, so no can do.'

'I know I am far too clumsy for this,' said Perrin. 'Listen, I promise, if you do this for us, for the rest of your life I will send my family's finest vintages to you every year at Christmas. I'm just so hungry. I need some food.'

'Well then, let's see how long that life will be after this harebrained scheme,' said Jox. 'I'm just not sure it's a terribly smart thing to do, tempting fate like this.'

Jox crossed to the shiny pile of ration tins. He peered closely without touching anything. He delicately placed the tied stone behind the canvas bag on which they were piled. He lay the string over the cans, making sure it didn't tangle with anything on his way back to the other two, who were hiding behind the ledge of the nearest sangar.

Jox and Beans kept their heads down, whilst Perrin gradually tightened the string. Once it was taut, they all ducked.

'Ready?' Beans said. Perrin nodded. There was a clatter, then a sharp snap, but no louder than a rattrap being set off. They gave it a few seconds and peered over the edge. The tins were scattered, two still intact, the third perforated and leaking what looked like blackberry jam. The Frenchman looked pleased with himself as he picked up the tins.

Jox smiled wearily. 'We got lucky this time. Those Schü-mines are hard to spot, but at least they don't do too much damage from a reasonable distance. If we cross another Bouncing Betty, we've had it. Look what happened last time; it took three of us out to differing degrees. Your string certainly wouldn't survive that.'

Perrin shrugged. 'We need more food.'

They headed steadily eastwards, and the rest of the morning was a sequence of spotting something of interest, setting up the string and stone apparatus, sheltering and seeing what happened. Not every 'find' was boobytrapped, and by lunchtime they'd gathered a reasonable collection of booty. On the negative side, they'd set off two more Schü-mines, one shredding the string. Perrin now sported a rather dashing scarlet cut across his cheekbone, thanks to a whizzing stone fragment. He took it all in his stride, saying it was worth it for what they'd accumulated: a number of water canteens, some holed and requiring quick consumption, but also rice, some cheese wrapped in paper and a tin of coffee powder. There was also a cast iron cooking pot, some silver spoons, a second kukri and a Webley MK VI Revolver from the body of a British officer who had no head. There were lots of ration tins from the British and Indian Army, but also quite a few from the *Deutsche Wehrmacht*, certainly enough to keep them going for several days.

Jox was grateful that Beans and Perrin carried most of the load, as his arm was becoming increasingly painful. While the other two were in high spirits, he was beginning to feel a bit feverish, and his arm had locked stiff, to the point where he refused to be involved with anymore 'string-pulling' operations. By then, the other two had perfected the procedure and were confident they could handle it on their own, notwithstanding the damage to Perrin's face.

At the bottom of a rocky gully they found an abandoned mortar position, full of empty ammunition boxes and bloodied bandages. On either side, steep slopes rose, providing good cover but limiting visibility other than straight up or down the narrow gulley. It was an ideal place for indirect fire but difficult to defend once pinpointed by the enemy. Lying around everywhere was evidence of recent action, including a medic's canvas satchel with a white circle and red cross upon it. A universally recognised symbol, in the hands of someone cynically minded, it was also the perfect bait to lure in an unwary victim. Jox was by now feeling wobbly and knew he could benefit from whatever medicine was in the bag.

'Look, it's worth the risk,' said Beans. 'You've put yourself in harm's way for us; now it's time for us to repay the debt. Relax, we can handle it, Jox. You take cover over there and we'll get you fixed up with whatever the doctor might have ordered.'

In the lee of a large boulder, Jox looked up at the sky, blue and infinite, marred only by some wispy cloud. It took a while for him to notice the high-altitude cross-hatching of vapour trails. He smiled. General Jimmy Doolittle's Twelfth USAAF were having another busy day. He could just picture the pugnacious face of the general, who'd played such a big part in Jox getting his first command. He owed him a great deal and would be honoured to serve with him again.

From the other side of the rock came Beans' cry of 'Fire in the hole!' followed by the sound of the falling stone attached to its twine. There was no explosion, just the two of them laughing at the game of it. Their laughter was joined by clapping and a woman's voice saying, '*Bravo!*' This was followed by the sound of rifle bolts being loaded and locked. Jox froze.

'Move slowly please, sahibs. Let me see your hands,' said a male voice. Jox sat up and immediately felt dizzy. 'I can see you too,' the voice said more loudly. 'Don't try anything silly.'

'I can't raise my arm,' Jox replied. 'I've been hurt.'

There was a quick exchange of Italian and the voice continued, 'Get up slowly, so I can see you properly.'

Jox did as he was instructed. Feeling light-headed, he was having trouble focussing, barely seeing the outline of Beans and Perrin with their hands in the air. The medic's bag was at the Frenchman's feet. Following the pair's gaze, Jox spotted two figures standing above them up one side of the gulley, with rifles pointed straight at them.

One was a petite, pale woman with freckles across her nose and cheeks. Her hair was covered with a red shawl, but otherwise, she was dressed like a man, with calf-high jackboots, bandoliers of cartridges over each shoulder and a green smock like those worn by the *Fallschirmjäger*. It was surprising she'd found one small enough, but there was no doubting she handled her scoped rifle with practiced ease.

Her companion was darker, had a full beard and was wearing a tattered British Army uniform. His beard was braided, the ends tucked up into a turban in the manner of the Sikhs. Jox recognised the red eagle on his shoulder as that of the 4th Indian Division, which he was aware included a bewildering array of troops from the Indian subcontinent, including Gurkhas, Rajputs, Jats, Sikhs, but also rather unexpectedly the Essex Regiment. The dead they'd encountered earlier could well have belonged to the same division, but somehow, they'd appeared fresher in death than this scruffy fellow, who could only be described as very well-worn.

'We're allied officers, escaped prisoners of war,' said Beans.

'Ah, you're an American,' the man replied in a perfect English accent. 'I can see you're not all officers; this one's a warrant officer, Free French, if I recognise the uniform correctly.'

'You have the advantage on us. Who are you, sir?' asked Beans.

The man lowered his weapon and came smartly to attention. '*Jemadar* Sad Singh, at your service, previously attached to 7th Armoured Division of the 8th Army, captured at Tobruk. A proud desert rat, sahib.'

Beans introduced them all, explaining they'd come from P.G. 35 and that they were exhausted, cold and hungry, and that Jox needed medical attention. He then asked the lieutenant for the name of his companion.

'My apologies, sahib. May I present Rosmarina, a partisan with the *Brigata Stella Rossa*, the Red Star Brigade under *Comandante* Lupo. I joined the brigade when I escaped from a camp further down south. They are a fine bunch, if a little excitable. They have been kind to me and there are several escaped prisoners amongst us, you will see. She speaks good English but is a little shy with strangers. However, please don't be deceived, *la coccinella* is deadly.'

At the mention of her name, Rosmarina smiled and pulled back her headscarf to reveal hair that was even more vividly coloured. Tactful as ever, Beans blurted, 'Hot dog, lady, well I never did see…'

Rosmarina glared at him.

'Please accept my apologies, Miss,' said Jox. 'My friend is being uncouth and has forgotten his manners. You are a vision to men who have not seen beauty for a long time. Why do they call you *la coccinella*? What does it mean?'

Singh replied for her. '*La coccinella* is the ladybird. You see, freckles like hers are unusual in Italy.'

Jox caught her eye. She blushed but gave him a shy smile which felt like a punch to the chest. He staggered but was caught by Beans. His head was spinning and the last thing he heard was Beans saying, 'We need to get Jox to a doctor, now!'

CHAPTER NINE

It was dark when Jox awoke. The air was musty and smelt vaguely of woodsmoke. He had no idea where he was and his arm was throbbing painfully, but at least he was no longer feverish. He sensed movement and asked, 'Where am I?'

'So, you're finally awake,' said Beans. 'For a little guy, you're damned heavy to carry up a mountain. I don't envy Whisky and the major hauling a big lump like Tex all the way back to the monastery.'

'Thanks, Bayou, I owe you one. Where are we? Have I been out long?'

Beans squatted beside the bedroll on which Jox was lying. They appeared to be in a grotto-like shelter, seemingly half dug into a hillside. It all seemed rather rough, but was at least warm, comfortable and out of the weather. There was clothing and equipment hanging from various pegs, along with bedding, stores, ammo boxes and weaponry stacked in the dark corners.

'Don't you worry. We're amongst friends,' said Beans. 'This bunch of partisans call themselves the Red Star Brigade. They seem to be a reasonable bunch despite apparently being commies. I met their commander and he's a straight up guy, ex-Italian Army sergeant-major who fought against us in the desert, but now leads his band against the Germans. Calls himself Lupo, as in the wolf.' He laughed. 'We sure do keep strange bedfellows in wartime. Guess it's a case of "my enemy's enemy is my friend".' He ran a hand through his shoulder length hair, which was looking distinctly unmilitary. 'So, how you feeling, buddy?'

'Not too bad,' Jox replied. 'The arm's still sore, but I guess I'm all right.'

'Good job we met up with those two when we did. They brought us back to the camp, and the woman's done a swell job of patching you up. She dusted you up with sulphur powder and put a fresh bandage on your arm. Gave you a couple of shots too, some kind of penicillin medicine against infection, out of relief packages.'

'The communists are getting Red Cross packages while we were still waiting for ours?'

'Apparently they're working with some outfit called Operation SIMCOL,' replied Beans. 'Not sure what it stands for, but it's part of the Office of Strategic Services — you know, those murky spy guys with all the connections. Actually, as soon as we got here, that Lupo guy headed straight off to get in touch with them. He was pretty excited to have a couple of aviator officer POWs joining his camp. It appears that SIMCOL has parachuted covert units all along the Italian coast, tasked with locating escaped prisoners of war and escorting them back to rendezvous points for evacuation by sea. It all sounds pretty good to me. Old Lupo says we're excellent bargaining chips in exchange for weapons and ammunition.'

'All smells a bit fishy,' said Jox. 'I'm surprised they've got themselves organised so quickly.'

'You have been out of the action for a couple of days. These plans have apparently been on the boil since before the armistice was signed. The partisans are keen and seem honest enough, if a bit rough around the edges. The Indian Army guy with the turban, Singh, says they sometimes get overexcited and just charge off on the attack, shooting up anything they can. Seems they're braver than they are skilful. That Singh's a top feller, though. He's been with them for several months, so he knows what he's talking about. Then there's that ladybird girl who fixed up your arm.'

'Oh yes, *la coccinella*,' said Jox. 'I thought perhaps I'd dreamt her up.'

'She's really quite something, ain't she? Apparently, she can take out a German's eye at over two hundred yards and is the best sniper in the whole damn unit.' Beans laughed. 'Singh was standing there in front of me, his head wobbling from side to side, saying, "Don't forget that though ladybirds are pretty, they can also bite", so you'd better watch out if you plan to tangle with that.'

Embarrassed to have been so transparent, Jox wanted to change the subject. 'So, tell me, what are these SIMCOL chaps all about?'

'We'll find out soon enough,' replied Beans. 'Singh says most are recruited from second-generation Americans who speak the local lingo. They've been trained to organise and equip the partisans, acting as the nuclei for new resistance cells. In the short term, their mission is to get Allied POWs back to our lines. There's apparently some kind of manpower shortage, especially for skilled troops, folks who can handle a landing craft, and technical experts like pilots, tankmen, artillery and engineers. With all the POWs that are out there, scattered across Campagna since the *Campos* across Italy opened their gates when the armistice was announced, hundreds of *Kriegies* have struck out on the their own. The Krauts have been furiously rounding them up, punishing any locals who help them. Operation SIMCOL is trying to organise the chaos and get the men back into the war effort. It's believed that RAF and USAAF guys languishing in Italy are a valuable military resource that shouldn't be wasted. Come to think of it, one of the guys here seems rather keen on seeing you.'

'Really, why's that?'

'No idea. I can't understand a word he says, but I think he knows you. All that can wait, though. What you need to do is to rest up and build your strength. I've got strict instructions from *la coccinella* to tell her when you're awake. I think she may have taken a bit of a shine to you and wants to check you over. You hungry?'

'Starving. I could eat a horse.'

Beans frowned, unfamiliar with the British expression. 'Not much chance of that, but I'll see if I can get you some mutton. Tastes kinda weird to a swamp gator like me, but at least it's meat for a change. Otherwise, it's pretty much standard compo rations all round, but I'll give it to that Singh feller, he's pretty handy at rustling up some decent chow. You take it easy, and I'll be right back.'

It was actually *la coccinella* who came to see Jox first. '*Signore*, are you strong?' she asked.

In the confines of the grotto, the air was suddenly filled with a fragrance, enticing and unsettling. Jox's head was spinning and he failed to reply.

'Let me smell your bandage to see if the wound is still bad,' she said forcibly.

Jox did as he was told, as she manhandled his arm from its shirt sleeve. As she came closer, her perfume grew stronger. She was brusque and more familiar than he'd expected, and he felt almost prudish as she sniffed. 'The bandage is okay.' Her pert, freckled nose then wrinkled. 'But you smell very bad. You must wash, to be clean for the wound.'

Jox was mortified but had to acknowledge it had been a while since he'd bathed, and his clothes were far from fresh.

Pink-cheeked, he dropped his head. She reached over and lifted his chin. 'Please don't be embarrassed. I will get Singh to heat some water. If you have trouble washing because of your arm, ask your friend to help you.'

Her English was peppered with the Italian habit of adding extra 'e's to every word. He found it endearing and smiled. Now it was her turn to look down shyly.

'You must be hungry,' she added. 'Singh will bring his speciality. He calls it "daal" and he makes it from, how you say, the lentil seeds. He serves it with flatbreads. It is very delicious.' She began to rearrange Jox's bedding. 'When he first came to us, we think what a strange little man, so hairy, with the plaited beard, long hair and big turban. But now, he finds us food, cooks and is an expert tailor, mending all of our clothes. He is such a good man, who prays every day, but is also a very fierce fighter. We love and respect *Signore* Sad Singh.'

Finishing her chores, she was set to leave and yet Jox was desperate to continue the conversation. 'Singh told us you were the sniper of the unit. How is it that a girl … I mean, a woman, is such an expert shot? How did you…?'

She smiled. 'My family makes cheese from the sheep's milk. You know *pecorino romano*? It is salty cheese from an ancient recipe. When the war came, my father and brother go to fight in Albania. My brother was killed and my father got so very sad, he caught the pneumonia, and he died too, somewhere near the *Klisura Passo* on the Greek border.' Her dark eyes filled with tears. 'The fascists tell us nothing. Our men die for them, and no one can even say where they are buried. They take everything from us and leave us with nothing. My mother and I tried to manage; she made the cheese and I took care of the sheep, but with the men away at war, the wolves became many.

So, I learned to shoot them. When the *Tedeschi* came, they are like wolves on our land too. The *Stella Rosa* tell me they take care of my mama if I come to shoot the wolves with them. I come and I shoot.' She grinned. 'Now, I follow our own wolf, Lupo, Mario Musolesi; he is our *comandante*. He's a good man and his betrothed, Livia, is my best friend. Altogether, we fight for our liberation. This is good, no?'

Jox was finding her direct, uncomplicated personality utterly charming and captivating. Was his reaction the result of months of incarceration, or were cracks forming in the layers of resilience and cynicism he'd developed over years of bitter war, personal disappointments and tragedies? He felt euphoric in her presence; quite why however remained a mystery. He swallowed down his confusion. 'Can you tell me of your proper name? I feel rude calling you *la coccinella*.'

She laughed. 'I don't mind.' She cocked her head like a bird, a clever red-headed jay. She smiled, tucking an unruly copper lock behind her ear. 'It is sweet you worry you offend me. I think maybe you are a British gentleman. We don't have so many here in this rough camp. My name is Rosmarina, after the sweet cooking herb. It means rose of the sea.'

'I suppose that must be rosemary,' replied Jox. 'A herb with a lingering perfume; that rather suits you. My name is Jeremy, but everyone calls me Jox.'

'You prefer Jox?' she asked. 'You can call me Marina. It is my name for those who are closest to me.'

Jox didn't emerge from his lair until the next day. It was a crisp autumnal morning with a nip in the air. Watery sunshine was cutting through grey clouds, dappling the camouflaged hovels, shelters and shacks making up the guerilla camp. The shelters were ingeniously fashioned from branches, grassy sod and tarpaulins to disguise any recognisable forms from aerial observation. The low cloud base masked the snow-tipped Apennine peaks above the camp, so mercifully reduced the likelihood of it being seen by any enemy reconnaissance aircraft passing overhead.

The previous evening, Jox had spent time in discussion with Singh over the meal that he'd prepared for him. The threat of detection was a constant, and the partisans had no anti-aircraft protection to speak of, so discovery would have severe repercussions for the lightly armed guerillas. They were particularly vulnerable to 'Jabo' fighter-bombers and long-range artillery, both of which the Germans possessed in abundance. Singh had explained that the partisans' war was one of rapid ambush and retreat. It involved precise sniping on the enemy or repurposing mines or improvised explosive devices to harm them at a distance, hopefully keeping their troops well clear of the inevitable retaliation from German forces.

Singh reported that several hapless villages in the vicinity of their attacks had borne the brunt of the *Tedeschi's* anger and frustration. He was a veteran soldier but was clearly haunted by how the brigade's actions were impacting on the local populace. And yet, they remained welcoming and tacitly supportive of the *Stella Rosa*, despite their suspicions over the unit's socialist leanings and having to bear the brunt of enemy's reprisals.

'The truth is only a few of the partisans are real socialists,' Singh had said. 'Most have just rallied to those colours as a matter of convenience. Even Lupo is just a professional soldier who wants his country back. He's bled for it and cannot accept it is being run by others. "There will be plenty of time for politics after the war is done," he says. "Now is the time to fight." He puts great faith in what the Allies can do to help, but there are some in the group, the more politically motivated and aligned to the left, who disagree. There is always the threat of traitors amongst us. This has always been Italy's misfortune, with politics and divisions fracturing national unity. The partisan brigades are infiltrated by political commissars from Marshal Tito's partisan army in Yugoslavia, and this has created further dissent and conflict. If I am honest, sahib, when and if this Operation SIMCOL gets former prisoners out of here, I will leave with a heavy heart but will be happy to escape the bloodbath between brothers that I fear is coming.'

Jox hadn't known how to react, but realised the kind-hearted lieutenant was deeply troubled by what he feared was in store for his adoptive homeland. Jox didn't fully understand the situation but could see Singh was worried.

Now, as Jox emerged, the camp was infused with the fumes of many campfires, ingeniously diffusing through layers of ferns and conifer branches to prevent detection. This explained why every habitation and all clothing smelt so damned smoky. For some, it was comforting and had become the smell of home and security, but its potency turned Jox's stomach. Still, once outside he could see that breakfast was cooking, bully beef and ersatz coffee by the smell of it, and he was hungry again, which must surely be a good sign.

Meeting his new campmates for the first time, Jox thought they seemed a rather motley crew. He'd somehow expected that their clothing might help distinguish the local villagers from the recently demobbed Italian servicemen and the Allied POWs, but in reality, it was hard to tell them apart. Everyone pretty much looked the same, like roughneck vagrants, long-haired and not a clean-shaven face amongst them. Jox, who was usually pretty fastidious about his appearance, realised he probably looked no different, despite finally managing to wash the previous evening, and he was feeling his unkempt state rather keenly. The diversity of attire was marked, with worn-out Allied uniforms, marginally fresher military garments of Italian and German origin, and an eclectic array of civilian clothing. Within this jumble, the partisans then seemed to compete with one another to look as outlandish as they could manage, with the only unifying garb being red scarves worn like boy scouts by some.

The exuberant style of one character in particular struck Jox. He was wearing a Chinese jade-coloured quilted jacket under a pale gilet of furry goatskin. He'd paired this with a balaclava then had a brown trilby hat on top. Jox stared at him incredulously, until the fellow turned suddenly and addressed him. 'How you doing, sir? I'd heard the name and had a notion it might well be you.'

Jox spluttered. 'I can hardly be expected to recognise you with a balaclava on…'

'Right you are — it's been fair nippy these last few mornings.' The man whipped off his hat then pulled up the hood to reveal a bright ginger beard, the badly set nose of a boxer and a mischievous dry laugh that plucked at Jox's memory.

'Well, I'll be blown, Flight Sergeant Patrick Kilpatrick,' said Jox. 'That is you, isn't it, Pat?'

'Aye, dead on. You're a sight for sore eyes, so you are.'

'Come here, you rogue,' roared Jox, embracing Kilpatrick, surprised at how emotional he felt seeing one of his Black Pigs again. They clapped each other on the shoulder, until Jox suddenly buckled. 'Steady on, Pat, I took some shrapnel in the arm last week.'

The Ulsterman's face dropped. 'For the love of God, why didn't you say so?' He caught himself. 'Begging your pardon, sir. It sure is grand to see you.'

Kilpatrick was one of two fighting Irishmen Jox had inherited when forming No. 333 Squadron, the Black Pigs, back in Malta. He'd been tasked with cobbling together a rogue bunch of men, some with legacy issues, into a fighting unit that had gone on to acquit itself well in Sicily. Turning a sow's ear of experienced but disparate men — some fresh out of hospital, others the glasshouse — into a silk purse hadn't been easy, but he was proud now to call them his squadron-mates. Leaning on a stout backbone of trusted Treble Ones, he'd collected the odds and sods stranded in Malta then added a number of replacements, bringing them to squadron strength and eventually to combat-readiness.

By far the toughest 'nuts' to crack were the 'Fighting Kilpatricks'. Pat was an Ulsterman from Londonderry, a staunch member of the Orange Lodge, and the other, Paddy, was from Kinsale in County Cork of the neutral Eire, and an equally resolute republican. Pat was about as ginger as they came, while Paddy was dark-eyed and tanned. By the time Jox was shot down for the second time in Sicily, the pair had become acclaimed fighter-bomber aces, particularly adept at taking out enemy armour.

'How the hell did you get here?' asked Jox, his eyes shining with pleasure.

'It's a long, dull story that does me little credit,' replied Pat Kilpatrick in his broad Derry accent. There was little doubt this was the fellow Beans had struggled to understand. 'It starts a week or two after you went for a Burton — and by the way, sir, we all thought you were dead, and Flight Lieutenant de Ghellinck had to take temporary command of the squadron.

'A little after you were reported missing, the squadron were assigned to provide air cover for XIII Corps as it crossed the Straits of Messina over to Regio di Calabria on Italy's toe. Opposition was light, so we were ordered to interdict some key roads and a bridge beside a mountain called the Aspromonte massif. We soon discovered it was held by Italian paratroopers of the 185th 'Nembo' Regiment, who unlike most of their pals, were in no mood to give up.

'We strafed their positions all day, and on one pass, I misjudged the height of the rock and didn't realise it was infested with AA guns. At that time, Paddy and I were having ourselves a little contest to see how many Eyeties we could beat up. I went in a bit too low, desperate to find a target, and got nailed good and proper. I lost all power and so tried to glide my way out of there, but I was too low to get very far.' His hand tracked his trajectory in the way all aviators tell a tale. 'I stayed up as long as I could, aiming for the mountains inland rather than heading for Sicily. I was getting desperate for somewhere to pancake and found a patch of flattish mountain heather. I belly-landed no bother and got out quick before she brewed up.'

Kilpatrick paused and ran a hand through his ginger beard. 'I was miles from anywhere and started walking, eventually running into an old shepherd. I couldn't understand a word he said, but he took me in for a spell.' He chuckled. 'The old feller must have got word out, because a day or two later a bunch of rough-looking types in red scarves turned up and took me in charge. I was worried when I saw him getting paid off, thinking these laddies must be bandits planning to sell me on to Jerry. Turned out they were sound as a pound, partisans of the *Stella Rosa* brigade.' Kilpatrick shrugged. 'Since then, I've been helping out where I can, but I have got to say I've been itching to get back into the fight. When I heard there was a Jox McNabb in the camp, I said to myself, "Pat, my boy, there's your man to get it done."' He patted Jox's shoulder, carefully choosing the opposite side to his wound. 'Can't tell you how chuffed I am to see you.'

'Glad to see you too, Pat,' replied Jox. 'Now, all we need to figure out is how to get back to our lads. I've heard encouraging noises about some OSS chaps due in soon. I'm told they may find us a way out.'

'Aye, I've heard rumours…' Kilpatrick was distracted by a commotion rumbling through the camp. Various partisans and former POWs appeared agitated, arming themselves and calling urgently to each other. Jox and Kilpatrick were joined by Beans and Perrin.

'What the hell's going on?' asked Jox.

'Apparently *les Boches* are coming down the road in the valley below,' said Perrin.

Singh and Rosmarina came out of the nearby hut, armed and looking serious. She had bandoliers of ammunition draped over her shoulders, crossing over her back. Her hair was covered by a navy-blue hood, which framed her pale face well. To Jox, she was as beautiful as any medieval donna in the Italian paintings he'd seen, despite her nervously fidgeting with the bolt of her Mosin-Nagant M1891 scoped rifle.

'Come,' said an anxious-looking Singh. 'We must run for the mountains. We will return when the danger is past. The *Tedeschi* are advancing on San Cristobal, the village in the valley which feeds and protects us.' He looked them over. 'Do you have any weapons?'

'I have a pistol,' replied Perrin. 'Not much use, unless we get close. Jox and Swampy have kukri knives but will need to be even closer to strike.'

'God willing that won't be necessary. We'll get you weapons, all of you.' Singh nodded at Rosmarina. 'We must be prepared to defend ourselves, and should it be required, sell our lives dearly.'

'I've got an old captured Mauser, but to be fair it's seen better days,' said Kilpatrick.

'Good, you and *Adjudant* Perrin can protect your officers,' said Singh. 'Airmen are precious to the war effort, and we've been ordered to get you all back.' He glanced at the partisans, now streaming away from the camp. 'Come, we must hurry. Will you take my binoculars, Jox? I must load my rifle.'

Singh was carrying a second sniper rifle, a bolt-action, magazine-fed Lee-Enfield SMLE with telescopic sights. He patted the wooden stock proudly. 'I learnt to shoot in the Hindu Kush mountains before war. I was just a young boy then, and the Pathans were our enemies on the Northwest Frontier. I was taught to shoot by an Englishman from East Sussex, Sergeant John Cook, a hard man and a tough instructor. We spent many long days sniping from the great heights of different peaks. A delightful game, but with deadly consequences. I was a young then, just a *naik* and didn't know, how you say, my arse from my elbow, but Cook, he knew and taught me well.'

Jox looked at the tough little fellow with renewed respect. He was clearly older than he appeared, and by the sound of things this was his second or third war. The conflict over the disputed Northwest Frontier of India had raged for a long time and had certainly been no picnic.

Jox slipped the lanyard of the binoculars over his head and checked that the kukri was securely attached to his belt. In the absence of his talismans, his doll's arm and switchblade, it would have to do as a good luck charm. In a tight corner, he supposed, it would certainly be more useful as a weapon, but for good measure, he taped the children's names on his bicep, wincing at the sudden stab of pain from his still healing wound.

After a twenty-minute scramble up the scree and boulder-strewn slopes, they set up observation posts. To the naked eye a column of vehicles was visible, some tracked, others wheeled, and in sufficient quantities to be transporting several companies or even a battalion of mobile infantry. There were no tanks, but the SD.KFZ.251 armoured personnel carriers were tracked at the back and had mounted HMGs to the front and rear, each carrying a complement of up to dozen *Panzergrenadiers*. Racing down the old Roman road that cut through the mountains, their tracks squealed on the ancient cobbles, throwing up prodigious amounts of dust. Through it, Jox glimpsed coal scuttle helmets and the tips of many rifles. Amongst the other vehicles in the column, he recognised the long snouts of several SD.KFZ.234 Puma heavy armoured cars armed with a 50mm KwK 39 cannon and a MG 42 machine gun. He'd seen these eight-wheeled behemoths before, and his heart sank at the memory.

He raised the binoculars as on either side of him Singh and Rosmarina lifted their scoped rifles, the trio observing the advancing column. Jox focussed the lenses on the lead vehicle, an older model SD.KFZ.231 armoured car with a smaller turret than the others and a curved frame antennae above it, indicating that it was a command vehicle. Under the wire ring he could see a black-clad officer, speaking into the mouthpiece of headphones clamped over his peaked cap.

Down the slope, a ragged line of partisans, visible thanks to their scarves, had chosen to engage and had opened fire. The enemy column skidded to a halt and a number of APCs disgorged their troops like the spooned stomach contents of a trout. Clearly well trained, they moved swiftly and confidently, providing each other with covering fire under the watchful eyes of the vehicles' HMG gunners. The Pumas sniffed the air, looking for trouble and signs of resistance. The partisans' desultory gunfire did little more than attract their attention, resulting in an intense barrage of counterfire from the well-disciplined, clearly very experienced German troopers. Such was the weight of fire that the reckless *Stella Rosa* partisans began to pull back, leaving a good number of the comrades lying prone in their wake.

Rosmarina's rifle barked, swiftly followed by Singh's. The HMG gunner of one of the APCs tumbled from his turret, flopping half in, half out, before sliding down the vehicle's exterior onto the cobbles of the ancient Roman road. Jox swivelled his glasses to the officer in the command vehicle. Something metallic glittered at his throat, and as he raised an arm to point, directing fire, his other grey sleeve flapped in the mountain breeze. His face was lean and skull-like, with high cheekbones that were unmistakable to Jox. There was no doubt it was *SS-Obersturmbannführer* Wolf Steiner, *Oberst* von Wella's 'pest controller' and expert at dealing with partisan 'problems'. By the look of things, his men were doing just that, with their opponents now retreating in the face of superior weaponry, efficiency and ruthless execution.

'Shoot him. That one, shoot him!' cried Jox, indicating Steiner and reasoning that his removal might blunt the grenadiers' murderous effectiveness and stall the decimation of the comparatively amateur *Brigida Stella Rosa* fighters. Singh, Rosmarina and eventually Pat Kilpatrick with his distinctly poorer weapon followed his instructions. 'The SS officer in the turret of the command car,' insisted Jox. 'Pale face, black cap with an empty right sleeve. Shoot him, he's their leader. The sooner you get him out of the picture, the better. Come on, hurry, shoot!'

They began firing carefully aimed shots, Jox watching for effect through the binoculars. He first saw Steiner react, then flinch a second time, as shots ricocheted off the armour of his turret. He glanced around, but not for long, further shots convincing him to shelter within the body of the vehicle.

'Blast, you missed him,' said Jox. 'Well, at least now he can't see to direct operations.'

'That is good,' said Singh. 'But we must pull back. They are far too strong. We can do nothing against them. Why these fools attacked such superior forces baffles me. If they catch us now, it will be a massacre.'

'I'm afraid it's already a massacre,' said Jox.

They scurried away, desperate to put as much distance between themselves and the pursuing Germans as possible. After an anxious retreat and an exhausting climb up steep slopes, what followed was a very cold night under an open sky, without the comfort of a fire. The darkness echoed with detonations, gunfire, screams and shouts, and the dull, spreading glow of fires in the valley. Something terrible was happening down there and it certainly wasn't just campfires.

CHAPTER TEN

Dawn brought with it the stink of damp ashes, the airborne particles providing the nuclei for a thick mist to condense and precipitate. It was a miserable awakening after a near sleepless night. Jox and his companions were wet and stiff but counting their blessings that they hadn't faced the fate of those caught down in the valley.

By mid-morning, they had cautiously made their way back down the slopes, to what remained of their camp. It had been laid to waste; Steiner's troopers, equipped with flamethrowers, had torched every shelter, large or small. The partisans' scarce supplies of guns and ammunition, abandoned in the hasty retreat, had been piled up and incinerated. Even more heartbreaking were the rows of wounded or captured partisans, who'd simply been lined up and executed. Their bodies had then been dowsed with flaming petroleum jelly and all that remained were shrunken, child-sized forms of carbonised flesh with grimacing faces, teeth exposed by the fierceness of the flames. They lay in a few forlorn rows, many in the stance of pugilists which burnt bodies often adopted, barely recognisable as humans, let alone comrades and friends.

This horror paled in comparison to the sights that awaited the returning partisans further down the hill, along the Roman road leading from the neighbouring village of San Cristobal. The settlement that had supported, succoured and cared for the *Brigata Stella Rossa* for long weeks and months had been reduced to burnt-out ruins. The road running through it was lined with modern timber telegraph poles, each of which now bore a grisly crop of villagers, hanged by their necks. Men, women, and children had all been strung up. There were grizzled farmers in their shirtsleeves and braces, ancient *nonnas* with black headscarves and pendulous drawers, up alongside grubby urchins in shorts and patterned summer dresses with dusty bare feet. This was the terrible price that Steiner demanded from those collaborating with the partisans.

The retreat back up into the mountains was in silence, apart from heavy breathing and muttered complaints over aching muscles and frozen joints. The *Stella Rosa* brigade had been decimated, and its survivors were shell-shocked and utterly dejected, with little more than a few dozen of them left.

As the dim, watery winter sun dipped behind the frosted peaks of the southern Apennines, clutches of exhausted partisans and former POWs began to stop, bunching up the few dry sticks they'd collected to light fires for some scant warmth and to heat up some evening sustenance. The prospect of a brew-up provided a powerful draw for the British and Colonials amongst them. The water, having been carried for miles, was finally set to the boil in multiple billy cans. At Jox's campfire were Rosmarina, Singh, Beans, Perrin and Kilpatrick, all equally desperate for a warming drink.

Very little had been said since leaving martyred San Cristobal behind. There hadn't even been time to bury the fallen.

'Who was the German you wanted us to shoot?' asked Singh, cradling his rifle like an infant.

Jox glanced at the lieutenant, who had a faraway look in his eyes. His hair and beard were uncharacteristically dishevelled after all the commotion of the day. The Indian Army officer lived up to his surname now, having previously explained that his name Singh meant 'lion' in Sanskrit. His long mane of hair had blossomed in a halo around his head and face.

'His name is Wolfgang Steiner. He's an officer of the SS who came to the P.G 85 to escort us to the monastery of *Certosa di San Lorenzo*,' said Jox. 'He's reputedly an expert at dealing with partisans, having learnt his trade in Russia, during Barbarossa and then the retreat from Stalingrad. His methods take brutality to another level. That's why I wanted you to take him out.'

'I see. Well, for all his cruelty he's an educated man, a student of history, if a cynical one.'

'What makes you say that?'

Singh gave a haunted smile. 'You recall the old road out of San Cristobal, the cobbled one with all those damned telegraph poles? It's actually part of the ancient *Via Appia*, one of the most important roads in the Roman Empire. When Spartacus the gladiator led Rome's largest slave revolt, he and six thousand of his followers were captured and then crucified all along the Appian Way, as a warning to all enslaved people. The recaptured slaves were made to carry crosses of timber along the length of the cobbled road for over a hundred miles and every sixty yards, a cross was erected, and a rebel was nailed to it. Can you not see the similarity in what Steiner has just done to San Cristobal? Using Roman cruelty as an example to others.' He held his turbaned head in his hands. 'I despair of the cruelty in this world. How can we do such things to one another?'

'I don't profess to know the answer, my friend,' replied Jox. 'I'm not as learned as you; I'm just a simple soldier. But I do know one thing: what we saw today tells me that I'm on the side of right, the side fighting against unimaginable cruelty, cruelty that shows utter disdain for mercy or human life. If nothing else, it makes me all the more determined to get back in the fight and help finish this damned war. If I can help bring bloodthirsty fanatics like Steiner and other such perpetrators to justice, if their dastardly actions can be banished to the ignominy of history's darkest annals, then I'll have maybe achieved something. I have no doubt they will be punished, and men like you and me are the ones to get that done. I make that a solemn vow.'

The two men held each other's gaze.

As the group huddled round the fire, Rosmarina leant against Jox. They shared the briefest of glances, then she wrapped his arms around her for shared warmth. It was a simple, practical solution to their predicament, but Jox hoped it was also a sign of the growing chemistry between them, hastened perhaps by the horror they'd witnessed earlier that day. Maybe it was all in his imagination, but he certainly hoped there was more to it.

It was Rosmarina's sharp eyes that spotted Lupo's men first, climbing towards the group's eyrie-like vantage point where they'd chosen to make camp. In the failing dusk, the climbers were drawn to the twinkling campfires, small enough to be invisible unless you knew what you were looking for. For the approaching partisans, they were as good as homing beacons.

There were about a dozen of them, bolstering the numbers of their depleted comrades and allied POWs who'd survived the day. Coming together would involve some tough conversations and shared pain over their losses. They approached, zigzagging up the slopes, observed all the while through several scoped weapons as the partisans watched for suspicious behaviour. The sentiment of 'once bitten, twice shy' was running high.

Jox hadn't noticed those approaching until they were a few hundred yards away. Rosmarina bounded up from their embrace and ran squealing down the slope to hug one of the advancing figures. The person was shorter and more obviously feminine than the rest. From the chatter between them, it became evident this was Lupo's fiancée, Livia Comellini, who Rosmarina had spoken of previously. A handsome, clean-shaven man stood grinning at them, and Jox assumed this must be Lupo himself, *Stella Rosa*'s leader.

In some ways, he looked a bit like Jox, with the same forehead and widow's peak, but he was taller and darker. He had a pointed chin, full lips and well-defined eyebrows, and was dressed in typical partisan uniform, an eclectic combination of military and alpine clothing. On the points of his collar there were enamelled red stars, symbolising his rank as the brigade's leader. Earlier, Singh had told Jox Lupo's story. A mature twenty-nine-year-old, he was one of eight siblings who had worked as a motor mechanic before becoming a professional soldier. He'd joined the Royal Italian Army in 1935 and had been posted to Ethiopia as an infantryman during the Second Italo-Ethiopian War to depose Emperor Haile Selassie. He'd shown talent and courage in combat but had then run into problems when expressing anti-fascist sentiments. He was stripped of his awards and reduced in rank to Corporal Major from that of Sergeant Major. He was redeployed into a new role as a tank driver in North Africa, and was subsequently captured by the British but managed to escape, reaching Italian lines after three parched days lost in the desert. He was then repatriated, weak and wounded, arriving home a few weeks before the Armistice, at which point he decided he was sick of the Fascists and joined the resistance.

Jox stood up to get a better view of the newcomers. They were carrying heavy packs, but otherwise most looked much the same as any of the other scruffy partisans. A few did stand out though, better dressed or equipped than the others, and Jox assumed they must be the SIMCOL operators. There was something familiar about one of them, a tall, bulky fellow with a full beard who wore a bulbous *coppola* flat cap on his head. He had his peasant shirt rolled up to the elbows despite the chill and was wearing pinstripe navy trousers with turnups, rather unusual and dandified for trekking in the mountains. Ahead of him, a thinner, slighter chap, was clean-shaven and with a suntanned face. He too wore a *coppola* cap that hid much of his face.

Behind them were two older men. One was large and balding, and the other was slimmer but still well-built, with receding greyish-blond hair and round gold-rimmed spectacles. As they got closer, the rotund fellow pulled out a spotted handkerchief and noisily blew his nose, then in an actor's voice with a touch of Oscar Wilde's farce, he boomed, 'I say, surely we must have arrived. Do tell me these are the fellows we're after.'

'That's them all right, Major, no question,' said the bearded man in the bulbous flat cap in a New York accent. He lifted his cap, revealing his eyes, a high, intelligent forehead and long hair brushed straight back. 'And that gentlemen is none other than Squadron Leader Jox McNabb.'

It took a moment for Jox to register that his name had been called. He was staring at the star-shaped tattoo on the man's right hand, between his forefinger and thumb. The slimmer man had one too and Jox recognised them in a flash. 'Well, of all the mountainsides in the world you had to pick mine, Giovanni Lomasso. Great to see you again, Glen. It's been a while,' said Jox.

Jox had first met OSS Captain Giovanni 'Glen' Lomasso and his superior Major Giuseppe 'Joe' Paolino in Malta. He'd first been tasked with dropping them deep in occupied territory in the middle of the night, for them to foment trouble on the ground before the ground assault on Sicily began. The pair were trained operatives but more importantly were New Yorkers with close ties with the Sicilian mafia, which ran most of America's cities and virtually all of Sicily. Jox had had a rocky relationship with them but recognised they'd played a part in getting him out of Sicily when he'd crash-landed on the island — well, at least the first time.

The slimmer of the two men removed his cap.

'Giulio Dennini!' cried Jox with real pleasure, seeing the young fighter who had plucked him from the Mediterranean Sea when he'd all but given up hope of rescue. 'What on earth are you doing here?'

'I work the radio and am a soldier now,' Dennini replied. 'I speak the English too.'

'You're doing well,' said Jox, impressed by the effort he'd obviously put in. 'How is your wife Elisabetta and little Violetta?' He rolled up his right sleeve, exposing the scab of his wounded bicep. Jox pointed to the *Stidda* tattoo on Dennini's hand. 'You once said, "Remember us, *amicu miu*. I will remember you."' In the pale moonlight and the soft glow of the fire, the names on Jox's arm barely luminesced, but were still clear enough to be read: Marguerite, Elias and Violetta. Dennini's eyes filled and he embraced Jox, kissing him roughly on either cheek.

What Dennini and Lomasso were doing in Italy was intriguing and somewhat concerning to Jox, but it wasn't really any of his business. Both men were strong characters, dependable but with divided loyalties to the mafia, who were always there lurking in the shadows.

'Once the war is won, you have to win the peace,' said Lomasso later. 'In Sicily, that was never going to be easy.' He and Jox had found a quiet corner by the fireside for a catch-up, after a poor meal of compo rations, the best Singh could rustle up at short notice.

'I wouldn't know about that,' replied Jox. 'I'm no politician and just fly planes for a living.'

'You're lucky not to be involved. I realised I didn't want to get bogged down when there was still plenty of war going on. I was more than happy to let the Sicilians get on with it.'

'That's surprising. I always thought Sicilian-Americans like to keep things "in the family".'

'That's true, but I feel more American than Sicilian. I lettered in college football for Christ's sake, and I suddenly found myself buried in some quasi-medieval village where they still believe in witchcraft and blood feuds. The longer I was there, the more I felt at odds with the local way of doing things. That feeling also became, how should I put it, limiting for my future health and prospects.' Lomasso sighed. 'It struck me that just allowing everything to go back to how it was before Mussolini and the Fascists, just didn't feel like progress. Nor was it bringing anything like American democracy to the island. I mean, why did we bother to liberate them, if all we do is plunge them back into the same feudal servitude they've suffered for centuries?'

Jox sniffed. 'I've got a friend called Jimmy Baraldi, who's the adjutant of my squadron, the Black Pigs. He's a Scotsman, but his family are of Sicilian origin. He'd be delighted to hear you express your doubts. Actually, you did meet him on the flight we shared from Tunis to Malta. He didn't take to your boss, Joe Paolino, no, not at all.'

'Yeah, Joe wasn't always the friendliest of guys. Not got a lot of friends and a whole bunch of enemies,' said Lomasso bitterly. 'I found that out to my cost.'

'Whatever did happen to Joe Paolino?' Jox had never much liked the bull-necked, thuggish and rather belligerent New Yorker. He'd always seemed suspicious about everything and was rather self-important. The pair had crossed swords a few times.

Lomasso had a sour expression on his face. 'We don't ask questions. Let's just say he disappeared.'

'What d'you mean?'

'Well, put it this way, he and Don Pietro Tramontin argued a lot, and you don't argue with the Don. When Joe came to Ragusa to be Tramontin's *consigliere* during the invasion, there was some confusion over who was in charge of who. Paolino bet on himself and lost. He should have known better than to go up against an old wolf like Don Tramontin. Like they say, "In the mouth of the wolf."'

'Where did that leave you?'

Lomasso laughed, flashing straight American teeth amidst his dark beard. Jox was still having trouble getting used to it. 'I had to get the hell out of Dodge as fast as I could. I was still on reasonable terms with Don Pietro, well, at least on the surface. He'd found me amusing at first but kept telling me to shut up because I talked too much. At first, he got a kick out of having a pet American, but now...'

'How does that explain you and Giulio being here?'

Lomasso grinned. 'I got two answers to that. Number one, I'm still a serving officer of the OSS and they needed guys who could speak Italian and know their way around, *capisce*? Operation SIMCOL needs to get POWs repatriated and back in the saddle, hopefully to rejoin the war. We've got some real tough campaigning terrain and weather ahead of us and our forces are being bled white. We're short of trained manpower, not least because many experienced troops have been sent back to England to get ready for the invasion of Western Europe they're brewing up for next year. Consequently, we're real short of trained technicians and experienced veterans to provide a backbone to a sea of raw recruits. Someone up high must have figured out that the pool of Allied POWs floating around the Italian countryside are a wasted resource.'

He held his hand before his face and put up a second finger. 'Number two, one day I'm reading the papers and come across a story about a bunch of high-profile Allied POWs enjoying the hospitality of old Adolf. In the accompanying pictures, who do I recognise but my old buddy, Jox McNabb. "Well, will you look at that," I said to myself and did some more digging. I discovered that a bunch of you were being used as some kind of human shield to protect a train loaded with who knows what. Our intelligence network confirmed that it had the highest levels of clearance from German high command. I did some research and realised that Reich Marshall Goering was involved, and that there was talk of looted artworks and treasures. So, I put my hand up and said, "I know that guy," and before I knew it, I was hauled out of Sicily and assigned to the two gentlemen you met earlier. I'll introduce them properly later.'

He gave a lopsided grin. 'As you can tell, they're not exactly soldiers, and are in fact art historians. The Brit is from the British Museum, and the Yank is a professor at Yale. The Limey's an expert in watercolours and prints, his American counterpart in oil paintings, or maybe it's the other way around. Anyhow, with peace or at least what they're calling peace, in Sicily, dozens of these old guys are coming out of the woodwork. It appears that after the wholesale looting and destruction of artworks on the island, someone on high decided something had to be done about it, before we started trashing things with the invasion of Italy. Sure, some of the damage in Sicily was down to the Krauts, but a good deal of it was us too, and we can't allow a repeat performance in *la bella Italia*. I think it was General Mark Clark, the new commanding general of the US Fifth Army who said, "fighting in Italy amounts to conducting war in a goddamn museum."

'Anyhow, these two fine gentlemen are part of the solution. They're called MFAA officers, and are responsible for Monuments, Fine Arts, and Archives on behalf of AMGOT, the Allied Military Government for Occupied Territories, which now controls Sicily and will do the same in Italy once it is liberated by the Allies.'

'Gosh, you Americans and your acronyms. How did warfare ever manage without them? I'm still trying to separate my SIMCOLs from my AMGOTs. Any idea how to keep it straight?'

Lomasso shrugged. 'Absolutely none. As long as things don't go SNAFU, I'm okay with that. What I can tell you is that the fighting troops call the AMGOT old timers "Aged Military Gentlemen on Tour" but occasionally use the more respectful expression "Monuments Men." I'm told the old boys refer to themselves as the rather more evocative "Venus Fixers."'

'Right, so what does that have to do with you, let alone me? And for that matter, why was Guilio Dennini dragged all the way here, away from his young family?'

'That's another reason Don Pietro let me leave Ragusa in one piece, on the condition that I take his nephew, and presumably his heir, out into the world to learn to speak English, get some experience of other cultures and most importantly get some combat experience. He asked me to make a man out of him.'

'And you're qualified to do that?' asked Jox, who'd always considered Lomasso a non-combatant, a rear echelon shadow warrior. 'Not exactly a combat veteran, are you?'

Lomasso's eyes narrowed. 'You got your way of fighting the war and I got mine.' He pointed at the black star on his hand, marking all 'men of honour' in their clan. 'Don Pietro says you owe Guilio Dennini a debt of honour for saving your life. If you owe him, you owe Don Pietro, and so you owe *la Cosa Nostra*, and we're here to collect.'

Jox felt a sudden chill, recalling Don Pietro promising him that one day that debt for saving his life would fall due. At the time he'd felt a frisson of fear, and it was back again. 'Me? What can I do?' squeaked Jox, higher than intended. 'I'm just trying to get back to the war and do my bit.'

'All in good time, buddy,' replied Lomasso. 'Don Pietro says the reputation of *la Cosa Nostra* would be greatly enhanced if we are seen to be helping to retrieve the great treasures of Sicily and Italy. As it happens, AMGOT agrees. So that's what Guilio and I are here to do, and we need you to show us where the treasures from the train actually might be.'

'How the hell would I know?'

'You got eyes. You're smart and nothing much escapes you. You must have seen it get loaded — how about when it got unloaded? You don't even need to have seen the actual stuff, just how the Krauts behaved around it, anything that might give us a clue. Think it over for a spell.'

Jox cast his mind back to the journey from *Campo* P.G. 85 to *Campo* P.G. 35 at the *Certosa di San Lorenzo* in Padula. He recalled how von Wella and his sidekick Steiner had stuck close to them all the way. 'The monastery is massive, and very recognisable from the air because of the Union Jack marked out on its lawned courtyard. Can't imagine any aviator would mistakenly bomb that. The place has huge cellars, which as far as I could tell were all empty. It did strike me as rather odd at the time. I can also remember the monks getting upset because they'd been kicked out of their rooms. The smaller rooms were used to cram in the influx of prisoners, but the larger, more luxurious ones were allocated to Steiner's troops. I remember somehow feeling that they were still around somewhere, although we didn't see them. Their vehicles were still parked in a nearby orchard and camouflaged under netting. That and the kitchens were constantly on the go, wafting over aromas that we never got fed. Drove us batty.'

'That would make sense, and if it wasn't prepared for you guys or the monks, then for who?'

'There were also whole areas of the complex which were strictly *verboten* to the *Kreigies*, with Italian guards posted at all entry points. They seemed less interested in keeping prisoners in the camp and more in keeping us out of those specific areas.'

'There you go — surely that's proof that there was something to hide.'

'Yes, but you're forgetting that all of that has probably changed by now,' said Jox. 'When the armistice was announced, the Italians disappeared, and the Germans were nowhere to be seen either. There had been talk of fresh German divisions coming down from the north and heading our way, and we saw plenty of troop movements when we were making our way through the mountains to get here. The big debate in the camp was whether to sit tight and wait for the Allies to arrive or to strike out on our own. Ironically, many of the men who'd been in the bag the longest were keenest to sit tight, but a bunch of us decided to go for it.' He laughed mirthlessly. 'For all the good it did us.' Something occurred to him. 'Let's not forget that the troops that destroyed San Cristobal were Steiner's paratroopers. If they've been deployed to anti-partisan duties, rather than guarding high-value prisoners, or even more valuable looted art and stolen booty, then logic would tell you that either or both have been shipped north. That would make sense.'

'That may well be, but we need to be sure. The Monuments Men won't accept that off chance, so we need to get to the monastery, and we're going to need your help for that.'

'Me? Why me?' asked Jox. 'Why can't Lupo and his partisans take you there? I've just spent the last few weeks trying to get as far away from there as I could, and in the process I have been blown up, lost friends, got shot at, witnessed a massacre, got wounded and then barely survived an infection. Why on earth would I go back?'

Lomasso had an odd expression on his face. 'Lupo's *Stella Rosa* are from far north of here. They tell me they don't know this region, and we've already got lost several times on the way here. You know the ground that you've covered, and I trust your navigation skills, but most of all, you owe a debt. Dennini saved your life, and what we're asking is a small matter in comparison to that. You don't have a choice.'

Against his every better instinct, Jox realised he would be returning to the *Certosa di San Lorenzo*. He was already dreading what they might find there.

'You cannot be serious, Jox!' cried Beans, covering his single eye and eyepatch with both hands. 'You were damned near killed getting here — so were we all. Old Shooter and Tex have certainly paid the price.'

'I've got no choice, Bayou,' replied Jox, wanting to agree with him but knowing where his obligations lay. 'You guys don't have to come. You can sit tight here, and we'll come back for you and then evacuate through SIMCOL. I've been told their first priority is the looted art and then getting us out is second. Who knows, we might even bust out a few more from the camp.'

'More than likely you'll run into that maniac, Steiner, again and end up dangling from a telegraph pole like a Christmas turkey. Not to mention the minefields and every artillery shell coming up from either side whilst they're shooting at each other. You're completely crazy.'

Pat Kilpatrick was listening to their exchange. He had a thunderous look on his face. He was toying with the brim of his trilby, running it through his freckled hands. 'I'll be going with the squadron leader,' he said. 'The Treble Threes would never forgive me if I found him, then went and lost him all over again. You can count me in, Jox.'

'You are determined to leave your skin in Italy,' fumed Perrin, equally furious at the idea of retracing their steps. He glared at Jox. 'I'll come, but I'm not happy.'

'Come on, Muriel, not you too,' whined Beans.

Perrin gave a Gallic shrug. 'We are *camarades*, so we must stick together.'

'You're all crazy,' said Beans. He stabbed a finger at Lomasso. 'And you, Mister, are going to get us all killed. You've no idea what a maniac that Steiner really is. If we run into him, we're done for, especially with two old guys in tow. No offence meant, sirs,' he added, lifting a placating hand in the direction of the bewildered Monuments Men.

'None taken, dear boy,' said the larger of the pair. 'I'll stick to my knitting, if you stick to yours. We're here to do a job, and that's to find out what Jerry has squirrelled away at Padula. We may not look like solders,' he added, slapping his paunch, 'but we still have our duty.'

'I can hold my own,' said the other, his glasses glinting in the firelight. His precise Connecticut accent was edged with anger. 'You young fellows ain't the only ones who can bring it in a fight, and *we know* what's at stake. We've studied these artefacts all our lives; we know what they're worth and would gladly sacrifice ourselves to protect them.'

CHAPTER ELEVEN

The expedition were due to set off at dawn. There had been a discussion about travelling at night instead — arguments that it would be safer and there was less chance of running into enemy patrols or reconnaissance aircraft. It was Jox, however, who pointed out that they'd be covering ground infested with mines and that the only reference points that he, Perrin and Beans had of their outward journey were visual ones. It was decided they'd wait until daybreak.

The group would consist of Jox, Perrin, Beans, Pat Kilpatrick, who had by now appointed himself as his CO's bodyguard, Lomasso and Dennini, with Singh and Lupo representing the partisans. The rest of the depleted *Brigata Stella Rosa* would stay behind to begin the construction of a replacement camp, continuing to gather whatever survivors may have escaped the attack on Steiner's troops and the subsequent massacre of San Cristobal.

Night fell early in the mountains and this one promised to be a cold one, the balmy nights of Tuturano now a distant memory. Jox laid out his bedroll and tried to make himself comfortable. He'd found a sheltered nook in the hillside, away from the others, who were all clustered around the campfire. His mind was filled with foreboding over what lay ahead.

Jox opened his eyes but could see no stars. The clouds were low, and it was a moonless night. The air smelt of the campfire and the faint sweetness of mountain heather carried on the wind. Somewhere out there, an owl called. He heard some feet scrambling on gravel, and he sat up at the noise. As a shadow loomed, his first reaction was to reach for the kukri under his folded clothing. That first flush of fear quickly disappeared when he was hit by a recognisable fragrance. The perfume grew stronger as his covers were lifted, and long, soft hair brushed across his face. Rosmarina whispered, '*Buona sera*, Jox.' She was still dressed, but her clothing loosened as she lay against his chest. 'I cannot lose you to this war so soon. You must survive and come back for me; can you make that promise?'

Jox hadn't been with a woman for almost two years. There had been no shortage of temptations in Tunisia, London and Malta, and even in poor, ravaged Sicily there were many hungry *bella donnas* willing to sell the only thing they had left, but that wasn't for him. His more roué comrades had teased him about his 'saintliness', but what they didn't know was that the thought of any closeness only brought him pain. The two women he'd loved had each in their own way dealt a dagger blow to his heart. Losing Alice without a trace in the Blitz had almost finished him off, then, when still fragile, he'd found new hope with Julianna in Malta, only to be betrayed as she ran off with one of his closest friends. For self-preservation, he'd shut himself off from interactions of that kind. Instead, he'd focussed his energies on the challenges of command, the welfare of his men and just getting on with fighting the war.

All that was about to change, here on this Apennine ridge, away from the others but surely not unknown to them. Jox rediscovered a part of life he'd locked away for many long months, voluntarily or not. It was like spring after a fallow winter, and his spirits now soared. The worries that had clouded his mind vanished, as he focussed on living in the present as vividly as he could.

Dawn had reached the jagged peaks by the time he and Rosmarina were asleep in each other's arms. It wouldn't be long before the hour of the planned departure. As quietly and discreetly as she'd come to him, Rosmarina awoke and slipped away, but not before a hungry kiss. 'We will not say goodbye. I'll be waiting for your return. We've not had long together, and I pray for more time. Come back to me. I know the war wants you and we must fight. Please remember a part of *Italia* will always wait for you in my heart.'

Despite his lack of sleep, Jox felt alert and keen to get underway. He'd packed a few belongings into a bergen rucksack, topped up his water bottle, checked his kukri and compass, and shouldered his new weapon. Lomasso had given it to him the previous night, presumably from SIMCOL stocks. It was a bulky M1 Thompson submachine gun with a polished wooden stock and a thirty-round box magazine. It was heavy, especially for lugging over mountains, but he could depend on its stopping power. Lomasso and Dennini had the same and were also festooned with American Mk II hand grenades. Each of the professors had a holstered pistol, worn on the left in the prescribed British Army manner. Beans, who wasn't much of a shot because of his eye, had opted for quantity over quality, so had a pistol on each hip like a cowboy. Singh had his sniper rifle, and Perrin a captured German infantryman's *Karabiner* 98k.

It was Pat Kilpatrick who had swapped his weapon for something more unusual. He was carrying an extraordinary-seeming contraption that looked a bit like a green pipe. It had a mushroom butt and an open barrel that was like a length of roof guttering. About a yard long, it was heavy and clumsy, and had the largest trigger Jox had ever seen, certainly large enough to fit through a gloved hand. He was also carrying a cardboard case across his back, made up of several foot-long tubes lashed together with a satchel strap.

'They've certainly got you loaded up,' said Jox. 'What the devil's all that?'

'Feel like a pack mule, so I do,' replied the Ulsterman, still in his collarless jacket and goatskin gilet. 'Mind you, I suppose I did volunteer. As it happens, I'm not a bad shot and can handle me guns, so I thought this might be a good craic.'

'Yes, Pat, but what is it?'

'They call it a PIAT Mk I, which stands for Projector, Infantry, Anti-Tank. In essence, it's a spigot mortar that lobs a two-and-a-half-pound shaped charge up to a hundred yards in a straight line and some three hundred and fifty when fired indirectly. The pointy bit can smack through four inches of Jerry's armour, a powerful punch if you're close enough. She's spring-operated, so there's no back-blast or muzzle smoke to give you away, but she's a devil to cock and kicks like a mule.'

'You seem to know a lot about it.'

Kilpatrick grinned. 'Had me a wee go with some Paras back in Sicily. Reckoned they owed us a favour for watching over them at Primosole Bridge. Come to think of it, wasn't that where you went down?' He laughed. 'At least the first time. You're making quite a habit of it, so you are.'

'Well, let's hope we don't run into anything that needs that kind of fire power,' replied Jox. 'You sure you know what you're doing with that contraption?'

'I've dealt with armour in our Spitfires and know their weak spots.'

They joined the others for a cup of acorn coffee, rather poor fare before setting off on a long journey, but up to the job of waking them up. After waving goodbye, they descended the steep hillside, heading west on an opposite tangent to that which they'd followed for the previous days. Lupo led the group, walking with Dennini, the pair determined to show the foreigners the way, despite their unfamiliarity with the territory.

They didn't stop for hours, walking towards the sound of distant guns, their tempo and volume increasing as they got closer. 'Whose guns are those?' Jox asked Lomasso.

The big New Yorker checked the date on his wristwatch. 'I guess we're in September now, so that'll be Operation Avalanche getting underway. We've opened a second front on Italian soil, principally to appease the Soviets and relieve the pressure on their troops. It's hoped the landings will get more German troops reassigned to the Italian front. I sure hope the boys landing at Salerno aren't expecting an easy life of wine, women and song. With winter coming in these damned mountains, it sure won't be sunny Italy and *la dolce vita* for any of us. The long, straight beaches at Salerno are pretty perfect for amphibious landings, but the Krauts know that too and they're overlooked by the Lattari Mountains, part of these same southern Apennines.' Lomasso combed a hand through his beard, a sign of anxiety that Jox was coming to recognise. 'That barrage there is either the Krauts shelling our boys, or our battleships in the Gulf of Policastro shellacking their positions up in the mountains. I suppose it could also be fighter bombers or medium bombers.'

Jox listened. 'No, they're not fighter bombers; the explosions are too regular and continuous.'

'Well, either way,' said Lomasso, 'someone's sure catching hell.'

They stopped for lunch when the old gentlemen were nearing collapse. There wasn't much to be had, just a few shared tins of pilchards and some dark rye bread, but it gave Jox the opportunity to quiz the art historians on what they planned to do if any treasures were found at the monastery.

The Englishman, the larger and more ebullient of the pair, had introduced himself as Edward Croft-Murray. He was tall, ungainly and corpulent, dressed in an ill-fitting uniform that was ringed with perspiration. Dark, yet mostly bald, he had a quick smile and twinkling eyes. Croft-Murray was a museum curator and a renowned expert on British and European artworks. He held degrees from Lancing and Magdalen Colleges, Oxford and was the Keeper of Prints and Drawings at the British Museum in London before the war.

His shorter, finer set companion was Deane Keller from New Haven, Connecticut, where he was a professor and lifelong Yale man. He had degrees in History, the Sciences and Fine Art, and completing his studies in Rome, he had won several prizes as a portrait artist before returning to his Alma Mater, where amongst other things he became the portraitist of the Yale faculty. He spoke fluent Italian, had a deep love for the nation and was anxious for the preservation of its masterpieces. Fair, with receding blond hair, he wore little round wire spectacles and at first seemed mild-mannered, but was actually rather short-tempered, twitchy and sometimes condescending. Despite their very different characters, the pair had a sort of Laurel and Hardy chemistry, often interrupting and finishing each other's sentences.

'You see, my boy,' explained Croft-Murray, 'it doesn't really matter if we find nothing but empty cellars. What's important is to reestablish a trace of where these precious things have been. That way, there's a trail for us to follow.' He smiled affably. 'This volume of artefacts isn't easy to hide or disguise, nor can it simply disappear into thin air, the present altitude notwithstanding,' he added with a guffaw.

His partner chipped in. 'What we're after is invariably beautiful, hugely valuable and highly desired, but not simply in monetary terms. Art is really the only way for one generation to communicate with another, and that is its true value. Human nature invariably means that its possessor wants to show it off. We've found that German bigwigs can't help themselves, and that's what we're counting on. We'll follow the trail and catch up with the artefacts when they emerge naturally. That, of course, presupposes that some overenthusiastic military types on our side don't accidently blow it all to smithereens.' He grimaced. 'There's been no shortage of vandals in the US Army, and you Brits did a hell of a job when bombing Palermo, wiping out some of its finest Baroque churches and their priceless contents. What I saw there broke my heart — just burned remains, mere ghosts of the ancient glories they once were. In my humble view, that is the very worst of war crimes.'

'So, if we find traces of the booty,' said Croft-Murray, 'we follow the trail, and if not, we sit tight until our superiors come ashore at Salerno and give us fresh orders. You chaps needn't worry about all that though. Just get us to Padula, then Captain Lomasso will take you back and get you evacuated. I feel sure he'll swing by the *Stella Rosa* camp, so you can reacquaint yourself with your charming companion.' He winked at Jox. 'Oh, to be a bright young blade again.'

'Say Jox, may I call you Jox?' said Keller. 'Would you mind casting your mind back to exactly what you saw when you boarded the train to Padula? I've spoken to the others —' he nodded to Beans and Perrin — 'but it would be useful to hear your recollection. Any light you can shed on the specific items we're dealing with would be very helpful.'

'Let me see,' replied Jox, closing his eyes and trying to picture the scene at Brindisi rail station. 'There were statues carved from light-coloured stone, maybe marble. I couldn't work out what they represented as they were wrapped up, but I did see their feet, long carved toes in sandals, some quite intricate. A few had what I thought were shinpads on their lower legs, a bit like cricket pads but thinner. I can remember thinking they were rather odd.'

'Ah yes, probably Roman greaves,' Keller confirmed, 'sheet metal formed to protect the shins and legs in combat. Simple legionnaires rarely merited them, but senior officers had ornately decorated ones. Statues representing heroes in military garb might well feature greaves. Alternatively, the statues could be of even more ancient Greek hoplites, who would almost certainly be wearing greaves. As for the toes, they sound like quite characteristic "Greek feet", with the second toe longer than the big toe, creating a distinctive pointed shape, quite prevalent amongst the Greeks and correspondingly their sculptures. Say, how tall were these figures?'

'Hard to tell,' Jox replied. 'Above head height — well, at least mine, which admittedly isn't exactly lofty, but several were on pedestals and the like.'

'Anything else you recall?' prompted Keller.

'Gilt and gold trim, lots of it. I got the sense of religious artefacts, but most of it was covered up. Then, of course, there were many paintings. Some were stacked flat and painted on wooden boards, but others, usually larger, were leaning up against the carriage walls, their canvas stretched on wooden frames. The interior of the carriages smelt of polish and something akin to castor oil.'

'That's probably from the pigments used,' Croft-Murray added. 'The boards will be older and the canvases more recent oeuvres, but no less precious. Anything else?'

'No, not really,' replied Jox. 'Just that there were twice as many freight carriages as passenger cars. Most were already sealed and had the *Luftwaffe* eagle on pasted sheets of paper with several signatures, including one that said, "By order of Reich Marshall Herman Goering".'

'Ah yes, the Fat One, the great magpie himself,' said Croft-Murray. 'Well, at least we know we're on the trail of good stuff. He doesn't mess around with mere trinkets.'

'Right, gentlemen, I reckon we better get going,' said Lomasso. 'Saddle up and let's get on out of here.'

'He's starting to get on my nerves,' grumbled Beans, still unhappy about being involved in what he considered to be a wild goose chase. 'That guy's been reading too many of them Western paperbacks you get for a dime. Full of cowboys with white hats and outlaws with black ones. Thinks he's some kind of sheriff leading a posse.'

Jox grinned at his grumpiness. 'Personally, I've always been partial to the adventures of James Bigglesworth — you know, "Biggles", the famous RFC fighter pilot. I know he's only fictional, but I've always rather modelled myself on him. He's certainly the one responsible for my becoming a pilot when I left school rather abruptly.'

Walking on, they breached the ridgeline above San Cristobal. It was late afternoon on a dull, grey day and the martyred village was unearthly still, apart from squabbling crows hidden from view somewhere. It didn't take much imagination to guess what they'd be fighting over.

The men stopped in the ruins of the village, the air still laden with the ashes of burnt-down dwellings. The main road through the centre of San Cristobal now looked like the gap-toothed smile of an urchin, with empty, smoke-streaked houses standing beside the blackened ruins of their long-time neighbours. Tiny, unidentified pieces of charred paper blew through the carnage like autumn leaves, on them the scribblings of everyday life, now gone forever. Where the villagers themselves were, remained a mystery. They'd obviously been cut down from the telegraph poles by someone, but there was no indication of where they'd disappeared to. It was likely that they were simply buried in a communal grave somewhere, Teutonic notions of efficiency and sanitation dictating that the disposal of the bodies be expedited.

Jox hadn't spoken with Lupo all that much, but from his hollowed-out expression it was evident he was struggling to control his emotions. Jox embraced him and could only say impotently, 'It's the war. It was their destiny; we cannot change that.'

Lupo nodded, biting his lip. '*Sì*, we are fighting for *our* destiny.'

They set up camp for the night in the garden of San Cristobal's *sindaco*, the mayor's house, who despite his Fascist leanings, had still been strung up along with his family and the other villagers. Evidently, for years the garden had been his pride and joy and was full of bountiful fruit trees and flowering plants, a stark and tragic contrast to the burnt-out husk of the family home. The men could pluck sweet, sticky figs straight from a tree, but soon found them cloying, nauseating even, given what had happened hereabouts. The logic for staying overnight in the devastated village was that having perpetrated such terrible things here and then covered them up, it was unlikely the Germans would return very soon. Nor, it was hoped, would they have had the time to sow mines and boobytraps, the usual *modus operandi* to interdict territory from the partisans or the encroaching Allies.

The night was cold and still, and after a poor supper and listless conversations, guards were posted and the rest tried to get some sleep. Tucked in their bedrolls, most slept badly, haunted by dreams filled with the ghosts of the recently departed.

CHAPTER TWELVE

Jox was up early. Everyone else was still dozing, sleep having come to them late. Even the two sentries meant to be on watch, Dennini and Lupo, were out for the count, slumped asleep against the two-hundred-year-old walnut tree that dominated the garden.

Jox felt he wanted to shave. It was his usual way of resetting, when marking a fresh beginning or if something was troubling him. When the day or mission ahead was challenging, he always found the mundane task was a good way to clear his thinking, sharpen his reactions and regain some focus. That said, his razor this morning was rather blunt, and he only had an old nub of soap and tepid water from his canteen to work with. Jox wasn't a particularly hirsute fellow, but this routine had been ingrained into him during his officer training. Being well-groomed demonstrated to others his self-discipline, confident leadership, attention to detail and control over his environment.

He smiled at how his example seemed already to be working, spotting first Perrin, then Kilpatrick following suit. The Ulsterman's ginger beard was more of a challenge than Jox's meagre affair, so he started by hacking away with some kitchen scissors that he'd found in the ruins. Jox watched as he snipped off several weeks' growth. Rubbing his own hand over his chin, he felt the sting. The blunt safety razor in his pack had proved too dull, so he'd instead tried using the sharp blade of his kukri but had done a poor job of it because of its size and his clumsiness. He now sipped the acorn coffee that Perrin had handed him. It was bitter, but somehow he had developed a taste for it, though he still longed for the American coffee he used to enjoy in Sicily, nectar compared to this vicious brew.

The stillness of the morning was suddenly rent apart by the throaty growl of an engine. Jox's first instinct was to look skywards, but he quickly realised it was coming in at ground level. He peeked through the garden hedge woven through with sweet-smelling honeysuckle. Up on the main road there was movement and a raised cloud of dust. Through it emerged the long barrel and pointed snout of an armoured car, which Jox instantly recognised as an SD.KFZ.234 Puma. He'd seen them as part of von Wella and Steiner's entourage, but also more recently during the deadly attack on San Cristobal. The vehicle was a mottled green colour, like the skin of a lizard, and had several black rings on its barrel, indicating its kills. Whether they'd been earned against armour, anti-tank guns or innocent civilians was unclear.

It was on its own, which was unusual as they usually operated in pairs, to provide mutual cover for one another. This one was presumably on a quick mission, perhaps ferrying supplies, ammo or personnel. It appeared unconcerned about being alone, driving confidently through the village with no expectation of threat despite the recent harsh treatment it and its companions had dispensed.

At the commander's turret, there was a flash of blond hair and Jox raised his head to get a better look. This moment of foolish inattention was rewarded by the sudden, barking report of the Puma's coaxial machinegun firing. The hedge behind which Jox was sheltering started to disintegrate. He dropped to the ground and made himself small, as shredded leaves and sweet-smelling yellow flowers fluttered around him, so out of place before the savagery unleashed. Across the garden, Jox's companions scrambled, swiftly alert and ready for action.

The Puma slowed, hatches slamming shut as the partisan's return fire began pinging off its carapace. The turret whirred as the main gun turned towards them, the striped barrel making Jox think of a monstrous wasp. It fired with a resounding boom, the powerful recoil making the vehicle judder. The round in the breech was presumably Armor Piercing rather than High Explosive, as it hit the two-hundred-year-old walnut tree with a loud crack. The tree that had provided shade and bountiful harvests to the mayor's family for generations shuddered at the impact. Walnuts the size of golf balls came tumbling down like green hail. Dennini and Lupo awoke with a start. Having struck the live wood of the ancient tree, the gun's round was stuck fast, deeply embedded and sizzling in sap seeping from the wound like dark blood.

Lupo screamed orders in frantic Italian, with Lomasso countering in his thick Bronx accent. Both were ignored as Dennini hammered away with his Thompson, making a whole lot of noise, but the .45 calibre slugs bounced harmlessly off the Puma's armour. The ragged tattoo did, however, distract the vehicle's crew long enough for Beans to crawl forward. He'd lettered as a quarterback at Louisiana State University, and amongst his many idle boasts was that he really could throw a ball. In quick succession, he lobbed a pair of pineapple-shaped hand grenades a prodigious distance. The first exploded harmlessly by the commander's turret, but succeeded in destroying the vehicle's radio antennae, which hopefully meant the crew couldn't report enemy contact back to their main force. The second dropped short and landed at the foot of the vehicle's outsized front tyres. The Puma's rear driver was desperately trying to reverse the armoured car around the corner when it detonated and sent razor-sharp fragments into the front two tyres on the left, shredding them despite their robust construction. The Puma's key strengths were speed and manoeuvrability, but both were immediately compromised by this damage, the reverse trajectory skewing into a banana shape, thereby exposing its less well armoured flanks.

Jox heard a hollow, metallic clunk behind him. It was the sort of sound that industrial apparatus made when finishing a cycle. From the corner of his eye, a half-shaved Pat Kilpatrick manhandled his T-shaped PIAT mortar. The spigot-launched hollow charge projectile travelled in a low parabola visible to the naked eye. It struck the rear of the turret, where the circular aperture acted as a socket. There was a second dull thud, followed by high-pitched fizzing, then the boom of a secondary explosion within the hull. The top hatch of the turret flew skywards, and the ragdoll form of the vehicle commander was flung into the air, like a cork exiting a bottle of champagne. The circular metal door struck the terracotta roof tiles of a nearby house, sending a deluge of orange shards sliding down the incline. The commander's body hit the roof with a splat, then slid down the grooved slope, landing in a crumpled heap at the foot of the white-washed wall. A scarlet slug trail streaked down both surfaces.

Despite the horror of the vehicle commander's fate, Jox knew it would be better than that of his three crewmates inside: the gunner and both drivers, who allowed the Puma to be driven equally successfully in either direction. All three were carbonised where they sat, leaving little to distinguish them from the tarlike sludge filling the hulk to a sticky depth of about a foot.

The violence that had shattered the early morning was followed by an unexpected stillness. The usual dawn chorus of songbirds remained mute, stunned by the fracas that had brutally replaced them.

'Everyone all right?' Jox asked the dazed men.

They got gingerly to their feet from the various nooks and crannies they'd taken cover in. Most nodded, but Kilpatrick was groaning, rolling around on the ground. He was clutching his arm across his body, one hand massaging his shoulder, his features screwed up in obvious pain.

'I've messed up me shoulder,' he gasped, breathing through his badly set pugilist's nose. 'I dislocated it years ago playing rugby, and it pops out every now and again. Hurts like all hell, but we can fix it,' he gasped. 'I'll need you to give me a hand, lads. Jox, take my jacket off, then slip it under the armpit of my hurt shoulder.'

'Which one is it?' asked Jox nervously.

'The right one, you eejit!'

'All right, all right.'

'I told you that PIAT had a kick like a mule,' said Kilpatrick through gritted teeth.

'Well, you did a grand job with it. That was a dead good shot,' said Jox, trying to distract him as he removed Kilpatrick's green silk jacket, to his evident discomfort.

'Ah well, maybe I've still got me uses,' Kilpatrick replied, eyes shut and jaw clenched. 'Now, lay me on my back and position yourself above my shoulder, then get ready to pull upwards with the jacket acting like a sling under my armpit to lift the shoulder. Mr Beans, I need you to grab my right wrist and get ready to pull downwards. When I say "go", both pull hard in opposite directions.'

Beans nodded, remarkably calm about what was being asked of him. Jox presumed he'd seen this on-the-field first aid when playing college ball. In contrast, he was feeling decidedly nervous about his role in the proceedings.

'Right, ready?' said Kilpatrick, licking his lips then gritting his teeth. 'Go!'

They both strained, and Kilpatrick gave a furious roar, his half-clipped chin jutting skywards. There was a loud pop, not unlike the sound of the PIAT firing earlier. He groaned a few times, his arms wrapped across his body, then went very quiet, before unexpectedly sitting up. 'That'll surely wake you up in the morning.' He looked worn out but managed a lopsided smile. 'Certainly puts hair on your chest.' He indicated the PIAT on the ground beside him. 'I'll not be able to carry that brute now.'

'I'll do that for you, Pat,' said Dennini, reaching for the heavy spigot mortar. His face immediately registering surprise at its sheer weight.

'No, it is my duty to carry!' cried Lupo.

The Sicilian and Italian began arguing, clearly both embarrassed that the group had been caught napping by the armoured car on their watch.

'Y'all can argue all you want,' drawled Beans. 'Me, Jox and Muriel are going over to check on what's left of those Krauts. We don't want any more surprises. Let's hope they didn't get the word out to any of their buddies.'

The trio shouldered their weapons and warily made their way towards the smouldering hulk. It smelt of kerosene, spent high explosives and nauseatingly of burnt flesh. There wasn't much left of the fellows inside the hull, but what was striking was the perfectly round, orange-sized hole where the hollow charge had punctured the side armour just below the turret. It was shocking to see the devastation that such a neat penetration had caused, the entry point looking so innocuous and apparently harmless.

Jox crossed to the crumpled figure at the base of the wall. It was clad in a green jump smock, which he recognised as belonging to a 'Green Devil' paratrooper. He had the triple-winged badge of a *Feldwebel* on his arms, a sleeve cuff that read *KRETA* and then the NARVIK shield dated 1940. This was clearly a seasoned veteran who had come through numerous campaigns before ending his days at the foot of this simple wall in Campagna. The body was obviously human, but the angles of the limbs and torso were all wrong, and had clearly suffered multiple fractures. When Jox turned him over, he saw that the face was intact, glazed blue eyes staring, mouth open to expose chipped front teeth. His hair was short and blond, and Jox recognised him immediately.

This was Schultz, the paratrooper sergeant from Munich who'd prepared smoked sausage, fresh sauerkraut and pilsner lager for the prisoners at Tuturano, prior to their transfer north. He recalled the burly *Feldwebel* warning him at Brindisi railway station that trying to escape would be futile, and also how he'd dealt swiftly and professionally with Darren Beans when he'd seen red and charged blindly at his nemesis, von Wella.

'Don't you recognise him?' Jox asked Beans, who'd come to stand beside him.

'Should I?' asked Beans, crouching to get a better look at the body.

'He's that paratrooper sergeant that took you out with the serving tray. You know, when you charged at von Wella like some demented wild boar. He got you right in the neck, as I recall.'

Beans rubbed his throat. 'Yeah, I reckon I do. Punched me pretty hard in the face too. But hey, look who got the last laugh? He sure didn't come out of this one the victor.'

'You've got to respect him as a soldier, though. He was tough as they come, and he saw a lot of action,' said Jox, pointing at the Iron Cross First Class on Schultz's chest and the ribbon of the Second Class at his button hole. Jox picked off Schultz's Iron Cross and pocketed it.

'What d'you want that for?' asked Beans.

'Don't want him to just disappear into the fog of war,' replied Jox. 'What they did here was awful; it shouldn't be forgotten, but nor should he.'

'Come on, boys, we'd better get going,' said Lomasso. 'With luck, they won't be missed for a while, but they will eventually, and we don't wanna be anywhere near here when that happens. Padula should be a day away, and you've said there's some scrappy, ravaged battlefields to get over before then. Crossing enemy lines was never going to be easy. This is territory that will no doubt be scattered with all kinds of nasty surprises set to catch out the unwary and foolhardy.'

The return to *Certosa di Padula* was an anticlimax. In war, events are often expected to build to a crescendo, but things rarely turn out that way. What is closer to the truth is that war mainly consists of long periods of boredom, punctuated by moments of sheer terror.

Navigating across the devastated landscape of Campagna, the men had crossed isolated farms, valleys of abandoned crops and endless overgrown pastures of yellowing grass. Filing through waist-high vegetation like lions in the savannah, they slipped from one enemy line to another. Passing mountain passes and rocky peaks, they found the slopes covered with the debris and chaos left behind by war. It was nerve-wracking to negotiate, as every blasted remnant of humanity, shattered piece of equipment, or even innocent animal caught up in the cruelty engineered by men, might prove potentially lethal.

Somehow, they negotiated the mine-filled 'valleys of death', eventually reaching the outskirts of the village housing the Padula Charterhouse complex. It was well past nightfall, and yet they could see the settlement was worn and beaten-up, the skyline ravaged. It was unclear whether actual combat, artillery fire or aerial bombardment was responsible, but Padula had suffered since their departure. At the time of the armistice, there'd been music and light from the settlement; now it lay silent as a tomb, apparently deserted.

The charterhouse loomed large and black against the night sky, devoid of illumination. As they stole into the grounds through familiar gates, the oppressive darkness soon halted their progress. They couldn't see where they were going, and imagined threats around every corner took a toll on their depleted courage. A long day spent navigating the fields of death had long since drained away their bravery.

CHAPTER THIRTEEN

Dawn came as a welcome release from a night that had been filled with imagined terrors. The chorus of songbirds helped soothe the men's troubled minds, inspiring optimism as to what the day would bring. Emboldened by the light, the little group ventured forward, splitting into threes so that each trio included a former *Kriegie* of P.G. 35, a red-scarfed partisan and a SIMCOL operative. Injured Kilpatrick would stay behind to rest and guard their packs, so that the others might travel light to cover more ground within the maze of monastery buildings and grounds.

Jox teamed up with Croft-Murray and Singh. The Englishman had lost weight over the last few days. His spirits were undaunted, though, and he'd grandly rechristened himself as 'a veritable Homer', after the 'odyssey' they had undertaken. Jox was unsure what he was talking about, the classics never having really been his forte.

Croft-Murray was keen to find any signs of stolen antiquities but also to discover the priceless baroque chapels, altar pieces, lavish staircases, mosaics and religious paintings that were to be found at the charterhouse itself. There was precious history all around them, and he feared for what was at risk.

Singh, on the other hand, was keen to find the kitchens, more focussed on providing his companions with sustenance after their long trek. He also wanted to find bathing facilities, to address his wild appearance after days of rough living. It was anathema for him to be unkempt, as he was usually so meticulous, devout and fastidious. As a Sikh, the ritual of cleansing, brushing out his hair and beard, plaiting it again and retying his turban, were more than simple matters of hygiene, and in some ways were like a prayer, symbolic of his devotion to his beliefs. This need was all the more urgent in a holy place like this, which had cloistered devoted Carthusian brothers for many centuries.

Jox cared little for such physical or spiritual matters; his need was to discover the fate of the comrades that he'd left behind. The monastery was deathly quiet and deserted, filling him with a deep sense of foreboding. He already knew it was most likely that the camp's prisoners had been transferred away, but after what he'd seen at San Cristobal, he was concerned about what he might discover. Reasoning that the camp's infirmary was a good place to start looking for clues, so he hastened the others to the building where it had last been.

Before entering, Jox paused, touching the large medieval doors; the ancient wood was reinforced with curved irons and studded for additional protection. He was wary of what he might find on the other side, so the trio agreed to breach it tactically. He listened at the latch and heard the low buzz of murmured conversation. Jox glanced at the other two, nodded and shoved the door hard, following it into the room beyond, covered by both Singh's rifle and Croft-Murray's pistol. His own 'spray and pray' Thompson submachine was at his shoulder, his eyes down the barrel as he entered.

Standing side by side were a pair of startled Carthusian monks in pristine white robes. One had his hood up, his face in the shadows; the other was uncovered, bespectacled and had a stethoscope around his neck. Both wore identical brown sandals, bare feet visible below the hems of their white habits that were cinched at the waist by knotted white ropes. The taller of two, with the hood up, folded it back to reveal the thin, angular face and haunted eyes of Brother Angelo. He and

Jox recognised each other straight away, the monk bowing and Jox lowering his weapon and coming to attention. The monk smiled and raised a bony hand to signal to his companion there was nothing to worry about. The other man was shorter and stouter.

'You gave me such a fright, *Signore* Jox,' said Brother Angelo.

'I'm so pleased to see you alive,' Jox replied warmly. 'Where is everybody else?'

'The peace we prayed for has not come easily to us. The *Tedeschi* have shattered our hopes and dreams.'

Assuming the worst, Jox's face dropped.

'*Niente*, nothing like that, my son,' said Brother Angelo, clasping Jox fondly by the shoulders with bony fingers. 'The *Tedeschi* have taken all the prisoners who waited here. The smart ones like you ran away. The others were caught up like fish in the nets. All have been moved to another *campo* in the north, maybe even shipped off to Germany by now. Many trains came to fetch them.'

'What about your brothers?' asked Jox. 'Where have they all gone?'

'They make the evacuation to a monastery some kilometres away. The *Tedeschi* say we must go; they do not want us to see what they are doing here.' The monks exchanged glances. 'But we have eyes on everything… God also sees everything. This is Brother Davide; he is a doctor, ministering to the sick and injured. He, myself and a few others with some medical training volunteered to stay, to take care of prisoners who are too sick or wounded to be evacuated. There were many at first, especially after the *Tedeschi* came back to make them prisoners again. Some chose to fight but had nothing for weapons. Many perished and were wounded, and some of them remain, the very sick, but thanks be to God some are also recovering in the doctor's care.'

Jox introduced Singh and Croft-Murray. Croft-Murray could barely contain himself and blurted out, 'What were the Germans trying to hide?'

'*Tresori*,' replied Brother Davide. 'The treasures of our nation that they have stolen from us. They took away what was stored here and then came back to rip out the precious valuables of the monastery. It is a disgrace, the wanton destruction of our holy relics. God will not forgive them and in time they will surely pay for it.'

Croft-Murray's moon face dropped. He looked utterly crestfallen, tears welling up and spilling down his fleshy face. Perhaps he was exhausted, but the two monks were touched to see a foreigner who cared so deeply about the loss of their national patrimony. Croft-Murray took a deep breath and shook himself like a wet dog.

'Right, well, my job here is to get all of that back. It may take time, it may take my lifetime, but I swear it will be returned to its rightful place. That is the sworn mission of the "Venus Fixers".'

'What is the "Venus Fixers?"' asked Brother Angelo.

'I'll explain later,' said Jox.

'Could I beg you to show me where these treasures were stored, and perhaps also where the monastery's own treasures were taken from?' asked Croft-Murray.

'*Sì*, I can do that. With a heavy heart, but I will show you that,' replied Brother Angelo.

'Singh, would you accompany the Prof and Brother Angelo? I want to have a look around and see if any of my chums are amongst the wounded. Means a lot to me to find them,' Jox said.

'Of course, sahib, my sacred duty will be to protect them. You find your friends and go with my prayers.'

The pair followed the white-clad monk from the room.

Jox turned to Brother Davide. 'May I accompany you on your rounds?'

'*Si*, of course,' he replied.

'Please forgive my weapon. I will hold it discreetly, so as not to distress your patients, but I must take it with me. I don't know what we may come across.'

The monk shrugged. 'I know how soldiers are. We had many here to start with, but not so many now. The lightly wounded were evacuated, and of course, the *Tedeschi* wounded were dealt with first.'

'Were there many of them?' asked Jox, unsure if the *Kriegies* had put up much of a fight.

'Not so many as amongst the prisoners, but there were some,' replied the monk. 'Now, we only have the serious cases and a few that joined us after the evacuation. Be warned, my son, some of what you will encounter is ugly.'

'Please don't worry, I've been through a lot of war,' replied Jox. 'But thank you for the warning. It's not something you ever get used to, is it?'

The monk shook his head and indicated the way forward.

The first room they entered held four beds. There were long drapes at the shuttered windows, hanging limply in air that was thick and foul. Jox recognised the sweet mousey smell of gas gangrene. In the beds were a pair of multiple amputees, swollen stumps blotchy and red-edged, the tips the colour of blackberries. Jox had seen the terrible progress of gangrene before, witnessing the heartbreak of successive amputations trying to halt the spread.

There was also a gut shot patient who looked only marginally better, his abdomen distended and his skin jaundiced. There were rubber drains coming from the wound, filling a glass demi-john on the parquet floor with a turgid dark liquid. Jox shuddered to imagine what it was.

'This poor boy has acute liver failure,' whispered Brother Davide, his hands pressed together beneath his chin. 'There is little we can do but pray.'

Jox looked across to the last bed in the room. On it was the emaciated body of a young man, skin as pale as a pearl and with the same waxy lustre.

'Poor Rafael has been in a coma for weeks. He has a head wound and is non-responsive. All we do is feed him intravenously. There are only so many times that Brother Angelo and I can give him our blood. He is fortunate that we are both O Positive, but we are running out of supplies.' He raised the sleeves of his monk's robe to show the needle marks on his bare arms.

'So am I,' replied Jox. 'I'd be happy to help. I'm sure the others would too.'

'Bless you, my son,' said Brother Davide and sighed. 'These are our worst cases. The others offer some cause for optimism. One was a penetrating wound to the abdomen — it was bad when he arrived, but by the grace of God, he has turned a corner. Now, the biggest problem we have is that he refuses to stay in his bed and is always hungry and desperate for cigarettes. He has some medical experience, so at least he helps us with the others, doing small jobs for them and keeping their spirits up. He is a good boy, an *Americano*, and a pilot like you. Come, let me introduce you to Gregory. He will take your blood. Don't worry, he is quite skilled.'

The monk led Jox to the adjoining room. Here the drapes were drawn back, and the windows were open, letting in the crisp morning air and streaming sunshine. Once again there were four beds, three made up and one with a folded striped bedroll sitting on the frame. Gathered around one of the beds three men were playing cards. They were pale but distinctly healthier than the men next door. One had stiff, greying hair and a bandage around his throat, another a huge walrus moustache and an arm in plaster from the wrist to the shoulder. The third had his back to them and was shirtless, with a bandage wound around his abdomen. All three turned as Jox and Davide entered, the bare-chested one revealing a thick beard, a cigarette held between his teeth and a bright yellow sheriff's star tattooed on his right pectoral muscle.

'Well, talk of the devil and look who turns up!' said Jox, recognising Tex Carver, in spite of the beard.

'Jox McNabb, you son of a gun,' grinned Carver. 'You came back! I sure hoped you would.'

Jox shook his hand. 'How on earth are you, Tex? You look in damned sight better shape than when I last saw you. Still a bit beat up, and that beard is quite something, but you look good, all things considered.' Jox cast his mind back to when they'd last seen each other. 'Where's the major and Whisky?'

Carver shook his head. 'They're long gone, Jox. God only knows where. I was still in bad shape when they got hauled off, and I got left here with these jokers.' His companions laughed. 'Oh yeah, sorry, this here's Toffee, on account of his sweet tooth. He's from South Africa and will be your pal forever for a piece of chocolate. This other feller with the Wyatt Earp moustache is called Teddy, from someplace called Weston-super-Mare. Say hi to Jox McNabb, fellers, a fine gentleman and the one I'm hoping is going to bust us out of here.

Actually, it was him who busted us out the first time too, but I got me a return ticket thanks to that little ball bearing in the gut.' He reached into his trouser pocket and held a metal marble in a clear plastic tube between his fingers and gave it a rattle.

The fellow with the bandaged throat hissed, 'Howzit.'

Jox said hello and laid down his Thompson. He rolled up the sleeve of his jacket and showed Carver the puckered scar on his bicep. 'I got hit by one of them too, same damned Bouncing Betty, but I never did get to keep the ball.'

A few hours later, the trios regrouped to discuss what they'd discovered. There were twenty-two sick or wounded prisoners in the infirmary, but only a handful of them could be moved. A skeleton crew of medically trained monks were caring for them but refused to leave the monastery. Otherwise, it appeared to be completely deserted.

Certosa di Padula had been extensively looted and wantonly damaged. Croft-Murray and Keller were disappointed that the stolen antiquities had moved on but were utterly devastated by the mindless vandalism to the monastery's cloisters and chapels. They had been daubed or scratched with swastikas, SS runes and various Teutonic exhortations to victory. Neither the delicately tiled Vietri ceramic floors, nor the inlaid marble works had escaped. It was heartbreaking and kindled an unexpected fury from the usually mild-mannered Monuments Men. It appeared that anything that couldn't be taken away had been defaced in ways that were painful to see, especially for scholars who had dedicated their lives to studying and saving them. They felt like they'd failed in their solemn duty.

'I'm real sorry for what's happened here,' said Lomasso, the SIMCOL leader. 'This is not the outcome we'd hoped for, but things are not always in our control. We're truly discovering the darkness that lies within our opponents, but I'm afraid this phase of our mission is complete, however unsatisfactorily. We need to start thinking about getting Jox and the other POWs back to Allied lines. We've got more guys to collect at the partisan base camp, and then there's the walking wounded to take along. It's going to be tough for them, but I don't want to leave anybody behind, especially if the Germans return.

'As for the fellers that are too far gone to move, the brothers say they are willing to stay and care for them, at least until our troops reach here, or things naturally resolve themselves.' He pulled a grim face. 'The beaches at Salerno aren't so far away. We've already heard the guns, so hopefully they'll get here in time, one way or another. The Profs want to try to establish contact with that radio which Giulio lugged over the damned mountains for us.' The young Sicilian raised a hand in recognition of the ragged cheer from his companions. 'He and Singh will stay here as their bodyguards, whilst the rest of us get the guys back to our lines. We'll be heading in the opposite direction, away from trouble and towards the Adriatic. We've got some hard miles ahead of us, but most of you have done the journey once before.'

'No, Glen, I am very sorry,' said Singh. Earlier, he had found the bathing facilities he'd been so desperate for and was once again his tidy, meticulously groomed self, beard plaited, turban in place and his tattered uniform as pressed and clean as he could manage. 'This I cannot do. I have reflected upon it, prayed, and have decided it is time for me to leave the partisans and return to the ranks of the Indian Army, with Jox and the others. I have been in these wilds for too long now.' He looked at Lupo. 'I'm sorry, my brother, our journey together is finished. I feel the draw of my people, and it is time for me to go. I will always remember my time with the *Stella Rosa* with great pride.'

Lupo nodded. 'I understand. I will miss you. You are always my brother, the fierce *leone* of *la Brigata Stella Rosa*.'

Singh nodded, touched by the tribute.

'Okay, in that case,' said Lomasso, 'Mario, will you stay here with Giulio and the professors until they make contact with those coming ashore? We'll catch up with you back at the camp, once we've done our round trip to Bari.' Lupo nodded his agreement. 'We've got a couple of fast Motor Torpedo Boats on standby there to get Jox and his mob back to Sicily. I hope we've got enough lined up, as our numbers are certainly growing. It'll be a quick overnight run to get you back, and then we can start sorting out who goes where. Our priority is to get the aviators back into the mix.'

He looked at Singh, cradling his sniper rifle as was his habit. 'Will you come with us?' Singh nodded. Grateful for the support, Lomasso ran a nervous hand through his dark beard. 'I know this feels like a bit of a wild goose chase, but it was the right thing to get our Venus Fixers on the trail of the missing loot. Future generations will thank you for it, but for now, we need to get back to our principal mission.'

Saying goodbye to Dennini was tougher than Jox expected. The 'made man' was pragmatic about partings, no doubt having seen many people come into his life and then disappear. It was an occupational hazard for a *mafioso*, but for Jox it was heartfelt. Dennini had once saved his life, and perhaps Jox had gone some way to repaying the debt.

Dennini laughed. 'What's the matter? Why you look so sad?' He reminded Jox that should they both make it through the war, he and his family could always be found in Ragusa, his hometown in the Sicilian hills. There would always be a warm welcome waiting with Elisabetta and Violetta. He added, 'Don Pietro, he always pleased to see you too.'

Jox smiled and wished him good fortune in the traditional Sicilian way that he'd heard many times: '*In bocca al lupo*, in the wolf's mouth.'

Dennini replied, '*Si, bonu, crepi il lupo*. Yes, good, may the wolf die.'

The Monuments Men were stern-faced when bidding their farewells. Their perceived failure was weighing heavily on their undeniably large minds.

'Mr McNabb, I want to thank you for your service and support,' said Keller. 'You've been quite the example to a crotchety old man who believed he had nothing to learn from young whippersnappers. Your ability to bring people together and work for the common good has been an education.' They shook hands and Jox heard a wobble in Keller's voice and saw an unfamiliar sheen behind his spectacles. 'God protect you, son.'

Croft-Murray was more effusive in his goodbyes, embracing Jox and booming, 'I do hope our paths cross again, McNabb. You're a fine young fellow. You can always track me down through the British Museum. Fair winds to you, my boy.'

CHAPTER FOURTEEN

The returning party reached the partisan camp by the evening of the following day. It had been hard going, especially for the wounded. Kilpatrick was still in pain, Carver looked pale and weak, and his two friends from the infirmary, Teddy and Toffee were both suffering. Toffee struggled with the weight of his cast, and Teddy with his breathing, occasionally spitting up blood from a not entirely healed wound to the throat. Jox and Perrin had appointed themselves as nursemaids and occasionally sheepdogs, trying their best to keep them moving. Lomasso was leading the party, navigating with a map provided by the monks, whilst Singh scouted ahead, pointing out hazards and ensuring the way ahead was clear. Beans was now tasked with carrying the PIAT, complaining most of the way up and down every wretched mountain.

The replacement partisan camp had grown in their absence. It was better camouflaged than it had been and blended perfectly into the landscape, despite containing a good number more souls. Various odds and sods, the flotsam of war had joined: more escaped prisoners, deserters from the Italian Army and survivors from various towns and villages ravaged by marauding German troops or victims of artillery fire or fighter-bomber attacks of unidentified origin. It is a truism of war that civilians carry the heaviest burden, and this made for a dejected, uneasy reception committee on their arrival, as most of the 'new' partisans were even more war-weary than Jox and his companions. It would certainly prove to be a challenge, pulling them together into anything resembling a useful fighting unit.

On the return journey, the one thing that had kept Jox going was the prospect of seeing Rosmarina again. Whilst away, he'd more or less managed to keep her from his thoughts, but now, as their reunion got closer, he could think of little else. Finally catching sight of her from a distance, he felt a flutter in his chest, and he chided himself for behaving like a besotted schoolgirl. 'For God's sake, man, get a grip,' he muttered to himself, and yet he was already imagining her in his arms. Any weariness he'd felt slipped away as he pressed on with renewed ardour.

'What was that?' asked Beans, switching the weighty PIAT from one shoulder to the other.

'Nothing,' replied Jox hastily, but he was feeling a little perplexed. Rosmarina had definitely seen him but had shown no sign of recognition. In fact, she'd turned away, resuming her conversation with Lupo's fiancée, Livia. The pair were laughing and Jox feared he might be the butt of the joke.

'There's nought fickler than women,' he'd once been told, and he could feel his pride already smarting. He wasn't all that experienced with women and perhaps he'd overthought what had happened between them. His hillside encounter with Rosmarina had certainly meant something to him, and although it was possible his feelings were partly due to it being such a long time in coming, he still felt it was significant. 'Maybe it wasn't to her,' he harrumphed. She still hadn't looked in his direction. 'Do get a grip,' he repeated to himself. 'And don't make a bloody fool of yourself.'

It was Livia who reacted first to their arrival, searching amongst them, then rattling away in anxious Italian. Lomasso replied reassuringly and her face brightened. Jox surmised she'd been worried that Lupo wasn't amongst them. Relieved, she smiled, then spotting that there were wounded men amongst them, ran forward with Rosmarina, sliding down the slippery scree slope to offer their help. Jox took this as a further rebuff, and like a petulant schoolboy stormed off, wanting to weather his embarrassment on his own.

'Hey, where the hell are you going?' said Beans as he strode off.

'Need some air,' he replied without looking back.

Jox knew he needed to cool off. He'd been sulking for about half an hour and was starting to feel rather foolish, when a little voice said, 'Why so angry, Jox?' His anger slipped away on hearing Rosmarina's voice. 'I bring you some soup.' She sat beside him and held out a metal mess tin. He took it but wouldn't look at her. He felt like such an idiot.

'Marina, why did you ignore me?' he asked.

Her eyes softened, and she smiled. 'It was Livia's idea. A test to see if you really cared for me. Maybe it wasn't such a good an idea. Please don't be angry with me, but you know, I don't really want the whole camp to know my love for the *inglese*.'

'I'm Scottish,' Jox replied petulantly, not having registered what she'd just said. It took a while for the cogs whirring in his head to catch up. His chest felt tight, and his spirits soared. She leant towards him and kissed him, and he was undone.

The night before the big departure for the coast, Singh was determined to commemorate the event with a feast. He managed to get hold of some goat meat and created a delicious meal of spiced stew, grilled vegetables, *daal* and his signature flatbreads.

After a glorious supper together, punctuated with toasts of fiery grappa followed by coarse red wine out of hairy leather bladders, they all sat around the fire, full and satisfied, starting to feel a little nostalgic. Pat Kilpatrick plucked at an Italian lute.

He began to tap a rhythm on the instrument's rounded back, making it sound like the call of a battle drum.

There were few peoples that could deliver a haunting lament better than the Irish, and Pat gave voice to the mood around the fire. 'You'll forgive me for playing an old favourite, but I'm thinking of chums that we've lost and those we've not seen for a long while.' He raised his tin cup in Jox's direction. 'Here's to Paddy Kilpatrick, a true rascal and rebel, and a dear friend of mine.'

He began to sing:
'Oh, Danny boy, the pipes, the pipes are calling
From glen to glen, and down the mountain side.
The summer's gone, and all the roses falling,
It's you, it's you must go and I must bide.
But come ye back when summer's in the meadow,
Or when the valley's hushed and white with snow,
Tis I'll be here in sunshine or in shadow,—
Oh, Danny boy, Oh Danny boy, I love you so!'

As he finished the first verse, guns began flashing against faraway peaks, followed by a low, deep rumbling. Livia took over when Pat Kilpatrick had finished, singing a sweet melancholic lament, by the end of which there were tears in her eyes and those of many of her fireside companions.

'What's that song about?' Jox asked Rosmarina.

She burrowed into him before answering. 'It is the story of two old lovers remembering their youth when they fought together in the revolution. How they once felt and how they feel now. She sings it for Lupo, who is far away but is always in her heart.' Rosmarina stirred in his arms. 'Can you hear the guns?' She touched his forehead gently, tracing the widow's peak he'd always found embarrassing. 'I will remember our starry night by this fire forever.'

Jox hummed along to Livia's sad song. He would never forget its melancholy melody, despite not understanding the words. He understood the feelings, sitting in the heady embrace of his Rosmarina.

She turned and looked him in the eyes. 'The bugles of the war are calling and soon we will part. For us, every hour, every minute must last. We've had so little time and I'm afraid of what fate has in store for us. We are young and full of life and yet must be prepared to die. We are like the stars tonight, shining bright for you and me, for liberty, *amore mio*.' She held his face in her hands. 'I cannot waste any time and have made a decision. In the morning, I am coming with you. That way we have more days together until we reach Bari. I have spoken with *Capitano* Lomasso; he agrees and says he will anyway need help with so many more former prisoners. The group is very big now, more than thirty. It will be difficult to lead these men safely through the mountains and not be seen by *il Tedeschi* patrolling from the sky. Are you happy for me to come?'

'Marina, you truly are remarkable,' replied Jox, reaching for her. 'Always surprising me, I never know what to expect.'

'Please, I must have your answer.'

'Yes, my answer is yes, of course it is. How could it not be?'

'Good,' she smiled. 'Now, you come with me, and we will waste no more time,' she added, a playful gleam in her eye. She got to her feet and led him into the darkness that still occasionally flashed with the light of distant explosions.

They didn't find trouble until the second day of their journey. They'd been following the undulating contours of Puglia, leading them down to Bari on Italy's heel, marching between vines hanging heavy with ripe fruit.

The previous day they'd crossed the Basento river, leaving behind the chilly highlands of the Southern Apennines, to the relief of everyone. The going was easier now, but simply following the vines cross-country was making Jox nervous. Their progress struck him as too predictable, their presence amongst the ordered rows likely to stand out and attract unwanted attention.

Being back in wine country, Perrin was in his element and kept up a running commentary on the *terroir* of this wine region called *Castel del Monte*, after the nearby 'Castle of the Mountain'. It was an area that produced blended wines, on which of course he looked down his Gallic nose, but did admit, 'They're not too bad for Italian wines.'

Purple grapes the size of pigeons' eggs hung from the vines in heavy clutches. Jox didn't know whether they had what it took to make a decent vintage, but his little band were certainly grateful to quench their thirst and boost lagging energy levels after a hot day's trek. Less welcome were the spidery ticks that dropped from the gnarled vines and their wobbling yellowing leaves. Perrin said they were from the deer that came down from the mountains to feast on the grapes. They were quite revolting but thankfully simple enough to remove with a cigarette or a sharp blade. One did, however, find its way into Teddy's cast, where it gorged itself to the size of a grape and was much the same colour. It then dropped to the ground, where the West Countryman quickly squashed it to a bloody splat.

As they crested a low hillock, a new panorama unfolded before them. In the distance a winding tarmac road snaked around a higher summit, but it was nothing compared to those they surmounted before crossing the river. What was most striking was the castle that sat upon it. It wasn't particularly large, but was an unusual shape, reminiscent perhaps of a crystal formation. From up there the view would undoubtedly be magnificent over the surrounding woodlands and the many rows of vines. In the soft evening light, the castle walls glowed biscuity yellow and Jox's fighter pilot's eyes caught movement, or at least something that seemed to be flashing.

'Freeze, everybody get down,' he ordered, crouching beneath a gnarled vine and hoping nothing nasty would drop down his neck. He focussed on the steep façade, scanning the castle walls dominating the valley. At the very top, there was definitely something flashing, and it was far too regular to be occurring naturally.

'What have you seen, Jox?' asked Beans, crouched amongst the fist-sized pebbles at the foot of a vine, crunching as he shifted his weight. Earlier, Perrin had explained they were there to absorb the heat of the sun during the day, slowly radiating it back to the vines overnight. This apparently led to optimal ripening and production of wines that aged well. Beans' head nudged a bunch of grapes hanging above him. He reached up and popped one in his mouth. Beans had always had a larger appetite than the rest.

'I'm not really sure. Something's not right,' said Jox, motioning over to Rosmarina and Singh, who were armed with their scoped rifles. He pointed at the castle then mimed focussing a telescope.

'What's that thing up there anyway?' Jox asked Perrin.

Beans was scouring the rough map that he'd copied from Lomasso. 'I think it's…'

'It's *Castel del Monte*, of course,' replied Perrin. 'The "Castle of the Mountain" I've been telling you about, a ruined thirteenth-century citadel of unique architectural merit, shaped like an octagonal prism with towers at each corner.'

'That's right,' said Beans, pointing at his map. 'Brother Angelo told me to look out for it, saying it would tell us that Bari wasn't too far away.'

Jox glanced at Rosmarina, who had pulled her eye back from her rifle scope. She held her hand in front of her face, opening and closing it in his direction. He frowned, not understanding what she meant. Singh then scurried across the pebbles to him and whispered, 'You have a good instinct for trouble, Jox. There's a heliograph up there signalling to someone.'

'What the hell's a heliograph?' asked Beans.

'Basically, it's a mobile mirror on a tripod,' replied Singh, rocking his head from side to side. 'Actually, it's an ingeniously simple way of signalling across a great distance if you have a line of sight. Whoever is up there can see for miles and presumably is reporting back to someone else. We used the same method on the Northwest Frontier against the Pathans and Afghans. Ideal for calling down artillery strikes.'

'Do you think they saw us?' Beans asked no one in particular.

'No,' replied Singh. 'We're quite a small group and well hidden by the vines. We've also been keeping quiet.' With remarkable stoicism, he added, 'But we'll find out soon enough.'

Rosmarina was now focussing on the road that curled around the base of the castle hill. There was a dust cloud above it. Singh followed suit. From the shadows in the lee of the slope came a convoy of half a dozen trucks, inexplicably with all their headlights blazing. They drove on, evidently unconcerned, and soon appeared larger and closer than they actually were. Rough engine noises reached Jox's ears, the low growl reverberating over the vineyards.

The air was suddenly rent by a shrieking sound, followed by several more. Directly above the first vehicle there was a loud crack, then a brief detonation followed by what looked like an inverted fan of rocket trails. Several more exploded up and down the length of the convoy, which stopped dead in its tracks.

'Airburst artillery!' shouted Singh. 'Take cover.'

Up ahead, vehicles had variously collapsed onto their axles or shed their loads like fly-tipped rubbish dumped by the roadside. Some had stopped dead, others careened drunkenly before coming to a halt, one up-ended into a drainage ditch, and another tangled in the steel wires holding up nearby vines. The carnage was too far away to see clearly with the naked eye, but the shocked expressions on the faces of Singh and Rosmarina spoke volumes.

She ran into Jox's arms, repeating, '*Che massacre*,' over and over again.

He tried his best to calm her as Singh, his eye still at this scope, said in hollow voice, 'No movement now. Those vehicles have been torn to pieces, perforated hundreds of times each. I can see blood oozing, like through the holes of a sieve. There are also small fires, but otherwise everything is still, deathly still.'

'Which side got hit?' asked Beans.

'Hard to tell,' replied Singh, panning across the devastation. 'Those trucks may well be 3-Tonner Bedfords, and that looks like a red jerboa painted on a wheel arch.'

'What the hell's a jerboa?' asked Beans.

'The emblem of the Desert Rats, the 7th Armoured Division,' replied Singh. 'I was one — no, actually, I am still one of them. Those fellows must be replacements. No desert veterans would cross open terrain as blatantly as that. What bloody fools.' He stood up cautiously, making sure his silhouette didn't breach the line of the vines on either side. 'It's my duty to go and see if I can help my comrades.' He gazed back at the group. 'Who is with me?'

'I will come,' said Perrin. 'Better than sitting waiting for something to happen.'

'Aye, I'll come,' said Kilpatrick.

'Yeah, me too,' added Carver. 'Maybe my medical training will be useful.'

'Thank you, my brothers,' said Singh.

'You two sure you're up to it?' asked Jox. 'You're both carrying an injury.'

'Aren't we all?' replied Kilpatrick. Apart from Rosmarina, they had all had been wounded at least once in the line of duty and by the look of things this war wasn't getting any nearer to ending.

'While you're off doing that, we'd better go take a look at that castle,' said Jox. 'We need to sort out the fellows who rained that merry hell down on our chaps. Can't just sit here whilst you lot do all the dirty work. Once you're done, come and look for us up there.'

Singh nodded. 'Right, if we're going to do this, let's go.' With him went almost half of the group, stealthily making their way through the trembling vines, heading towards the devastated convoy. Their progress was hidden in the fading light, the sound of rounds cooking off amongst the devastated convoy masking the crunching gravel under their feet.

As they disappeared, Jox chewed on his lip. 'Let's hope there aren't too many Jerries up there in the castle. I can't imagine there would be, as more than likely, it's just an observation post. In this fading light, they'll be losing their line of sight and may well have stood down. They're probably already celebrating giving the *dummkopf* Tommies such a good kicking.'

He glanced up at *Castel del Monte*, its octagonal walls seeming to glow in the last of the light. 'We should have the advantage of coming out of the setting sun, with stealth and surprise on our side, plus Rosmarina's long-range firepower acting as overwatch.' He turned to Teddy and Toffee, one rather red-faced and having trouble breathing, the other pale from the exertion of lugging his plaster cast around, as well as the blood loss from the tick. 'You boys are excused from games,' said Jox, raising a smile from each. 'There's no shame in it; you're just not fighting fit.' They nodded, relieved to be let off the hook. 'Once we know what's what, we'll come back and get you. In the meantime, lay low and try to get some rest.'

Jox patted each on the shoulder. 'Right, it's the three of us: me, Bayou and Marina. Bayou, we'll try to sneak up to the castle, while Marina finds a position to protect us from. Only fire if you have to, otherwise it'll warn them something's up. Everyone understand?'

Beans and Rosmarina nodded.

'Bayou, we'll have our sidearms and I've got my Thompson, but we don't really want to go in there with all guns blazing and making an almighty racket. Who knows what other troops are within earshot? We need to get up there as stealthily as we can.' He took a deep breath. 'I guess it's time to find out if we're worthy of carrying these things, and more to the point if we have the stomach to use them.'

Jox pulled out the kukri blade from the leather sheath at his belt. Beans had one too, picked up from the battlegrounds they'd crossed to get here. The American nodded but looked decidedly nervous at the prospect of what lay ahead. He checked both of the pistols he wore in cowboy fashion, and confirmed he was ready.

The broad, bent blade of Jox's kukri shimmered in the dim light. As they advanced towards the castle, Jox whispered, '*Ayo Gorkhali*, the Gurkhas are upon you,' to himself. It was the famous battle cry of the Nepalese fighting men that Singh had taught him. He only hoped he could do the weapon justice, and that it would protect him rather better than it had its previous owner.

They rapidly climbed the gravelled slope towards the 'picture perfect' *Castel del Monte* surrounded by its peculiar octagonal towers. As they got closer, it became obvious the ruins were occupied, with the sound of music coming from an open window giving onto a balcony above the main door. On it was positioned the heliograph they'd spotted earlier, and above that, at the top of the fifteen-metre-high castle wall was a sand-bagged gun emplacement from which jutted the fluted nose of an MG42 machine gun, mounted on a stand. Channelled as they were between rows of vines, if they'd been caught by the gun in the open, the fire would have been murderous.

Towards the top of the hill, the vines gave way to a wooded thicket, which provided better cover for their approach. A track led up to the main door and a flat, open area around the base of the castle walls, from which budded the eight identical octagonal and windowless towers. The castle looked surprisingly modern despite its ancient origin, reminding Jox of the fortifications in some parts of the Atlantic wall that he'd seen in France, especially the terrifying flak towers.

There were two flights of steps rising up on either side of a stone isosceles triangle that lead to the open door of the dilapidated citadel. Judging by its small size, it was probably never more than a hunting lodge, but it was evident that it was well-worn by the passage of time. There was no roof left on the top floor, but the main entrance was still rather grand with an ornately carved stone pediment and thin fluted pilasters on either side of a vaulted portico.

First, they found Rosmarina a position under a low bush, but with a clear view of the front entrance, the open window and the machine gun nest above it. As they left her, she whispered, 'Stay alert, *amore mio*.'

Jox and Beans headed towards the castle, heads low and shoulders hunched. The music was loud and there was laughter within, but it was hard to tell from how many and where exactly they were. He recognised the husky tones of the song on the radio. It was the anthem of the desert war, Sicily and now the Italian campaign, 'Lili Marleen,' sung in the original German by Lale Andersen.

With their kukris held at the ready, Jox and Beans took the steps up either side of the open door, two at a time. Inside, they found a central courtyard open to the sky, the darkening heavens forming a cobalt-blue octagon above their heads, shedding little light into the interior. The eight Moorish-influenced towers provided access to the rooms of the castle, which on the ground floor were high and vaulted, meeting up in a four-arched apex. There was little or no furniture, and it was clear that many of the fixtures had been looted long ago. The place was deserted save for the music and some quiet conversation on the floor above. The pair crept up the spiral stairs of one tower, heading towards the music. The stairs were of the type designed for sword fighting, so as to give the right-handed defender retreating up the stairs the advantage. Jox didn't suppose the castle's builders could ever have imagined the property being defended by an MG42 and stalked by a pair of airmen with Nepalese butcher blades.

Jox was first to reach the open door to the room with the music. He could smell cigars and the fug of men who'd been in their clothes for too long. He wasn't any less fragrant himself after the day's long trek. There were two men sitting at a table with glasses and a bottle of wine before them. One was writing in a logbook, the other smoking a stubby cigarillo, his eyes closed and his jaw chewing as he listened to the music. He was a chubby-faced artillery officer with dark blond hair in a severe side parting, long on top and very short at the back and sides. It must have been a recent haircut, as the shortness didn't match the tan on his neck and ears.

The other was a slim corporal with pen and paper in hand. He had the red lightning badge of an artillery signaller or spotter on his arm, and wore little round glasses. The tip of his tongue was out the side of his mouth as he concentrated on what he was writing, presumably an after-action report. On the table, there was a rectangular *Wehrmacht* issue torch with a large silver lens, plus a penknife, half a loop of dried salami and some cheese wrapped in paper.

Jox nodded towards the officer and pointed at himself, then the corporal, silently indicating to Beans, 'That one's yours.' The American's jaw twitched anxiously. Neither of them was particularly well trained in hand-to-hand combat, beyond a few rudiments imparted by Singh. Theirs had always been a 'long distance' war where they rarely even caught sight of their human opponents, let alone spilt their blood at close quarters. Jox swallowed hard and nervously raised his kukri.

The movement must have caught the blond *Oberleutnant's* peripheral vision. He turned towards Jox, his pale eyes widening and his mouth dropping in abject terror. A ball of half-chewed salami fell onto the table as he reached for the penknife, uttering an anguished, '*Nein!*'

The bent blade stuck the left side of the *Oberleutnant's* neck, immediately severing his carotid artery. It was so sharp that little withstood it. The Gurkhas were known to routinely decapitate their adversaries; Jox's inexpert strike failed to do so, but was no less deadly.

A crimson arc pulsed through the air, followed by a second, then several weaker gushes. The artillery officer fell like a dead weight into his supper, a red tide racing across the table. His eyes were glassy in seconds and the air filled with the smell of the cigarillo extinguished by blood.

Beans' blow to the back of the *Gefreiter's* head was even less well delivered. He struck so hard that the signaller's glasses flew across the room and the blade was stuck fast, imbedded in the bones of the man's neck. Reflexes made him jump and let out a mighty moan, before collapsing to the flagstone floor, where he flopped like a fish, rough boots scraping the thirteenth-century stones.

They'd attacked noiselessly, until Beans was violently sick, the horror of what they'd done turning his stomach. He retched so loudly that a voice called down from above. There were footsteps, then the sound of the MG42 being cocked and loaded. The stand it was on was noisily manhandled with much scraping and thudding.

In a desperate bid to escape the sight and smell of the recent butchery, Beans plunged onto the balcony, still projecting half-digested grape pulp. The machine gunner upstairs must have glimpsed Beans and let rip, but the bulky American was fortunate that the weapon couldn't be depressed sufficiently to reach him. Jumping back like a scalded cat, he leapt into the room, promptly slipping on the hapless *Gefreiter's* spectacles and landing in a heap on the blood-covered floor.

Outside, there was a single echoing shot and the characteristic ripping sound of the rapid-firing MG42 stopped. There was a cry, and something heavy landed on the balcony with a dull thump. The body bore a startled expression and had a red maw where the bridge of its nose should have been. Jox had once heard that Rosmarina could take out the eye of a German at a hundred metres — not this time, but it was close enough. Above, there was more clattering, and the gun fired again, presumably now crewed by the gun's loader, who'd taken over his predecessor's role. He was firing short, precise bursts at what could only be Rosmarina's sniping position. There was another rifle report, but it must have missed, as the automatic fire continued.

Fearing the worst, Jox wiped his kukri on the *Oberleutnant's* jacket and sheathed it. The time for stealth was over. He pulled the hefty Webley revolver from its holster and charged towards the door. Beans was still on his knees in the sticky mess of vomit and blood. His eyepatch had slipped off his head with the violence of his retching and lay in a wet mess by the corporal's smashed glasses.

Jox scrambled up the steps of the nearest turret. He had no idea what he'd find up there, caring only to get at whomever was firing at Rosmarina. Reaching the top, he spotted the rear of the sandbagged gun emplacement. Within it, the dome of a coal scuttle helmet was hunched over the weapon. The gunner was facing away from him, firing in measured bursts, oblivious to Jox as he approached. Jox levelled his pistol and fired twice. The first round punched a neat hole through the helmet with the sound of a cracked bell. The second missed, as the gunner was already falling, then lay slumped at the bottom of the gun pit amongst dozens of spent cartridge cases. He was young, and again had the startled look of someone dying in an instant. His eyes were open and pale, and he had a large nose, full lips, red hair and freckles across his face. Because of the heat of the day, he was wearing shorts — not long, baggy ones like those issued by the British Army, but smaller, tighter ones, like something an overgrown schoolboy might wear.

Exhausted, Jox dropped to his knees, panting and desperate to catch his breath. Adrenaline coursed through his veins and his head was pounding. He dropped the pistol and stared at his hands, finding it hard to believe what he'd done. The burn scars from long ago were smothered by congealed blood. He now had the hands of a butcher; never again could he hide behind the pretence of killing 'remotely', a skill at which he'd become so adept as a fighter pilot.

He needed to find out what had happened to Rosmarina. He picked up his pistol and got to his feet. Reaching the sandbagged wall of the emplacement, he peered down, trying to find her. He spotted a crumpled figure amongst the vegetation, rolled in a tight ball and lying very still. His heart sank as he called down and received no reaction. Terrified at what that might mean, he charged headlong down the spiral stairs, feeling dizzy and a little disoriented as he reached the ground floor. He passed by a now recovered Beans, who ran after him, still covered in gore.

CHAPTER FIFTEEN

When they found Rosmarina, she was still tightly clenched. Jox touched her shoulder delicately and was rewarded with a groan. All the shrubs around her had been shredded, the prickly bush she'd been hidden beneath barely hanging together and oozing sap. By some miracle, she didn't appear to be seriously hurt. The butt of her rifle had been struck by a 7.92 mm round from the MG42. The transferred momentum had made it buck, delivering a powerful blow to the side of her face, the impact like a punch to the jaw from a heavyweight. Still dazed from the blow, her eyes were tightly shut, her freckled cheek bruised, and her lip cut and swollen.

Recognising Jox's voice, she muttered, 'It hurts.' She opened her eyes cautiously and gasped. The men were a frightful sight, both drenched with blood.

'It's all right, it's not mine,' soothed Jox. Reassured but still looking horrified, Rosmarina relaxed a little, uncoiling herself to sink into his arms. She tensed as he returned her embrace, revealing that she'd been slashed from elbow to wrist by a stone fragment that had ricocheted. The cut was superficial but deep enough to hurt.

'We better get her up there,' said Beans, picking up Rosmarina's discarded sniper rifle. His bloodied eyebrows rose at the sight of the inch-deep divot in its varnished stock. 'That was a helluva close call. Let's get back to the castle and I'll see if there's a first aid kit knocking around. We should probably be ready in case all that shooting attracted any attention. Better to be holed up there, I guess, in a solid defensive position rather than exposed out here.'

Once back within the walls of *Castel del Monte*, they prepared for all eventualities but made a point of avoiding the gory tableau in the 'radio room', heading straight for the gun position on the roof instead. Beans dragged the body of the red-headed boy soldier away and checked that the MG42 was still operational. There were additional ammunition belts in lidded boxes at the rear of the emplacement, more than enough to put up a decent fight. Downstairs, the radio was still playing and lively accordion music drifted up through the door to the balcony below. It sounded vaguely obscene, given what was down there.

'I'll turn that off,' said Beans. 'And I'll take a look around, see what I can find. I'll get cleaned up too — I must make quite a sight, given *la coccinella's* reaction.'

Rosmarina smiled and pressed an affectionate hand against his bloodied face. 'Yes, you smell bad and look terrifying, but I'm happy you are not hurt. Your eye, it looks not so good.'

He grinned self-consciously; he wasn't wearing his usual eyepatch. 'Oh, that's an old wound. Looks worse than it is.' He looked back at them and took a deep breath. 'You know, that was so awful...' He held up his hands. They were shaking. 'I don't know how I...'

'I know, Bayou, I know,' said Jox. 'Take comfort that we've made it through. It's not over yet. We need to keep on our toes.'

'I'm okay. Honestly, I'm fine.' He shook himself like a wet dog. 'I'll be right back, looking more presentable, I promise. Maybe I'll even find some food. All this fighting's given me an appetite.'

'An appetite? Good grief, Bayou,' said Jox. 'You're unbelievable.'

'Hey, a man's got to eat, especially big fellas like me. Tell you what, you stay here. Let *la coccinella* catch her breath. You'd better get on that gun in case any unexpected visitors turn up, at least until it's dark. Come to think of it, we'd better go and find Teddy and Toffee too. They'll be scared out of their wits with all the noise and are probably panicking.'

Beans didn't take long. He returned with a first aid kit and set about dressing Rosmarina's wound. He'd cleaned himself up and had even found a bottle of Perrin's 'not so terrible' *Castel del Monte* DOC wine. It was very welcome and even had a pleasant chill from the cellars. After a final swig, he checked his pistols and headed off to find the wounded pair they'd left behind.

Fortified by the wine, Rosmarina said she'd watch for trouble. 'I can see further with my rifle scope than your naked eye. Please, *amore mio*, now you go and get washed up too. It is upsetting for me to see you covered in blood like that.'

Jox returned to the radio room and saw that Beans had tidied up. The bodies of the two German artillerymen had been dragged out of sight, red trails visible on the ancient flagstones. He'd wiped down the table, but it still bore signs of its recent drenching, with crimson in the cracks and crevices of the wood. Jox found a steel pail that Beans had used to wash down the room. He filled it from a hand pump down in the courtyard, the rusty mechanism and slender metal arm shrieking like a hurt animal as he pumped.

Stripped to the waist, the ice-cold water stole his breath, coming as it did from an underground cistern deep within the castle's foundations. Jox focussed on getting his face, ears, hairline, hands and nails clear of blood. As he scrubbed, the words of Lady Macbeth came to mind from his far-off schooldays: *Out, damned spot! Out, I say!* He sponged down his grubby uniform as best he could, then once satisfied, rinsed off his Gurkha boots. Finally, he turned his attention to the kukri, washing then drying it off meticulously. The knife hadn't let him down, nor he it, getting the blade well and truly blooded. It had been a horrifying experience, and now it felt somehow important to get it pristine again.

Returning to the radio room, Jox found the salami and cheese, the German officer's last repast. Beans had helped himself to a portion of each before heading off. They had surely been drenched with blood, as they were on the table at the time, but Beans must have rinsed them off. The idea of ingesting any of their victims' blood made Jox shudder, but it occurred to him that Rosmarina really needed some food to rebuild her strength, reasoning that what she didn't know wouldn't hurt her. He immediately felt guilty about the deception, but surely, it was for the greater good.

Searching around the room, he saw the discarded torch that had been knocked to the floor. It lay beside the German corporal's smashed spectacles. Jox placed both by the radio set on the sideboard. He knew it was a chunky *Wehrmacht* Military Radio 15 W.S.E.B Field Transmitter, but only because it said so in large white letters on the front, under the only other word Jox recognised, 'Ark'. There was a large central knob below a glass window with black calibrations, half printed on a white background, half on a red. Three smaller knobs were underneath. It occurred to him that the artillery spotters could easily have spoken to their guns by radio, but probably preferred the heliograph during the day as it was quick, silent and couldn't be monitored or interfered with. Jox could find his way around his onboard R/T set, so he decided to have a go at turning the big beast on. It came alive with a long buzz and then a blast of lively brass band music which made him jump. He dived for the volume control, reducing the German *Volkstümliche Musik* to a more reasonable level.

He twiddled the frequency knob and after a good deal of whistling and distortion, the cutglass received pronunciation of an Englishman said, 'London calling, London calling. This is *Radio Londra* broadcasting to Italy on the BBC World Service, Colonel Stevens at the microphone. Here is your tuning signal before a few special messages for our dear friends.' The radio began pulsing with a repeating pattern, three rapid pulses followed by a longer one: 'Dit-dit-dit-dah.' It was the letter V in Morse code. V for Prime Minister Winston Churchill's triumphant raised fingers, V for the letter daubed by patriots on walls across the occupied countries of Europe, and V for the victory that they'd been striving after for all these years. The signal was repeated over and over.

'Dit-dit-dit-dah,' the broadcast continued at a relentless pace. It gave Jox an idea. He picked up the *Wehrmacht* torch. It was a pale green rectangle with a round silver lens with three sliders that controlled the colour of the light emitted. Green was for map-reading, amber for directing traffic and red for discreet use at night. He switched it on and was blinded by the powerful beam. He pulsed the light along with the signal. He saw that outside it was quite dark now and it occurred to him that a red light signalling V for Victory would make a useful homing signal for Singh and the others making their way to *Castel del Monte*.

On the radio, Colonel Stevens, who Rosmarina later said was known as *Colonnello Buonasera* by the partisans, began reciting his 'special messages' for various resistance groups. He spoke in Italian and English, and repeated each message twice. He droned on and on, '*Patrizio è triste*: Patrick is sad. *La mia barba è rossa*: My beard is red. *Mio fratello sta domendo*: My brother is sleeping. *Il tucano vola*: The toucan is flying.'

Jox switched *Colonnello Buonasera* off and climbed up the spiral stairs back to the gun position on the roof. He took the cheese, salami, torch and his Thompson with him. Any anxiety about the tainted food he put to the back of his mind.

Rosmarina ate hungrily. 'This salami tastes quite liverish but is excellent. *Grazie, amore mio*.'

Jox was grateful for the darkness, so she couldn't examine it too closely.

'I'm going start signalling,' he said, partially to distract her. 'Hopefully, it'll lead the others to us.'

She stopped chewing. 'Is that wise? What if the *Tedeschi* see?'

'I'm hoping it won't mean anything to them beyond a curious red light. To our men out there, it should be recognisable as V for Victory.'

'I understand,' she replied. 'I hope it does not bring us trouble. Still, if it comes, we have the guns, a height advantage and this view, although it is dark.' She gazed up at the new moon shedding beams of silver light. '*Allora*, we can try.'

Jox turned to face the direction from which he estimated Singh and his companions would be coming from. He began signalling, curious as to what news they'd bring of the shattered convoy. They would no doubt have heard the exchange of gunfire between Rosmarina and the MG42 and would be correspondingly cautious when approaching the castle. Jox hoped his signal would work, reassuring them that the castle was now in friendly hands.

Where the devil have Beans, Toffee and Teddy got to? Surely, they should be here by now, he thought.

Rosmarina scanned the darkness with her scoped Mosin-Nagant M1891 as Jox continued flashing his signal. They heard the crunching of gravel, followed by some unexpected bawdy singing. As it got louder, Jox recognised the words to a drinking song he'd sung more than once.

'Show me the way to go home,
I'm tired and I want to go to bed,
I had a little drink about an hour ago,
And it's gone right to my head,
Wherever I may roam,
On land or sea or foam,
You will always hear me singing this song,
Show me the way to go home.'

'Will you lunatics please shut up?' Jox hissed from the top of the castle walls. 'Don't you know there's a bloody war on?' He got a guffaw in response.

Once at the castle door, he found a trio that wouldn't stop giggling. 'I'm sorry, Jox,' said Beans, trying to keep a straight face. 'It's been like herding cats. I took a couple of bottles of that wine with me, and it's gone right to their heads. I guess they must have been dehydrated or something.'

'Jockey on the oche!' cried Teddy in his West Country accent, waving his outsize plaster about. His South African partner in crime, Toffee, burst out laughing.

'Come in, and for Christ's sake keep your voices down,' growled Jox.

The convalescents were 'well refreshed' and after the long day's trek and having only eaten a handful of grapes, the alcohol had clearly hit them hard. As recent medical patients, not to mention POWs, they wouldn't have touched drink for months, and it showed. Rosmarina was finding their drunken antics hilarious, a welcome tonic to her spirits after the events of the day, especially when Teddy swept her into his arms, plaster cast and all, and spun her around in a jaunty polka.

Worried for her wounded arm, Jox scowled, as things were getting out of hand.

'Come on, boys, leave *la coccinella* alone,' said Beans, seeing Jox's eyes narrow. 'Let's go and see if the Krauts have any coffee stashed someplace. You two could certainly do with some.'

'Coffee, boo,' hissed Toffee. 'We want more wine. Now that would be truly *lekker*.'

'Liquor?' replied Beans. 'We ain't got no liquor, more's the pity.'

Toffee and Teddy laughed a little too loudly, in the way drunks do.

'*Lekker*, man, not liquor,' wheezed the South African. 'Means something's good or tasty in Afrikaans.'

'Well, shoot,' said Beans, in his Louisiana drawl. 'How the hell am I supposed to know that?'

'All right, let's all calm down,' said Jox.

Teddy stumbled over to the radio, turned it back on and tuned in some big band music.

'*Brava*,' cried Rosmarina. '*Amore mio*, now you must dance with me.'

Jox was reluctant, but it didn't seem like he had much choice, especially with the baying encouragement of Teddy and Toffee. By the time the music came to a climax, he was rather enjoying himself.

The honeyed voice of an American woman came on air: 'Hello there, suckers, that's the sound of Bruno and his Swinging Tigers, brought to you exclusively by the "Jerry's Front Calling" show, broadcasting on Radio Italia from Rome on 47.6 metres Short Wave and 491.8 metres Medium Wave.'

Jox recognised the voice immediately.

'This is your Axis Sally with a very special message for the boys of the Fifth Army currently engaged in Operation Avalanche on the not so sunny beaches of Salerno. You were hoping to surprise us, but now, how are you all enjoying the ring of fire from our artillery and the special warm welcome from the 16th Panzer Division? Is it hot enough for you now, boys?' She laughed demonically. 'Seems like my signature tune, from the divine Cab Calloway, is even more appropriate than usual. Here for your pleasure then is "Between the Devil and the Deep Blue Sea":

'I don't want you,
But I hate to lose you,
You've got me in between,
The devil and the deep blue sea.'

The men all looked at each other as her words sank in. Everything that Axis Sally said had to be taken with a pinch of salt, but she was rarely inaccurate. Her real name was Rita Zucca and she was a renegade Italian American, so had a vested interest in delivering bad news, but it was clear that things were not going well at Salerno. The barrages of artillery they'd heard when crossing the mountains had sounded ominous enough, but it appeared they had heralded even greater carnage than imagined.

'Someone having a party?' cried a voice from outside the window. 'It's kinda rude not to have invited us.' Jox recognised the accent as belonging to Tex Carver. He went out onto the balcony and counted four figures in the darkness below him, and was relieved that they'd all made it back in one piece.

'Great to see you, chaps. It's really not much of a party, but maybe if old Bayou rustles up some more of that wine, we can get one started. After a day like today, we certainly deserve it.'

There was a good deal of handshaking and backslapping and rather forced bonhomie, but it was evident that the newcomers had been through an ordeal. Beans was sent off to hunt for said wine, and Perrin, keen to get involved whenever wine was mentioned, went with him.

After a few drinks, the exuberance of their reunion was exhausted, and Rosmarina had danced with each of them. It was time to make her excuses, as she wanted to wash up. The men gave her some privacy, promising to stay away from the downstairs rooms with the high arched ceilings, so she could bathe. Singh and Beans drew some fresh water for her, then rejoined the others in the radio room.

The music on Axis Sally's radio show had mellowed, this new section of the programme designed to reach out to lonely Allied servicemen in damp trenches, isolated airfields and on the ocean waves, getting them to feel sad and melancholic, dreaming of the homes and sweethearts they'd left behind.

'You can be sure, boys, that while you're out here in your foxholes, some 4F Romeo is keeping your darling nice and warm back in the States,' she said, her voice dripping with sarcasm. 'How many more "Dear John" letters will be arriving on the next mail call, I wonder? Till then, so long, suckers, and as ever, my show is sealed with a loving kiss from your Axis Sally.'

The men sat at the table, passing around a fresh bottle of DOC *Castel del Monte*. There weren't enough chairs for everyone, so some sat on the floor with their backs up against the wall. Piled all around them was a mass of weapons, bed rolls and packs.

'So, how was it really?' Jox finally asked Singh, who was sitting cross-legged on the floor. 'What kind of shape did you find the convoy in when you got to it?'

Singh sighed and was terribly still for a moment. His eyes burned with fierce intensity. 'I've never seen such devastation,' he whispered. 'I know artillery can do terrible damage to soft-skinned vehicles, but these must have been some kind of new airburst munitions. The carnage was beyond belief.' He drummed his fingers on the floor absentmindedly. 'There must have been at least sixty men lying around, more than enough for two platoons. And we couldn't find a single one of them alive. Their bodies had been struck dozens of times and were piled on top of each other in the back of lorries like carcasses in a butcher's van, or else like discarded roadkill by the side of the track. Drivers were still at their steering wheels, and I saw one very tall captain, who was presumably in command of the detachment, hanging from a front cab window, his arm and head missing. Maybe he was the fool responsible for leading them blindly into that ambush.' He ran a hand through his shaggy beard. 'There was nothing we could do. There were too many for us to bury, so we had to leave them. only hope our advancing troops will find them before there's nothing left.' He was staring at the wall, seeing things that only he could see. 'Do you know the worst of it? It was the silence, the absolute silence, a deathly quiet with only the wind whistling through holes punched through the hulks of the lorries. Then there was the awful hissing sound of dripping blood meeting fire or hot metal; the smell was nauseating.'

Jox swallowed his bile, remembering the *Oberleutnant's* extinguished cigarillo.

'What happened up here was nothing like what you saw on the road,' said Jox, 'but it was no less awful. Bayou's cleaned up, but there was blood everywhere.'

Singh ran a finger along a join on the table. A dark residue was left on his fingertip. 'He didn't get everything,' he sighed. 'It'll take a long time to cleanse away what was spilt today.'

'It was a hell of a shock for me to get right up close to the enemy,' said Jox, his eyes smarting at the memory. 'To see him, hear him, smell him and kill him. If that's what you infantry face every time, you're bloody welcome to it.'

'Infantry?' asked Singh, taking a swig from the bottle and passing it on. 'Yes, it's always the poor bloody infantry. Even when I transferred to armour, I was still in the poor infantry. When it comes down to it, killing the enemy as you're holding onto his belt buckle, is when we're all reduced to poor bloody infantry. It's war at its most basic, brutal and instinctive. We become little more than animals, ripping at each other's throats.' Singh wiped his eyes with the sleeve of his jacket. 'I'm so tired of all this.' He rested his turbaned head and arms on his raised knees and asked, 'Did you see the carved figures downstairs, the ones holding up the arches in the room where *la coccinella* is bathing?'

'Yes I did,' said Jox, surprised at the sudden change in topic. 'Impressive carved knights on horseback, each made from different coloured stone.'

'They're not actually knights; they are the *Quattro Cavalieri dell'Apocalisse*, the four horsemen of the apocalypse. Each is identifiable by his colour.'

'How so?'

Singh raised his head. 'In your Christian faith, the horsemen herald the opening of the seven seals that will bring the end of days. Each of the horsemen provides two interpretations of the curses that befall men. The first wears a crown and carries a bow. He rides a white horse and represents war of conquest, or alternatively, the curse of pestilence. The second, the red horseman, has a mighty sword, representing the fratricide of civil war and mass slaughter. The third is on a black horse and carries the scales of justice, representing famine, but also oppression. Finally, the pale green horseman, the colour of a cadaver, is death, representing the end of empire.'

'I had no idea,' said Jox.

'Can you not see that all of those maledictions are already upon us?' Singh looked back at Jox. 'War of conquest, pestilence, fratricide, slaughter, famine, oppression, end of empire and then death, always death. Haven't we seen all of that in the last few months, let alone years?'

'Yes, but surely that's not unique to our generation,' replied Jox. 'The ancients recognised it in their time, hence the carvings, and now it's simply our turn. I fear it was ever thus.'

'Ever thus,' Singh repeated. 'The curse of man is ever thus.' He lowered his head back onto his arms.

CHAPTER SIXTEEN

'Get up, quick, there's someone outside!' said Singh. Jox sat bolt upright at the sound of roaring motor engines outside. Rosmarina, still asleep beside him, groaned with discomfort from her arm and from sleeping on a hard floor.

'Who's on guard?' Jox asked no one in particular.

'No one, we all fell asleep,' replied Beans, struggling to pull on his boots. 'You'd think we'd have learnt our lesson from the last time. Damn it all.'

'Blast,' said Jox. 'We need to get someone on that gun upstairs. The rest of us can hold them off with personal weapons until then.'

'Right, I'm on it!' cried Kilpatrick, always up for a fight. 'Snipers, with me. Frenchie, you happy to serve as my loader?'

Perrin bounded after the Ulsterman up the spiral staircase of the tower. Singh followed them, scoped rifle in hand, then Rosmarina, sleepy-eyed but no less aware of her duty.

Jox cocked his Thompson, as did Carver. Beans had his pair of pistols at the ready, whilst Toffee had acquired the German corporal's Mauser 98k rifle, and Teddy, the artillery officer's Walter PP handgun. Watching all of them get set for action, Jox couldn't help imagining this was like getting prepared for the gunfight at OK Corral, the wild west story he'd once read about. He only hoped this contest would turn out better than that one had.

'By the sound of those engines, unless we get the MG 42 going, we're going to be massively outgunned,' said Carver.

'Pat'll do whatever he can,' replied Jox, crossing to the window giving onto the balcony.

Roaring up the road to *Castel del Monte* were a trio of green scout cars, four-wheeled but with a spare set of tyres mounted on either side of their waists. Each had a vicious-looking main gun which looked to be at least 20 mm in calibre, far heavier than anything they had. Jox was no expert, but at least these weren't blasted Pumas, like those that had massacred the villagers of San Cristobal.

A tinny voice came from a tannoy speaker mounted on the lead vehicle, speaking in accented Italian. He repeated what he'd said in equally poor German.

Upstairs, Rosmarina's shrill voice replied in Italian. Her reply was met by silence, the courtyard falling quiet and still, apart from the armoured cars' throbbing engines.

Jox glanced out the window to see the top hatch of the lead vehicle open, and a brown beret with a crimson band emerging with headphones clamped over the top of it. A voice with a home counties accent called out, 'Right, you lot, identify yourselves, or I shall be forced open fire.'

There was a clatter from the stairwell. It was Singh, wide-eyed and excited. 'They're Desert Rats; those are Cherry Pickers, the 11th Hussars (Prince Albert's Own).' He leant his rifle against the wall and crossed over to the window. 'Do not fire, sahib. We are friends!' he shouted.

'Identify yourself,' repeated the voice.

'*Jemadar* Sad Singh, late of the 7th Armoured Division, captured at Tobruk. I am a desert rat like you, sahib.' He went out onto the balcony with his arms raised, beaming from ear to ear.

'Well, I'll be blown, it's a sepoy officer. What-oh Johnny, what the devil are you doing up there?'

'I'm an escaped POW. What a sight for sore eyes you are, lieutenant. We are many here.' Singh turned to the room. 'Come on, they're friends, our rescuers.'

'Take it easy buddy,' said Beans. 'A friendly bullet kills you just as well as a hostile one.'

'It's probably time to take that leap of faith, Bayou,' said Jox. He placed his Thompson on the floor and followed Singh out onto the balcony, his arms raised in the air.

The hussar looked up at them, shading his eyes with the palm of his hand. 'And who are you?' he demanded, as the hatches of the other vehicles lifted behind him and more brown berets emerged.

'Squadron Leader Jeremy McNabb,' replied Jox, irritated by the impertinent tone of the young officer. 'Commanding Officer of No. 333 Squadron. Is it no longer customary in the 11th Hussars to salute a superior officer? Your name is…'

'Yes, of course, sir. Cornet Rupert Stamper, at your service, sir.'

'Good to see you, Stamper. Now, be good enough to post your guards and get up here so I can introduce you to the rest of my mob. I hope you've got some teabags in that tin can of yours. After many months behind the wire, we could properly murder a good brew.'

Stamper grinned. 'I'm sure we'll manage that, sir. To be honest, a cuppa really wouldn't go amiss; it's bally thirsty work, rolling about in these things.'

'I did mean to ask,' said Jox. 'What exactly are they?'

'Humber Mk. 1 armoured scout cars, sir. Brand new and really rather whizzo.'

'Looks like great fun. Come on then, up you pop.'

After introductions, they shared the much longed-for cups of tea. 'A spot of milk would have been nice,' said Stamper absently. He was cornered by Jox, Beans and Singh, who all quizzed him relentlessly on the progress of the war. It emerged that the cornet, whilst well-meaning and essentially solid, wasn't exactly the sharpest tool in the box. He was the sort of well-connected home counties lad who simply joined the regiment because generations of his family had done so before him. He did what he was told and didn't ask too many questions, and everything was either a 'wizard prang' or a 'dashed poor show'. He'd recently crossed into Italy during Operation Baytown, fording the Straits of Messina to Reggio di Calabria. Then, as fast reconnaissance troops, his regiment were tasked with linking up with the British 1st Airborne Division, landed by sea at Taranto as part of Operation Slapstick. Since then, the cherry pickers had advanced up the Adriatic coast, until they'd reached Bari earlier in the week. They'd run into some stiff opposition and were now increasingly finding the terrain hard going, with many fast-flowing rivers and sharp ridge lines running at right angles to their direction of advance. Beyond that, all he knew was that the Salerno landings were in trouble, the Germans now occupied Rome and that some German paratroopers had been dropped in by glider, freeing Benito Mussolini from imprisonment. He was currently believed to be in Germany.

When Singh enquired about the convoy they'd seen, Stamper became subdued. 'Yes, I'm afraid that was a chum of mine, Seb Rhodes. Went to school with him, actually — he was always a rather headstrong sort of chap who never listened to instructions. I'd often joked he was too tall for a recce regiment and that one day he'd stick his head out of a hatch and cop a bullet.'

Singh grimaced. 'If it's the poor fellow that I saw, he caught more than a bullet.'

'Yes, that was rather a poor show,' replied Stamper, looking thoroughly miserable. 'Actually, my troop was up ahead scouting for his detachment, but I took a wrong turn and got stuck up some blind valley. Never was much good at map-reading.' It struck Jox that surely map-reading was a requisite for reconnaissance troops. 'Poor chap, but there you have it, couldn't be helped.'

'So, what are your orders now, Stamper?' asked Jox.

'Secure the castle, set up an observation post, then head back to Bari.'

'In which case, Cornet Stamper, you may well be heaven-sent,' replied Jox. 'We have a long overdue appointment at Bari. Would you be good enough to give us a lift?'

'That would be my absolute pleasure, sir. Happy to oblige.'

'Are you Sub-lieutenant Brodie?' Jox asked the slim Royal Naval Volunteer Reserve officer standing on the quayside once they had reached Bari. Brodie was wearing a tan duffel coat with ropes and toggles, his weathered face topped by an outsized cap that made him look rather like a lollipop.

'That's right, sir, Iain Brodie,' he replied in the lilting accent of Ayrshire. 'Might you be Squadron Leader McNabb's party? We've been expecting you for a while.'

'I'm sorry about that. We got rather waylaid on the way here.'

'That's nae problem, sir. We're loading the last of our supplies and hoping to make a run back to Sicily tonight. To catch the tide and the darkest portion of the night, we'll be heading off at 2200 hours. I'll be needing your party aboard by nine, so perhaps you should have an early supper beforehand, say your goodbyes and please report in good time. As you're a party of landlubbers, be warned that MTBs move at a fair old clip and things can get choppy.'

'Thanks for the warning, Brodie,' replied Jox, looking over at the motor torpedo boat moored alongside the quay. 'Do you know, I rather expected more vessels to be ferrying us back.'

The sailor smiled. 'This is only a third of our flotilla. Two of us waited here for you, and the other four have already gone ahead with the rest of the POWs brought in by that Yank captain.'

'Captain Lomasso?'

'That's right — shady sort of fellow.'

'Comes with his line of work, I'm afraid.'

'Wouldn't know about that, sir. We small boat types don't ask too many questions, but I will say we're glad to be of service getting you and your chaps back into the game. We should be safely back in Sicily by dawn.'

'Really?' replied Jox. 'You've no idea how reassuring that is to hear. We've rather been through the grinder. So, tell me, how fast do these things go?'

'We're capable of forty knots, but generally tend to motor along at about twenty. Like I said, fast and bumpy, but I suppose it'll be nothing like the speeds you pilots reach, although we are known as the "Spitfires of the Seas".'

'Sounds exhilarating. She's a real beauty,' said Jox as the matelot's face coloured with pride.

'Well, this is MTB 80, a Type II Vosper-built 73-footer with a crew of thirteen. She has three engines delivering 4,200 horsepower under a flat, planed tail which displaces forty-nine tons.'

Crewmen were carrying ammo boxes, coiling ropes and fiddling with the craft's bristling guns. They looked awfully young in rimless navy-blue hats and thick, roll-necked Arran jumpers.

'We have two 18-inch torpedo tubes, plus a quick-firing six-pounder gun on a powered mounting, twin 20mm Oerlikon guns aft and two .303 Lewis guns forwards. We pack quite a punch, but as you can see there's not a lot of room.' Brodie pointed to the motor torpedo boat moored alongside, which looked much the same, but had the number 81 painted in white on its grey bow. 'That there's Laurie Strong's craft, which has four torpedo tubes to our two, but he has less firepower than us. Mind you, each Mark 8 torpedo has a 466-pound warhead and a range of 16,000 yards when travelling at 36 knots. Anything we hit, we take out,' he added proudly before checking his clipboard. 'So then, how many in your party, sir?'

Jox quickly counted them up in his head. 'Eight.'

'Are any of them senior service men?'

Jox considered the question. 'Afraid not. There are three pongos, and the rest of us are airmen — two Brits, two Yanks and a Frenchman.'

'Right, we'll have to split you up. Half will come with me and the other half with Laurie. I can't promise it'll be roomy and like I said, it will be choppy.'

'Roger that. Let me see … I'll stick with you, Brodie, so that'll be McNabb, Kilpatrick and Perrin, all three RAF, then Beans, who was RAF too, but is better listed as USAAF moving forward. On MTB 81 will be Singh, Carver, and … wait a minute, I don't even know their real names.' Jox turned to his companions still clustered around Stamper's scout cars which had driven them down here and were still parked up on the quayside. 'Teddy, Toffee, let Sub-lieutenant Brodie here have your surnames and unit details. It's for his ship's manifest.'

Brodie grinned. 'Well, we really do need to know who's onboard, just in case we sink.' It was meant as a joke, but Jox hoped the jest wouldn't prove to be famous last words. He'd come too far to fall at the last hurdle.

Looking back towards the quayside, he caught sight of Rosmarina, standing amongst the men, shorter but obvious thanks to her red partisan scarf and brightly-coloured hair. Only Singh was about her height, but his turban made him seem taller. Beside him she seemed petite and pale, but he knew that disguised her strength of character and steeliness. The moment of their separation was approaching, and he didn't feel ready for it. It was inevitable, they both knew that, but it didn't lessen the pain within.

'We'll see you at 2100 hours, Brodie. I appreciate what you're doing for us. It's been an extremely long haul for many of us, and this is the final furlong. Good to be back amongst friends.'

'Righto, sir. If you're interested, there's a good fish restaurant called *Al Pescatore* in the old town. They usually have excellent squid ink pasta. Looks revolting but is really top-notch. Just don't overdo it — remember the bumpy ride.'

Despite Brodie's warning, they were all determined to enjoy their final meal together, the former POWs, their partisan friends, plus Cornet Stamper and some of his Cherry Pickers, who'd brought them to Bari. Rosmarina had caught up with some of the other *Brigata Stella Rosa* partisans, those that had accompanied the earlier groups, and she would be returning to the mountains with them after their departure. There were gentle arguments over who and how they would pay for the meal, but that was settled by the former prisoners offering up a few long-hoarded gold coins from their Escape and Evasion kits. The lustre of yellow metal ensured that the restauranteur made the very best of everything on the menu available.

After many long and lean days, in captivity and then trekking across the mountains, it was inevitable that some would overdo it. Almost predictably, Teddy and Toffee were front and centre, with Jox fearing what shape they'd be in by the time they boarded. He counted his blessings that at least they wouldn't be on the same vessel as him. Singh, too, seemed rather affected, but not by high spirits, instead feeling rather low, maudlin at the prospect of leaving the partisans he'd been through so much with, especially Rosmarina, who he was evidently very fond of.

Before the time to report back arrived, Jox and Rosmarina went for a walk around the port as dusk was falling. The harbour facilities had clearly suffered under Allied bombing, but also from the explosives that had been rigged to go off once the Germans had evacuated the city. The failing light did much to disguise the damage, with all the raw edges softened, and the orange reflections of the quayside lighting danced prettily on the black surface of the water. It was an idyllic setting for their heartbreaking goodbyes.

Neither had the right words to say, the silence hanging heavily between them. As ever, Rosmarina took the initiative, taking Jox's hands between hers and looking into his eyes. '*Amore mio*, it is time for you to turn from me and walk away. I will do the same and we will not look back. If fate decides that we see one another again, that is good and all I could possibly wish for, but if not, what can we do? *Che sarà, sarà*. What will be, will be.'

With a heavy heart, Jox nodded, kissed her one last time and turned away, walking towards whatever fate held in store. He would never forget Italy, and Rosmarina would always be part of his soul.

Once they'd pulled out of the harbour, the wind picked up, and the ocean turned to veined marble. Driving spray drove the 'spare parts' on deck down below, but Jox was permitted to remain in the glass-fronted navigation room before the helm as a nod to his rank. He brooded over his and Rosmarina's goodbyes as the twin craft left the reassuring pool of light in safe harbour, venturing towards whatever dangers the darkness of night might hold.

For most of Brodie's crewmen, taking shelter wasn't an option. They manned their guns despite the spray, swarming like dark wraiths across the deck and wearing bulky rubberised oilskins and sou'westers. The swift MTBs headed southeast, on a parallel course less than a hundred yards apart, like competing fillies on Derby Day. They followed the Adriatic coast until they were through the Strait of Otranto, clearing the heel of Italy off Santa Maria di Leuca and its world-famous lighthouse. Forty-seven metres high, the three white pulses it emitted every fifteen seconds pierced the gloom, the sole source of light from a coastline still under strict blackout. It struck Jox as a stark contrast to lit-up Bari, and he asked why that was.

Shouting over the throbbing Packard 4M V12 engines, Brodie replied, 'The Boche are still active around here. We're well within range of the *Schnellboote* or E-boat squadrons based out of Corfu. When the Italians packed it all in, their fine *Torpediniere* boats became the property of the *Kriegsmarine* and they've been causing merry hell with them ever since. We don't want to get caught by any of those tiger-hulled devils, I can assure you of that.'

Jox could picture the tiger-camouflaged attack boats. He'd come across them in Malta, or rather what was left of them after the famous raid on Valetta's Grand Harbour. 'I saw them in action in July of 1941!' he shouted back. 'I was stationed in Malta during the siege and saw the aftermath of the MTB and frogmen attack which destroyed some shipping as well as the St Elmo Bridge. As I recall, it was a rather foolhardy attack that cost them dearly.'

Brodie looked impressed. 'That was the great raid by the *Decima Flottiglia Motoscafi Armati Siluranti*, undoubtedly ill-advised but nonetheless very brave. That's the Eyeties all over. I didn't realise you'd been in the region for quite so long.'

Jox smiled wearily. 'Off and on, but yes, for a long time.'

The lighthouse pulsed steadily on their starboard side and guided them along at a bracing, thumping pace. Through the windows of the wheelhouse, Jox observed the moonless night with its bruised sky filled with deep purple, steel grey and anthracite black.

'We're motoring over the deeper reaches of the Ionian Sea now,' said Brodie. 'There's always a chance of running into a Jerry U-boat recharging its batteries on the surface at night. That would certainly be a prize plum for us to pluck. Those bastards have been nipping into Sicilian waters, off the eastern ports, picking off our transports willy-nilly. I'm afraid the war at sea is still very active, especially with Jerry so pissed off that we're getting the upper hand in the air and a firm toehold on the Italian mainland. Out here, though, it's a far from a done deal.'

The radio crackled from the tiny radio room situated behind the helm. The operator stuck his head out of a hatch, exposing tousled red hair under headphones and a mouth mic. 'Message from Lieutenant Strong, sir.'

'Well, shout it out then, Chalmers,' replied Brodie. 'I can't be expected to read in the dark.'

'Right you are, sir. Says "DASHER 81 calling DASHER 80. Radio check. Ask Brodders what on earth these pongos have been eating. One of them is pebble-dashing the inside of my crew room with what looks very much like tarmac. OVER."'

Brodie looked horrified and turned to Jox.

'Is it the chap with the walrus moustache and the West Country accent?' asked Jox.

'Pass the question on, Chalmers,' said Brodie.

The radio operator nodded and complied. 'Lieutenant Strong confirms the moustache, but not the accent. He says the subject is currently rather green and appears to be talking in tongues. Wants to know whether he should treat this as a medical emergency; he says it looks like black worms.'

Jox guffawed. 'No, that'll be Teddy after over-celebrating his freedom with too much *vino collapso* and platefuls of that squid ink pasta you recommended. What was it called again?'

'*Spaghetti al nero di sepia,*' replied Brodie, now grinning. 'I did warn you about *le mal de mer.*'

'Old Teddy was never going to heed that warning. Poor chap's been locked up for two years and very nearly lost his arm. He was always going to celebrate.'

'He won't be celebrating now,' said Brodie, then addressed the R/T operator. 'Let Laurie know there's no need to worry. It's nothing a bucket and mop won't fix.'

Jox wondered how Beans was faring down in MTB 80's wardroom. Back at *Castel del Monte* he'd shown he had a strong appetite but a weak stomach. A repeat performance would not endear them to the MTB's crew, who were already looking at them with bemused pity.

The radio man added, 'Lieutenant Strong says, "The fellow's stunk out my crew room and I can smell it all the way up to the ward room. I've had to take refuge at the helm to get away from the stink. This is even worse than sharing with you, Brodders."'

Sub-lieutenant Brodie laughed. 'Och well, they do say war's hell.'

'So, you know Lieutenant Strong rather well,' said Jox.

'Aye, he's a good lad. We went to Torpedo School at HMS *Jackdaw* at Crail in Fife together. In such a wind-blasted place there wasn't much else to do but become pals. He's from down south — Bognor Regis, I think he said.'

'I know what you mean about the wind,' replied Jox. 'Got my wings at Montrose, another godforsaken, wind-blasted spot. Scotland seems rather full of them.' He glanced at his scarred hands. 'That's where I got these.'

Brodie looked down. 'Aye, well, there's no doubting you've been through the wars, Squadron Leader. You'll have earnt a wee rest after all of your adventures. A nice spot of leave will surely be on the cards.'

CHAPTER SEVENTEEN

They had been bombing along for several hours, having cleared the 'arch' of Italy's boot, slipping past the sleeping city of Crotone on the Calabrian coast on the starboard side. The jerking rhythm of the planed hull bouncing on the swell had calmed a little, and Beans, Kilpatrick and Perrin were asleep in the cramped wardroom.

Jox couldn't sleep, thinking about Rosmarina. Had he let happiness slip through his fingers? It wasn't his choice, rather the call of duty that had forced the separation, but that didn't make him feel any less forlorn. He longed for an eventual reunion, but from long and savage experience he feared it was unlikely. There was so much pitted against them, and it was a realisation that stuck in his throat like a stone. He couldn't sleep so opted to keep a vigil beside Brodie and the other officers aboard MTB 80.

They formed a tight-knit trio, interacting easily and with the rest of the crew, speaking in a shorthand that was a little hard to follow. Jox had seen similar chemistry amongst bomber crews and had always been amused at how when on leave they still travelled in packs. Fighter pilots tended to be more solitary creatures, but he was intrigued as to whether it was the same for the crews of these 'Spitfires of the Seas'. He suspected it probably was.

MTB 81 was a little ahead of their vessel, barely visible in the darkness, save for the natural luminescence of her wake churned up by her three powerful engines. Jox wondered if the rest of his mob had settled down after their initial seasickness.

He was grateful that at least his stomach appeared to be holding up.

A sudden burst of white light rose before them, swiftly followed by a second. In the brightness, Jox's contracting irises ached and his night vision was shot. More flares arched away from MTB 81, each following the next like a blazing comet. Almost immediately, tracer rounds roared from the boat, the rattling of twinned .303 Vickers K machine guns on the portside of the wheelhouse, followed by the clanking of the 20mm Oerlikon cannon on the raised platform at the boat's stern.

'Bloody hell,' said Brodie, forgetting all pretence of radio procedure. He grabbed the transmitter from the stunned R/T operator and barked, 'Laurie, what the hell's going on?'

The seconds it took to receive a response felt like an age.

Aboard MTB 80, one of Brodie's subordinate officers shouted, 'All hands, action stations!' In the resulting scramble, Jox almost missed the reply from the other vessel.

'Brodders, there's a bloody great sub out there, right to the portside.'

'Where away?' asked Brodie, straining to see through the spray-splattered window to his left. 'How do you know it's not one of ours?'

'I just saw him, right there, with a bloody great V painted on his nose and a red bear on the conning tower. It also had a shield with a crossed torpedo and palm tree.'

'Christ, did you really get that close?'

'Yes, practically rammed him. He's gone past me now, but you should be right on top of him. Get some flares up, quick — he'll be diving like the clappers by now.'

'A V painted on the nose — that's the 24th Flotilla. He's a long way from home.'

The radio crackled in response. 'Well, he's right on our bloody doorstep now, so find him. We can't let him get away. You're to engage aggressively and buy me some time to get my tin fish ready and circle back after him. Come on, tallyho, tallyho.'

Up on deck, MTB 80's 57mm quick-firing 6-pounder Mark IIA gun began firing with a series of deep booms that shook the laminated wood structure of the boat. Earlier, Brodie had explained that like the old Hurricanes Jox had flown during the Battle of Britain, motor torpedo boats were primarily of wooden construction, strips of light-coloured ash and dark sipo mahogany glued together to produce an incredibly strong and light outer shell, but one that was susceptible to fire, if for example a fuel tank was punctured and set alight. Much like the old Hurri, MTBs could absorb a lot of punishment, with most rounds passing straight through if they didn't strike anything important along the way.

Off to the left, Jox saw what might have been twinkling return fire, and at about the same time the vessel was struck by several ominous thuds. There was some furious splashing, like rising mackerel flopping on the surface of the flint-coloured sea, on either side of the leaning vessel as she pulled round. In the glow of yet another sodium flare, the low cloud lightened and Jox sensed movement on the water. Tendrils of tracer fire flailed towards them from the dark, looming silhouette of a U-boat conning tower. It looked like a giant dorsal fin of some primaeval shark, taller than the MTB's wheelhouse, with a rampant red lion painted on it. It was definitely a lion and not a bear — somehow to Jox that detail seemed important.

There was a loud bang inches from Jox's head. The glass of the wheelhouse shattered, peppering him with translucent shards. His face was stinging where he'd been nicked and he tried to shake the jagged pieces from his hair, failing as it was soaking wet.

Outside the wheelhouse, the portside Vickers gunner had disappeared. Fire from the U-boat's conning tower had presumably swept him aside and the twin barrels of his guns pointed uselessly towards the sky. Jox rushed to the side, catching sight of the matelot's head and yellow lifejacket disappearing into the gloom.

'Man overboard!' he screamed, as a white-jumpered rating brushed past him with a grappling hook and coiled rope in his arms.

'You, man that gun, Jox!' cried Brodie. 'No need to aim, just fire at the bloody sub.'

Confronted by the ungainly twin-barrelled contraption, bulky circular magazines and double stocks, Jox spluttered, 'I don't know how.'

'Lord's alive, let me do it,' said Kilpatrick, who'd come up from the crew room because of all the commotion. The Ulsterman manhandled his CO out of the way, keen as ever to get into the fight. Jox was relieved, since Kilpatrick knew his way around guns much better.

'Thanks, Pat,' mumbled Jox. 'I'll go help get that chap back on board.'

He stumbled to the rear, the deck heaving under his feet. He could feel the knocking reverberations of more rounds striking home. How much more punishment could the little wooden boat take? He ducked under the raised platform where the Mark II 6-pounder was banging away and reached the stern to find the sailor who'd rushed past him earlier. He was desperately hanging on to a rope that disappeared into bucking darkness.

'I've got a hook into him, when we swung round,' the man grunted, face pale with exertion. 'We're going too fast. I can't haul him in on my own.'

Jox grabbed the wet rope and together they began pulling. For every foot they managed to reel in, a fresh acceleration of the boat's powerful engines stripped it back out again, and each time the rope burned through their hands. All the while, the guns fired and Kilpatrick roared into the wind and spray, like a half-mad Captain Ahab. His double Vickers were the high note to the tenor beat of the twin 20mm Oerlikon aft and the deep bass of the 6-pounder at the rear.

The pair kept hauling in the stricken gunner, but it was taking too long. By the time they finally managed to get his sodden body over the gunwale, it was limp and lifeless. His sodden hair lay across his forehead like seaweed. Blue-lipped, his face was the colour of oystershell. Driven by hope rather than reality, his crewman pumped his back, trying to clear his lungs.

'Come on, Matty, come on…' he begged.

Jox felt helpless and looked down at his rope-burned hands. They'd tried, they really had, but in the end, it was the sea that won. It was little comfort when they discovered a fist-sized hole in the front of the sailor's kapok lifejacket where he'd been struck mid-chest. Dragged behind the boat's wake like trolled marlin bait, he'd been exsanguinated in the flint-coloured water. The pallor of the dead man's skin told Jox everything he needed to know, and he placed a comforting hand on the crewman's shoulder. 'All right, mate, he's gone. We did what we could, and now we better get him stowed away and go back to our duties.'

He looked bereft for a moment but nodded. 'Aye-aye, sir.'

They returned to the wheelhouse, soaked and sore, getting another dowsing on the way. Lieutenant Strong's MTB 81 had pulled across their vessel and was very nearly struck by outgoing fire as it sent an arch of spray over Jox, Kilpatrick and the crewman. Over the R/T, Strong said, 'All engines full astern. I need sea room for my tin fish to arm.' The craft slowed and unexpectedly went into reverse, and Jox saw a pair of torpedoes fly from the tubes on either side of the deck. Eighteen inches in diameter, they were twice a man's height and leapt away like greyhounds at the track. At first, they ran submerged beneath the frothing grey brine, but then began porpoising as if checking their trajectory onto the target.

The run couldn't have been more than a minute before a bright flash pierced the gloom, followed by a growing ball of orange flame. Whatever had been struck, whether bear or lion, at least one of Strong's tin fish had struck a mortal blow. A ragged cheer went up from both MTBs and all firing ceased, MTB 80's engines slowing to a burbling idle. A spotlight at the bow came on and swept across the dark surface of the sea, floating oil iridescent where thin but lathered in gloppy clumps where thicker.

The explosion had broken the U-boat's back. The bow end was burning as it plunged to the depths, and as unlikely as it seemed, fire was swelling up from beneath the surface, illuminating the water like a submerged volcanic spout. The larger stern portion, with the weight of the conning tower and engines, tipped up, arse-end exposed with the copper propellors still spinning as the vessel plunged to its doom. As she sank, cargo and other buoyant material was disgorged to float to the surface. As the flames receded, amongst the oil-covered flotsam were the flailing figures of several men.

Jox grabbed the crewman beside him, the one he'd helped earlier. 'Get your grappling hook out to those poor fellows.' The matelot coiled the rope over his arm and searched for a target. He began spinning the hook before launching it towards a struggling submariner.

Brodie's voice roared, 'Belay that order, Jenkins! We need to make a run for it.'

'There are men in the water!' cried Jox. 'Surely, we must help them…'

In the distance, the horizon was pierced by several red flares rising through the brume.

'We need to get the hell out of here, Jox,' said Brodie. 'Those lights are the attack signal of the *Kriegsmarine's* E-boats. The tiger-hulled devils will be on us in minutes, if we don't get away. The *Torpediniere* boats they nicked from the Italians are bigger and faster than we are, and we've taken damage too. Those chaps in the drink are not our responsibility, and with any luck might even slow the E-boats' pursuit. Come on, get in here. We need to get moving. Hold on tight — it's going to get bumpy. If it makes you feel any better, we're running for our lives and we better pray that our engines hold on until daybreak, when we can get to air cover in the straits.'

MTB 80's idling Packards roared as the revs picked up, drowning out the screams of desperate U-boat crewmen struggling in the water. Jox feared he'd hear their anguished cries for the rest of his life.

In the confusion that followed, they rounded the toe of Italy, turning northwards towards the narrowing Straits of Messina. As Brodie had predicted, with daylight came succour and their pursuers dropped away, the threat from Allied airpower growing with proximity and the dawn of a new day. With it, the damage to the vessels became clearer.

Strong's MTB 81 was running alongside, swift and parallel to her sister ship MTB 80, trailing a grimy line of smoke. The damage to her hull was considerable. Jox was reminded of the USAAF bombers he'd seen landing in Tunisia after running the gauntlet of flak and enemy interceptors, having come the long way over German territory from Blighty. At the time, he'd been struck by the extent of the damage: ripped and gouged aluminium panelling, chewed ailerons and tailfins, and even gaping holes in the wings themselves. He'd marvelled at how they'd ever managed to make it back. The hull of MTB 81 looked no different than those battered B-17s, and it was a wonder she was still afloat. Dark rivulets of blood had oozed from ragged holes in the boat's decking and laminated wooden structures, the wind sweeping it back into gory wings. Jox doubted their own vessel looked any better, but they'd been fortunate to have suffered only a single casualty. From the trail of gore down her sides, MTB 81 appeared to have fared rather worse.

'That doesn't look good,' Jox said to Brodie.

'Aye, you're right,' he replied, chewing his lip anxiously. 'I'm gonna have to ask, but I'm not sure I want to hear the answer.' He reached for the mouthpiece of the radio. 'DASHER 80 for DASHER 81. Sit rep, please. You're in a hell of a mess there. Any casualties to report?'

'DASHER 81 receiving,' replied Strong's tired voice. 'Yes, I'm afraid two of my chaps are hurt, McClintock seriously. The poor fellow may be blind.'

'Christ, sorry to hear that. That's a tough break, Laurie,' he sighed. 'But hey, listen, congrats on the kill. That's a really top effort.'

'Joint endeavour, Brodders. You know that. It was you distracting him while I lined up the shot that got it done. Don't look too clever yourself, by the way. Anyone hurt at your end?'

'Aye, we lost Palmer — shot in the chest and then fell overboard. We managed to get him hauled back, thanks to Jenkins and Squadron Leader McNabb here. Another good effort, but sadly to no avail. At least we'll be able to give him a decent burial ashore. I'll make a point of it once we're back on Sicily. There'll be no "we commit his body to the deep" this time for one of my boys. It's the least we can do for him.' Brodie fell silent, and then perhaps wishing to change the subject, he added, 'Laurie, you ought to get your kill pennant up before we get back to Messina.'

Strong chuckled wearily. 'I wouldn't worry about that. I haven't got much of a mast left to hang a jolly roger on anyway. It's a miracle the R/T's working at all.'

Jox nudged Brodie, who nodded. 'By the way, the squadron leader is asking after his chaps.'

There was an awkward silence at the other end. 'Yes, I was meaning to say. I'm afraid one of them has copped it and another has lost a foot.'

Jox's heart sank, immediately worried for Singh who had done so much for him over the last several months.

'Who was hit?' he asked. Brodie relayed the question.

'The pongo that was spewing all over the place earlier. Poor fellow had such rotten luck, his arm already in plaster and then sick as a parrot, so I sent him below. Should have been safe down there but got hit in back of the head. Came straight through the planking and he was out like a light. Made a hell of a mess, but he won't have felt a thing.'

Jox winced at the picture in his mind.

'What about the other chap?' asked Brodie.

'Quiet South African, calls himself Toffee. I'm afraid his foot's gone, but that little Indian fellow has done a marvellous job taking care of him. My two hurt boys too, for that matter. I've a mind to put him in for a gallantry award.'

'Thanks for the gen, Laurie. I reckon there's a good chance of tea and medals all round. It's not every day we bag ourselves a U-boat. That one definitely wasn't one that got away, a real flamer.'

'Yes, poor sods. I hope the Eyeties picked some of them up.'

'Couldn't be helped. It's a cruel sea for all of us out here. You should focus your energy on getting to home port.'

'Roger that,' Strong replied. 'See you back on dry land, DASHER 81 out.'

Brodie turned to Jox. 'Speaking of medals, that marvellous Irishman of yours did a hell of a job. Lieutenant Strong said that we distracted the Hun, but in truth it was mostly down to your fellow. I'm not exactly sure what the procedure will be with such a motley crew of ex-prisoners, but I intend to recommend him for a Distinguished Service Cross. It's generally awarded "in recognition of an act or acts of exemplary gallantry during active operations against the enemy at sea". I don't believe what Kilpatrick did could be better described than that.'

Jox smiled. 'I'm delighted to hear that, but it shouldn't be too complicated. You see, whilst I'm unconnected to all the others, I am actually Pat Kilpatrick's commanding officer. He's one of my "Black Pigs" of No. 333 Squadron. I'd be delighted to endorse any recommendation you put forward. It's been a honour for us serve with you in this recent action.'

'Aye, well, the feeling's mutual, Jox,' said Brodie. 'What Kilpatrick did was well beyond the call of duty, showing real courage in adversity. I want to see that recognised, and what you did trying to save Palmer shouldn't go unrecognised either. The Royal Navy needs comrades like the two of you.'

'I only wish the outcome had been better. Actually, Jenkins deserves a good deal of the credit,' replied Jox. 'I'd be happy to tell Kilpatrick, or would you rather do it?'

'Oh, I think it'll be better coming from his Commanding Officer.'

Not long after daybreak, the battered pair of motor torpedo boats and their exhausted crews and passengers pulled into the port entrance of Messina. It was four hundred metres wide and faced northwest into the straits, a large natural inlet with an inner port protected by a curved breakwater shaped a bit like a crab claw. The quiet waters of the inner harbour were dotted with blue-grey warships of varying shapes and sizes. A soft sea breeze was blowing, with gulls gliding in the thermals, their squawking providing a plaintive soundtrack to what would have seemed a perfectly peaceful scene if it hadn't been for the ominous multitude of warships.

As the boats headed towards their moorings, Jox stood with Kilpatrick and Beans watching the crews guide their battered craft between the sullen behemoths, heading for the portion of the marina reserved for the fast attack boats.

'Happy to be home, boys?' asked Jox.

'This ain't exactly home,' drawled Beans, 'but I'll be happy to be back on firm ground at least.'

Jox put his hand on the American's broad shoulder. 'You're not wrong there, Bayou. I guess we'll soon be parting company. Pat and I are going to track down our lads, and Muriel has asked to tag along until he finds his Free French mob. What are your plans?'

'I don't rightly know,' Beans replied, frowning. 'It's been a spell since I was under military authority. I've no doubt by now this island is hooching with all kinds of official types, but the question is how quickly I want to get wrapped up in red tape. I might want to live it up for a spell, after all this time away. Not going AWOL as such, but, you know, timing my return to the colours.' Jox nodded, not necessarily agreeing but understanding what he meant. 'As you know, I've also got my concerns regarding Morlaix and then my, shall we say "forced assistance" to the Axis cause before coming across you. Yeah, I'm gonna have some explaining to do.'

'I don't believe you've got anything to reproach yourself about. You can always count on my recommendation. It may not hurt to have a squadron leader in your corner, if things get sticky. Please don't ever hesitate to get in touch. I'm your friend and comrade, and always will be, so you can depend on me.'

'I appreciate that, Jox,' replied Beans, looking wistful, his single pale eye distant. 'You've no idea how much.' He smiled. 'Hell, if wasn't for y'all, I'd have given up the ghost a long time ago and probably still be stuck behind that damned wire.' He smiled. 'Not to mention missing what has proved to be the adventure of a lifetime, popping back and forward across enemy lines like some demented yo-yo, and seeing Italy from not exactly the most scenic of routes.'

Jox snorted at his pronunciation of 'routes', making it sounding like English 'routs' rather than 'roots.' An example of two nations divided by the same language, yet united by a common cause. He smiled at his friend. He would certainly miss him.

'Seems almost a shame it's all over,' said Beans. 'What have I got to look forward to now? I'm just a washed-up, one-eyed aviator with no real prospects.'

'Don't be so daft, Bayou. Flying isn't the be-all and end-all. You're smart, a great leader of men, and people like you. I remember back at Debden, the station commander old Duke-Woolley even said you ought to go into politics one day. You've certainly got the gift of the gab and all the right connections, and you're rich to boot. You'll be fine, I'm sure of it.'

The wounded from MTB 81 were being carried down the gangplank on bloodied stretchers. Toffee was ashen-faced, keeping the bandaged stump of his leg elevated. He gave them a weak smile and waved. He was followed by a second stretcher with a shrouded body, carried at one end by an exhausted-looking Singh.

'Is that Teddy?' asked Jox.

Singh nodded. 'I did my best, but he stood no real chance. I can't stop; we must get these injured sailors and Toffee to a hospital. I'll stick with them until I know they're all right. I'll try to catch up with you. Good luck to you, my brothers.'

There was no time for protracted goodbyes, and before they fully realised what was happening, the wounded and Singh were bundled into an ambulance and driven off the quayside to the nearest hospital in Messina. How typically selfless of Singh to put others first, rather than considering himself. Jox really hoped to see the brave Sikh warrior again, but who knew what the vagaries of war held in store? He'd not meet finer again, of that he was he sure. An old Scottish toast came to mind; it might even have been from Robbie Burns. 'Here's to us, and those like us,' he whispered to himself. 'Damn few, and they're all dead, more's the pity.'

Starting to feel a bit melancholic, Jox turned to Kilpatrick, hoping he'd cheer him up. 'How about you, Pat? Looking forward to seeing the boys again? Things'll no doubt be different from when we left. Who knows what we'll find? I fear there'll certainly have been losses.'

Kilpatrick nodded, running a hand through his salt-encrusted hair. 'Sure, no doubt, but it'll be grand to be back. What I'm really looking forward to is seeing the look on their faces when I walk in with you. It'll truly be the return of the prodigal son.'

'That may be, but actually that reminds me: I've got a bit of a surprise for you.'

'Have you now? Not sure I like them all that much.'

'You'll like this,' said Jox. 'Now listen, I know you're a bampot old Paddy who likes nothing better than getting into a good scrap. Our friends in the Royal Navy don't and somehow believe you've been rather brave, doing a grand job shooting up that U-boat, whilst wailing like a banshee into the wind.'

'Aye, well?' said Kilpatrick, eyeing him warily.

'In their wisdom, the commanding officers of these two fine vessels have decided to recommend you for the Distinguished Service Cross for gallantry. I have been pleased to endorse that recommendation. My sincerest congratulations to you, Flight Sergeant Kilpatrick.'

'Well, ain't that something?' said Beans, slapping Kilpatrick on the shoulder. Perrin gave him Gallic kisses on either cheek. The blushing Ulsterman grudgingly accepted their congratulations and then began to chuckle — first quietly to himself, then letting out loud, howling laughter. It was perplexing but also somehow infectious. After many months of captivity and all the trials of their journey to freedom, it was a glorious release. With tears of laughter pouring down his cheeks, Jox finally croaked, 'What on earth's so damned funny?'

'I'm just picturing the look on Paddy's face when I waltz into the room with a DSC pinned to my chest. That old rascal's going to be as sick as a parrot, so he will.'

Jox laughed even louder. Pat wasn't wrong. It was good to laugh, but it wouldn't last. There was still a lot of war before them.

Jox was tired, perhaps more tired than he'd ever been, but his job wasn't done. With winter here, Italy's vertiginous mountain ranges and the enemy's formidable defensive lines lay before them, and this campaign was far from over. It had certainly proven to be no 'soft underbelly of Europe' as had been expected. There would be tough times ahead, and Jox knew he would play his part. He always did.

EPILOGUE

London, 1992

Melanie McNabb was watching the television screen as the guns marked the end of the two-minute silence. The royal party began laying wreaths on the cenotaph steps, followed by the Chiefs of Staff, politicians and Commonwealth High Commissioners. The burr of conversation returned to the room as ever more dignitaries stepped up to place their crimson poppy wreaths.

'Did your grandfather always march with his RAF boys?' asked Nancy.

'He usually did, but varied it between different squadron associations, then the groupings for the various campaigns in which he participated. He was never short of invitations to march with one chapter or another, but yes, mostly with the Treble Ones or the Treble Threes, and sometimes also the Wing and Group he went on to command. Of course, Uncle Pritch was a Treble One too. On certain anniversaries, though, my grandfather would choose to march with the former prisoners of war, the *Kriegies* as he liked to call them. He particularly enjoyed those reunions and I can remember how diverse a group they were, chaps from all over, from different services and regiments. I always found the RAF gatherings rather samey, all similar types, albeit from different countries.'

On the screen now, there were a trio of figures advancing towards the cenotaph steps already covered with dozens of fluttering paper wreaths. These were the last of the officials before the march-past by the veterans. One was a heavily braided senior policeman with service medals, representing the Metropolitan Police Service, the second, an equally well-decorated member of the London Fire Brigade. Finally, there was a Sikh gentleman with a long grey beard and a blue turban wearing the comparatively plain uniform of a Transport for London tube driver. Each of these services had played a vital role during the world wars, especially during the Blitz, and had been given the honour of laying wreaths.

Melanie recognised the Sikh gentleman at once. 'That's Mr Singh!' she said. 'He served in Italy with my grandfather. He used to visit us. Such a lovely man. Looks rather sombre on the telly today, but he was always so jolly when we met up. Grandpa lost touch with him for a while after the war, but was absolutely delighted when they reconnected.'

'It is good you remember him,' Nancy said wistfully. 'We old-timers often get forgotten. There'll come a time when none of us are left and all the memories will fade. Schoolchildren barely know about the Second World War these days. So, how did Jox meet this Singh fellow?'

'They were both *Kriegies*, but I don't think they were in the same camps. Mr Singh was part of a band of partisans who came to Grandpa Bang-Bang's rescue when he was on the run. I know they fought side by side in Italy for a while, went through some savage combats, and were then evacuated back to Sicily through something called SIMCOL. Sadly, they then lost touch, until a chance meeting on Horse Guards parade after the march-past one year when I was still a girl.'

'Partisans, you say?'

'Yes, I did some research into them,' said Melanie. 'Things didn't really turn out too well. Apparently, they were a Communist-inspired group and went by the name of the Red

Star Brigade, *la Brigata Stella Rosa*. The Germans considered them to be the worst kind of terrorists.'

'One man's terrorist is another man's freedom fighter,' said Nancy grim-faced.

'I believe Grandpa and Mr Singh were fortunate to get away from them when they did. Things turned rather bad for them afterwards. Apparently, the unit was led by a rather dashing former Italian Army Sergeant-Major called Mario Musolesi, with the *nom-de-guerre* of *il Lupo*, the wolf. All sounds rather dramatic, doesn't it?'

'I had a *nom-de-guerre*, you know. *La souri blanche*, the white mouse. Doesn't have quite the same impact, does it?'

Melanie chuckled. 'Well, I'm not sure that's true, but anyway, it appears that after the Salerno landings, the *Brigata Stella Rosa* moved up north to take the battle behind the enemy's defensive lines, during the stalemate of the Cassino and the Gustav line. They operated in the region of Sasso Marconi, near Bologna, north of Rome. They made such a nuisance of themselves to the occupiers that eventually the whole of the *16th SS Panzergrenadier Division Reichsführer-SS* launched a massed operation against them. I couldn't find out too many details, but what I did discover indicated that the *Stella Rosa* were wiped out, along with a great many civilians that were accused of assisting them. There were a number of massacres and Lupo was killed, as was his girlfriend, Livia Comellini, along with her mother and brother as they attempted to break out of an encirclement. I don't think there were many survivors.' She paused. 'The impression I got was that Grandpa knew all about this and was very sad when talking to Mr Singh about their time with them.'

'It's always tough talking of lost comrades. You feel so guilty that you survived and they didn't.'

'Yes, of course. The odd thing was seeing Grandpa so sad, but Mr Singh remaining so jolly. That's when he insisted that Grandpa and I come to dinner at his home in Southall, later that same week. I was still too young to fully understand what was going on, but I can remember being quite excited. Mr Singh said that he and his wife would prepare us a special Indian feast. He promised to also prepare some of the Italian dishes that would remind them of their time in Italy. Grandpa said that Mr Singh was always a superb cook, so I was really looking forward to it.

'When they met us at the door of their home, Mrs Singh was green-eyed and extraordinarily beautiful, wearing a traditional green dress embroidered with gold thread. Her hair was remarkable, bright red with just a few grey streaks but contrasting with the green material of her outfit. I was completely bewitched. She was very kind and made a great fuss of me, and I suppose I was distracted by the lovely present they gave me, a wonderful set of Ladybird books about the great women in history. All the while, my grandfather was strangely quiet, his eyes wide and filled with tears.

'Mrs Singh spoke with an extraordinary mixed-up accent, and I later learnt it was Italian, English and Southeast Asian all jumbled up. She called my Grandpa "*amore mio*", which I didn't understand at the time, but I later found out it means "my love". Grandpa didn't give me too many details, but there was great affection between them, and it turned out Mrs Singh had also fought alongside Grandpa and Mr Singh before they were married. There was a lot of hugging and crying, which scared me a little at first, but Grandpa said not to worry, everything was all right, everyone was very happy.

'I remember Mrs Singh said to him, "It was such a dark time back then. I was lost and alone, wounded and frightened when my *Leone* came to the rescue." She sighed and smiled, gently touching her husband's grey beard. "Life has so many forks in the road, and we must not regret the paths we took, whether by choice or necessity. We can only look back with warmth, affection and love. I am so happy we have found each other again. We have lost so many others along the way. We must take comfort in our reunion."

'With her other hand she touched my grandfather's face, and the three of them hugged for a long time.'

'It's so lovely that they found each other again,' Nancy sighed. 'There are so many lost comrades from my war that I so wish I could see one last time.'

Melanie took her hand. 'I'll do what I can to help you find out what happened to them.'

'You're so very kind, dear.' Nancy squeezed Melanie's hand in return. 'Sadly, I know what happened to them. You visiting me is enough. You'll never know how much I look forward to our visits.'

Melanie felt a tear come to her eye as they fell into companionable silence, reflecting once more on the anniversary of the devastating war that had impacted both of their lives in so many ways.

A NOTE TO THE READER

The Jox McNabb stories are of course works of fiction but in them I do try to follow the trace of history, whilst allowing our Jox to participate in as many momentous events as I can. On occasion, this requires stretching or compressing timelines, which I hope the reader will forgive me for. Invariably, there may be some mistakes, particularly on certain technical aspects, for which I beg your indulgence. I am however always happy to hear from readers and will endeavour to correct any mistakes in the historical narrative or in technical matters in subsequent editions.

Jox McNabb and many of the characters he meets in his adventures are the product of my imagination, often an amalgam of real historical figures and people I've met and known, and occasionally, with fairly typical author's conceit, there's a bit of me thrown in there too. With them, I always strive to tell a story that is authentic, compelling, reflective and hopefully moving.

I hope you've enjoyed reading Jox McNabb's latest adventure. The challenge of telling this particular story was that much of the action was on the ground, and often confined to the limited perspective and rather finite world of the *Kriegie* or Prisoners of War. I thought, though, it was a worthwhile challenge to explore this lived experience of so many servicemen during the Second World War and indeed other conflicts.

Broadly following the narrative of this novel, but otherwise in no particular order, here are a few historical notes and character details that I hope you may find of interest.

Operation *Lehrgang*, the German and Italian withdrawal from Sicily across the Strait of Messina to Calabria in Italy took place in August 1943. It involved the evacuation of over 100,000 troops and 14,000 vehicles during what came to be known as 'Germany's Dunkirk'. The straits themselves and the vessels crossing between the two shorelines were guarded by some 500 guns, more than 300 of which were anti-aircraft guns. Allied fighter and bomber crews are said to have described the flak over the Messina corridor as the thickest they had ever experienced in the entire war.

Overseeing the defence was indeed *Oberst*, later *Generalleutnant* Ernst-Günther Baade. Described as tireless and omnipresent in his duty, *Generalfeldmarschall* Albert Kesselring, Commander-in-Chief South himself, is said to have observed of him, 'he seems to have overlooked virtually nothing and to have provided virtually everything.' Personalities like Baade are heaven-sent for the novelist, and if I'd invented him, he would barely be believable. Legendary from his exploits in the desert with the *Afrika Korps*, he was a noted equestrian athlete, an Olympian and a noted Caledonophile, who was known to go into battle wearing a kilt and carrying a claymore sword. We will undoubtably meet General Baade again.

As a boy, I watched many great black and white war movies, some of which involved plucky prisoners of war being captured and incarcerated in *Stalags* and *Stalag Lufts*. My own grandfather was a *Kriegie* at *Stalag XV11-B* at Krems in Austria. In these films, they invariably learnt that their days of freedom were at an end with the immortal words, 'For you, Tommy, the war is over.' I therefore couldn't resist referencing those words in Jox's latest adventure, indeed using it as a goad to keep him restless and always looking for the opportunity to escape.

For me, researching the world of the *Kriegies* has been fascinating. Learning about the conditions in the various camps, how they were organised and what prisoners spent their time doing or indeed obsessing about was truly a voyage of discovery. The treatment of non-white POWs was invariably bad, as noted, and they were often kept separately from other prisoners. Generally speaking, conditions were poor, especially as the war progressed and the camps became increasingly crowded with all the associated challenges of accommodation, nutrition, sanitation and illness. Boredom and listlessness also took their toll.

Unlike the Germans, I discovered that Italian camp authorities did not separate prisoners from the Allied air forces, army and navy. The sheer diversity of the fellow inmates that Jox meets is reflective of three long years of a global conflict on several fronts and between often very different belligerent forces. Many of Jox's fellow *Kriegies* are either real or amalgams of the various personal war stories that I've discovered. For example, Mieczysław 'Whisky' Wyszkowski is real, and was a member of the vaunted Polish Fighter Team 'Skalski's Circus', which in only five weeks became the most effective unit in all the Desert Air Force in North Africa in 1943. Fifteen Polish pilots shot down twenty-five of the enemy with the loss of only one — 'Whisky' Wyszkowski. Taken prisoner, he was evacuated to Italy, where I have him meet Jox, and he was later sent to *Dulag Luft* near Frankfurt am Main and onto other camps. He survived the war, ending his service with the RAF in 1949, after which he returned to Poland. Like many Poles who served with Western Allied forces during the war, Wyszkowski was viewed with suspicion by post-war communists but ended up flying for the national carrier LOT Polish Airlines. By the war's end he was said to have flown 1,850 hours on 44 different types of aircraft, a remarkable record, considering the amount of time he also spent behind the wire.

Fokke De Boer is fictitious, but his unit, the Kittyhawk "Billy Boys" of No. 1 Squadron South African Air Force are real, as is their squadron's "*Jou Bielie!*" war cry, giving rise to their nickname. His 'flak-happiness', deafness and foul mouth are hopefully illustrative of the state POWs arrived in to the camps after the trauma of combat, ditching and capture, and were in a parlous state, affected physically or psychologically, and often both.

Some the 'high profile' prisoners that I have described Jox meeting are fictitious, but others are very real. Notably, Capitan Richard Carver was General Montgomery's stepson and was captured during the advance from El Alamein. Similarly, Colonel John Waters was General George Patton's son-in-law, captured at Sidi Bou Zid in Tunisia. I have made both pass through Jox's orbit, something that is entirely conceivable, but their actual stories also read like fiction. Capitan Richard Carver spent time in several POW camps in Italy, before escaping at the time of the Armistice, much like Jox and his companions. He made a trek of some 500 miles back to Allied lines and was 'on the run' for some four months. When he was finally reunited with his famously acerbic stepfather, Monty is reported to have said, 'Where the hell have you been? What took you so long?'

Infamously, General Patton's reaction to his son-in-law's incarceration was rather more 'hands on', as might be expected of 'Old Blood and Guts'. In late March 1945, he ordered Task Force Baum on the ill-fated and controversial mission to penetrate fifty miles behind German lines to liberate the *Kriegies* of *Oflag XIII-B*, near Hammelburg in Bavaria. His hapless son-in-law knew nothing of the rescue attempt, and was wounded in the process, but recovered to become the commandant of cadets at West Point, then deploying to Korea as Chief of Staff for I Corps. He successively became Commanding General for the 4th Armored Division, the V Corps and the 5th United States Army. He finally retired in command of the U.S. Army, Pacific, based in Hawaii, having arguably had a military career that eclipsed even his illustrious father-in-law's.

The *Campos* of P.G. 85 at Tuturano, south of Brindisi and P.G. 35 at the *Certosa di Padula*, south of Naples where Jox and his companions are incarcerated were both real and much as described. They are amongst forty or so other *Campos* or *Prigione di Guerra* right across mainland Italy, including Villa Orsini on the outskirts of Sulmona in the Apennine mountains, which as described was used to accommodate Allied Generals above the rank of Brigadier. There was also the 'naughty boys' camp in the fortress at Gavi known as the 'Italian Colditz', where amongst others, David Stirling, the founder of the SAS was kept once captured.

A detail I discovered purely by accident regarding P.G. 35 at the monastery of *Certosa di Padula* was the 'Union-Jacked' lawn enclosed within the cloisters. Viewing the site on Google Maps, I couldn't help but notice a very obvious British flag that would certainly have been spotted by any aviators flying overhead. This was too good a 'factoid' not to include in my story.

Another aspect of life in the camps, and indeed during Jox's arduous journey through the mountains, is Italy's sights, sounds, smells and even tastes. I reference *grano arso*, burnt grain Puglian cookery, and also squid ink pasta later in the book, both authentic flavours of their regions. *DOC Castel del Monte* is an excellent white wine which Perrin, of the real Perrin family of French wine growers, turns his Gallic nose up to. An exploration of tastes also includes the contents of the *Kriegies'* lifeline, their Red Cross packages. They were discussed at great length, and were the subject of huge inmate focus and attention, and subsequently I have tried to be as factual as possible when detailing their contents.

A key turning point for the *Kriegies* in the Italian camps was the announcement of the Treaty of Cassibile, named for the Sicilian town where it was negotiated. When Fascist Italy capitulated, prisoner of war camps across the country were abandoned by their guards and the POWs faced the dilemma of whether to sit tight until liberated (the standing orders from British High Command) or to venture out into the unknown and undoubtedly dangerous Italian countryside. The implications of this decision could be very serious. On one hand there was the risk of being 'on the run' in an active warzone, with all its associated risks from both sides of the conflict, weighed against staying put, which for a good many actually resulted in extended incarceration and eventual transfers north to Germany, as Italian camps were overrun by German reinforcements.

Once Jox and his companions made their decision, they encountered some of the real dangers waiting 'out there' and were fortunate to run into the partisans of *la Brigata Stella Rosa*. They were one of many such bands that sprung up after the armistice, with the Red Star Brigade being led by a dashing former Sergent Major Mario Musolesi known as *Il Lupo*, the wolf. One of his men was the real Sikh soldier, Sad Singh, a former Indian Army officer and POW who joined the *Stella Rosa* partisans, fighting by their sides for several months.

The OSS's Operation SIMCOL was tasked with rescuing and evacuating POWs. Equally real were the Monuments Men whose mission was to find and preserve the cultural heritage of Europe, as it faced widespread looting and the threat of destruction through bombing and battle. General Clark of the US 6th Army is known to have complained that fighting a war in Italy was like fighting in a museum. The two Monuments Men I have referenced, Edward Croft-Murray and Deane Kelly are both real and as described, venerable art scholars who survived the war having done a great deal to help preserve many of Italy's greatest treasures.

As the war became more desperate, bombing raids were more frequent, and Italy's suffering increased exponentially. Italians remained divided and conflicted over the prospect of losing the war, how to react to the armistice and how to cope with changing sides. The frequency of massacres and outrages against civilians, but also actions against partisan forces, increased in savagery and scope, often executed by veteran shock troops drafted in from the Eastern Front. These troops were outraged by the perceived 'cowardice' and duplicity of their erstwhile Axis allies. I have attempted to illustrate some of the savagery of this fratricide, but have barely touched on what would become a terrible hallmark of the Italian campaign as it continued to the war's weary end.

The radio broadcasts from Axis Sally and *Colonnello Buonasera* were also much as described and provided the soundtrack to the Italian campaign.

Finally, the return of Jox and his companions to Sicily on motor torpedo boats is accurate, and was the preferred evacuation method for SIMCOL POW returnees. MTB 81, commanded by T/Lt. Laurence Vezey Strong is real and was in fact responsible for sinking U-561 on the 12th July 1943 in the Straits of Messina, somewhat in the manner described. Only the U-boat's 26-year-old commander Fritz Henning and four of his crewmen survived, and Strong was subsequently awarded the Distinguished Service Cross (DSC) for the action on the 21st December 1943. I feel sure Strong wouldn't begrudge Jox and Kilpatrick a share of that glory.

After his return from imprisonment, Jox could perhaps have expected to have earnt a rest, but his war in Italy is far from over. What the Allies had hoped would be a quick campaign against 'the soft underbelly of Europe' had proved to be anything but. The weather, the arduous terrain and the dogged determination of the beleaguered and increasingly desperate German forces will mean he and his comrades will face many more challenges ahead.

I hope you will join him in what will prove to be some of his most hard-fought adventures, and given Jox's already very long war, that's got to be saying something.

I really hope you've enjoyed reading my fifth Jox McNabb novel. As ever, reviews and / or ratings are very important to authors, so if *The Wire and the Lines* has touched, entertained or thrilled you, I hope you would be willing to post a review on **Amazon** or **Goodreads**. Readers can also connect with me on **Twitter (@P33ddy)** and via **my website**. Also, for anyone who may be interested, I have loaded some images on **Instagram (jox_mcnabb)** that inspired me to write the story of Jox's remarkable war. Until the next time.

Per Ardua Ad Astra.

Best regards,

Patrick Larsimont

patricklarsimont.com

Sapere Books is an exciting new publisher of brilliant fiction and popular history.

To find out more about our latest releases and our monthly bargain books visit our website: **saperebooks.com**